For the Sake of Love

For the Sake of Love

Dwan Abrams

www.urbanchristianonline.com

Urban Books, LLC
97 N18th Street
Wyandanch, NY 11798

ISBN 13: 978-1-60162-744-5
ISBN 10: 1-60162-744-0

First Trade Paperback Printing June 2014
Printed in the United States of America

10 9 8 7 6 5 4 3 2 1

Distributed by Kensington Corp.
Submit Wholesale Orders to:
Kensington Publishing Corp.
C/O Penguin Group (USA) Inc.
Attention: Order Processing
405 Murray Hill Parkway
East Rutherford, NJ 07073-2316
Phone: 1-800-526-0275
Fax: 1-800-227-9604

For the Sake of Love

by

Dwan Abrams

To Nia and Carrington

Acknowledgments

I have to thank God for blessing me with my seventh published book. My latest book was inspired by my novella titled, *Only True Love Waits*. That was my first attempt at inspirational fiction. Initially, I planned to expound upon the story, make major changes to the storyline, go deeper with the characters, and create a full-length novel. Of course, it didn't work out that way. The storyline took on a life of its own, completely changing the original premise and the characters. *Voilà* . . . a new story was born.

I want to thank Alex for being so supportive of me and my career. A special thanks to my daughter, Nia, for giving me the time and space to write and think. I love the two of you more than words could ever express.

To Ireana for not just being my sister but my friend. I love you so much, and thanks for blessing me with my adorable little niece, Carrington.

To my mom, Ms. Gwen, for giving me so much love and a listening ear whenever I need it. I love you more than words could ever express.

To my auntie Wanda and aunt Gail for calling me just to see how I'm doing. I love you for that.

To my Sisters In Literary Kinship—I appreciate our sisterhood.

A special thanks to Shameka Powers and Jessica Barrow-Smith for your opinions, suggestions, and wonderful input. I appreciate it so much.

Acknowledgments

I have been fortunate to have connected with many wonderful people during my literary journey and have been blessed to learn something from all of them. To all of my author friends, whether self-published or traditionally published, I appreciate you!

To all the book clubs that have supported me, I owe you a debt of gratitude. Thank you for the good food, lively conversations, fun retreats, and lots of laughs.

Peace & Blessings,
Dwan Abrams

Charity Is Love

Charity suffereth long, and is kind; charity envieth not;
charity vaunteth not itself, is not puffed up,
Doth not behave itself unseemly, seeketh not her own, is
not easily provoked, thinketh no evil;
Rejoiceth not in iniquity, but rejoiceth in the truth;
Beareth all things, believeth all things, hopeth all
things, endureth all things.
Charity never faileth: but whether there be prophecies,
they shall fail; whether there be tongues, they shall
cease; whether there be knowledge, it shall vanish away.

~1 Corinthians 13:4–8~

One

Atlanta, Georgia

Spade couldn't prove it, but if someone asked him, he'd swear even his dreams were in music. He woke up in the morning to the sound of "Live Your Life" by T. I. featuring Rihanna on his cell phone alarm. As he got dressed, music played on his surround sound in his two-bedroom condo. He found himself bobbing his head even when no music was playing aloud; there was always a song on rotation in his head. For him, music was like food; the very sustenance that kept him alive.

Spade had just gotten home from a strenuous workout at the gym when his cell phone rang. When he saw his manager's name appear, his heartbeat sped up. "What you got for me?"

"I have some of the best news of your life. The negotiations are complete, and we're ready to sign the recording contract with Big Ups Records. We have a quick meeting scheduled with the label today at 4:30 p.m. to sign the papers."

He dreamt of this day ever since he was a kid. He used to sneak and listen to the hip-hop greats, Run–D.M.C., Public Enemy, Eric B. & Rakim, LL Cool J, Boogie Down Productions and the Beastie Boys. And he used to mimic their rhymes. When he felt like being extra rebellious, he listened to Ice T. and N.W.A.

Spade spent countless hours writing lyrics, listening to beats, and rehearsing his stage presence. Most nights he'd stay up until three or four o'clock in the morning laying down tracks. The extra bedroom in his condo had been converted to a studio. He knew that in order for him to be a success, he needed to work while everyone else was sleeping—especially if he was going to be the first Christian rapper to reach legendary status like Jay-Z, Tupac, and the Notorious B.I.G.. Like the mogul P. Diddy said, "If you're chasing your dream, you're not running fast enough. Run faster!"

Spade was very fortunate in the sense that when his grandmother died, she named him as the sole beneficiary on her life insurance policy. His mom didn't appreciate it, but she hadn't been all that responsible back in the day. Being that she had been a crack addict for a number of years, her mother always had concerns that she may one day relapse, even though she never did. Since Spade was her only grandchild, making him her heir seemed the most responsible thing to do to ensure his future. So, as long as he lived modestly, he could afford to work his music full-time.

"For real?" Spade questioned, being cautiously optimistic.

"For real," he repeated. "You know I don't kid around, especially when it comes to money. I'll text you the address. And be on time."

"Of course. Thanks, man."

Once he hung up the phone he could hardly contain his excitement. He pumped his fist in the air as he whooped and hollered in the privacy of his condo. He checked his watch and saw that he only had an hour and a half before the biggest meeting of his life. At three o'clock in the afternoon he felt confident that his neighbors were at work, so he felt free to get as loud as he wanted.

"Woo hoo!" he shouted. He hurried up and put his arm down after getting a whiff of the funk emitting from his armpit. Good thing he came straight home after the gym. He would've been embarrassed if he had stopped off somewhere smelling like stinky cheese.

He hopped in the shower, planning to get in and get out in less than five minutes. He stopped dead in his tracks when he noticed a doughy-to-the-touch golf ball-sized lump on his lower torso. It didn't feel tender, but Spade was confident the lump hadn't been there before. At least he hadn't noticed it. He immediately got out of the shower smelling of sandalwood. He grabbed the handheld mirror sitting on his bathroom countertop and studied the lump. Pressing it, he couldn't help but wonder what it was.

Far from being a worrywart, Spade didn't think the lump meant anything. He figured he probably had a small cyst that could be easily removed, so he called his doctor to make an appointment.

The physician's assistant on the other end told him, "Would it be possible for you to come in today?"

Not a snowball's chance in a volcano. His meeting today was too important. Not that his health wasn't, but the lump wasn't bothering him. It didn't hurt. Whatever the lump was, Spade was certain waiting a few more days wasn't going to make a difference.

"Sorry, I can't. I have an important meeting scheduled. I can't miss it."

The PA seemed reluctant. "Okay, but you really need to get this checked out ASAP. What about first thing Monday morning?"

"I can do that."

The PA scheduled the appointment, and Spade went on about his business. He brushed his freshly cut Afro temp with a curly look to it and got dressed in a suit and tie. As hot as it was outside in the month of May, Spade sacrificed his comfort in favor of professionalism. He figured Jay-Z and Diddy wouldn't show up at a business meeting with the bigwigs looking thugged out, so neither would he.

Thinking about what this meeting could mean for his future put a huge smile on his face. He went to his meeting feeling like the shot caller he aspired to be one day.

When he arrived, his manager and attorney were already there waiting. He noticed that the record company was laid out with expensive furniture, paintings, sculptures, and a huge fish tank filled with piranhas. It was obvious that an interior decorator had hooked that place up. He had been there before, but he was so nervous about auditioning for the label execs that he hadn't paid much attention to his surroundings. Now that he was there to seal the deal he could relax somewhat.

When Kerryngton Kruse, the CEO of the parent company of the label signing Spade, entered the room, everyone stood up. He was like a combination of Tommy Mottola, Suge Knight, Russell Simmons, and Jay-Z all rolled up into one. He had this air about him that could intimidate even the hardest thug on the street or locked up. People called him a pit bull. Not to his face, of course, but that was his reputation. Spade noticed how everyone called him Mr. Kruse out of respect and jumped every time he made a move. Dude reeked of money. He looked like he wiped his butt with hundred-dollar bills.

"Spade," Mr. Kruse said, "I've heard so much about you that I had to come over here and meet the man who people are saying has the lyrical genius of some of hip-hop's greatest." He shook Spade's hand. "I listened to your demo, and I was very impressed with you. I've worked with some of the biggest names in the industry, and I'm personally going to help produce your debut CD. The fact that you can sing too . . ." He nodded like he was impressed. "That's what's up."

Spade felt highly favored at that moment. He knew that was nothing but God directing his career. "Wow. I'm honored. Thank you." He tried not to smile too hard. He didn't want to appear soft, because he had worked too hard to establish his swag and tough guy image.

"Gentlemen, I'll let you get back to business." His tone was professional, confident, and in control.

"Let's get down to business," the record label attorney said. He showed Spade every place he needed to initial and scribble his John Hancock.

After initialing each page and signing the last page of the lengthy contract, Spade received a check for his hefty advance. The record company gave him the upfront fee to cover the costs of recording, producing, mixing, and mastering the record.

"Congratulations," the record label attorney told him. "Welcome to Big Ups Records."

"Thank you."

The attorney placed the documents in his briefcase. "Have a great day."

Spade's attorney waited until the mahogany door closed behind the record label counsel before saying, "If there's any money left over from the advance after all the costs of recording are paid for, *those* coins can end up in your pocket."

His manager chimed in, "Yes, that's why we negotiated you such a high advance. It's in your best financial interest to keep recording costs low. You already know it's very common for artists to never see any royalties from sales unless the record becomes a major seller."

"I understand." Spade sounded confident. He had heard too many artist horror stories and refused to be another statistic. Many of his friends were established artists, and they warned him about the perils of the music industry. That's why he listened attentively when his lawyer had told him that "Artists aren't actually paid any royalties from sales until the label has covered or recouped their expenses from making the CD." He explained that some of those recoupable expenses can include the artist's advance, recording and producing costs, the costs of promoting, marketing and advertising the record, tour support, video production, packaging, manufacturing, shipping, warehousing expenses, and mechanical royalties paid to songwriters. And that wasn't even all. There were more reasons for the record company to withhold money and negatively impact royalty payments.

So, when Spade said, "I understand," he really did.

"You thought you worked hard before," his manager said, patting him on the back. "You haven't seen anything yet. The label knows that playing live shows has proven to be a great way to build up a fan base and has a direct effect on sales, so we included a provision in the contract to help cover some of the costs associated with touring."

"I remember." He knew the advantages of performing live firsthand. That's how he got discovered. His mix tape had been moving a lot of units, and one of his songs got some airplay on Atlanta's biggest radio station. He had even been written about in a national magazine as an up-and-coming artist to watch. Locally, he performed at hot spots around the city and established a cult following. He had generated so much buzz that record companies A&Rs attended his shows to see what all the hype was about. He was definitely no stranger to hard work.

"Great," the attorney said. "Do you have any questions?"

"No, you guys did a pretty decent job covering me on the particulars during the negotiation process. I feel good about everything," he said sincerely. "Now let's get this money." He rubbed his hands together.

The attorney stuffed some documents in his accordion-style briefcase. "Absolutely." He shook Spade's hand.

His manager said, "It's been a pleasure. Give Bria my best."

Spade couldn't wait to go over to his fiancée, Bria Murray's, house to share the news with her. "I will."

Finally, Spade was free to go. No longer an independent artist, he was officially signed to a major record label, and that felt real good to him. He couldn't wait to release his CD and go on tour. With the financial backing of a major label, Spade felt his career could go all the way to the top.

On his way out, he waved at the model-looking receptionist sitting behind her desk. She returned the gesture.

Once outside, he looked up to the heavens and thanked God. He paid particular attention to the baby blue sky with just the right touches of white sprinkled throughout. Spade smiled to himself as he thought of God as the ultimate artist with the whole world as His canvas. Designing the sky was probably just His pastime.

He stopped off to get a large Mellow Mushroom pepperoni pizza, a liter of Dr. Pepper, two Blu-rays from Redbox—a horror movie for both him and Bria and a romantic comedy for her—and a fresh bouquet of colorful flowers for his girl. He knew that she liked flowers, and they both enjoyed pizza and movies on Friday nights. That had become their ritual.

Before he even got to Bria's house in Lithonia, he had made the decision to tell her about his recording contract but not the lump he'd found. Bria had a tendency to worry enough for the two of them, and he didn't see any point of getting her all worked up over something that would most likely turn out to be nothing.

When he arrived at Bria's two-story brick front house, he tucked the soda bottle underneath his armpit, balanced the warm pizza box in the palm of his hand like a pizza delivery driver, with the flowers and Blu-rays resting on top. He then pressed his back against the doorbell and the love of his life came to the door looking fit and sexy in a long, figure-hugging striped dress. Bria—a few months younger than Spade—had a curvaceous body that turned heads whenever she entered a room.

She grabbed the box and let him in. "The pizza smells good."

He followed her into the traditional-styled kitchen. They placed all the items on the island.

"You know you short, right?" Spade teased as he reached out to hug her, noticing that she was walking around barefoot. She usually wore four- to six-inch heels, which made people think she was much taller than her five feet four inches.

She pretended to smack him. "Shut up," she said, laughing. They hugged and briefly kissed. "Do you like this toenail polish on me?" She held up her foot and flexed, showing off some red-looking color.

"It's cool." He didn't care about her polish. He just knew she had some suckable toes.

She picked up one of the movies, opened the case to read the title, and smiled. "Good choice." She then did the same thing to the other Blu-ray and nodded her head in approval.

Bria retrieved two plates from the cabinet before picking up the bouquet and inhaling the scent of the fresh, gorgeous gerbera daisies in vibrant assorted colors and placing them in water.

Spade grabbed two glasses, filled them with ice, and poured their bubbly drinks. "We need to raise some glasses," he announced.

"What's up?"

"Your man over here," he patted his chest, "just signed his first major record deal."

"Shut the front door! Baby, I'm so proud of you. Congratulations!" She left the flowers on the counter next to the sink and hugged her man again. She then planted kisses all over his clean-shaven face.

He loved the way she smelled. Clean like a body wash with a touch of Tommy Girl cologne. He especially loved the way she made him feel like he was the greatest man on earth. Like she believed he could do anything, which made him feel as though he could do anything. He could tell that she was genuinely proud of him.

"We've got to do something to celebrate," she said. Her face lit up.

"Just being with you is enough." He meant every word.

They stood facing each other, holding hands. She touched the side of his face and showed him her even, white teeth. "That's sweet, just like the flowers, but this is worthy of a celebration." She backed away from him and took the lid off the pizza box. "Mmm, pepperoni, my favorite."

He knew it was her favorite; that's why he got it. "Baby, let me change." He went out to his car and grabbed a change of clothes; then he went into her bathroom and put on a baseball cap, a clean bright white T-shirt, loose-fitting jeans, and a pair of white-on-white sneakers so clean snow would've gotten jealous. Feeling more comfortable, he left his clothes in the bathroom and joined Bria in the kitchen.

She picked up a slice and the gooey cheese dangled until she removed it with her finger. "Tell me everything. What label signed you? I want all the details."

She acted like she was talking to one of her girlfriends. He wasn't about to give her details. He didn't like to talk that much. She'd be lucky to get the CliffsNotes. "Big Ups Records," he told her.

"That's huge." She sounded impressed.

He grinned. "Yeah, I think so. It's all good." He left it at that.

"Okay. How about Six Flags this weekend?" she suggested, taking a bite of the warm pizza.

Spade stacked three large slices on his plate. "Sounds like a plan."

Bria inserted the horror movie in the Blu-ray disc player. They took their food into the family room and ate on folding TV tray tables. While the previews showed they talked about their upcoming wedding.

"I found the most adorable white flower girl dress for your cousin," Bria told him, her enthusiasm evident.

"Hold still," he said as he kissed and licked away a string of cheese from her chin. Once it was gone he leaned back.

"Before I forget . . . We have a cake tasting and meeting with the caterer to sample the menu."

He smacked his lips. When she mentioned the word *cake,* it reminded him of the Rihanna and Chris Brown song, "Birthday Cake." He couldn't wait until their honeymoon so that he could have his cake and eat it too. "You know as long as there's food I'm there. Just let me know when."

"While my mom and I were out looking for the mother-of-the-bride outfit, which we didn't find, we saw a really nice suit for your mom. I took a picture of it on my phone." She got up to get her phone and showed him the elegant-looking outfit with rhinestones on the lapel.

He took the phone from her to get a better view. It looked like something his mom would wear. "I like it. I think my mom will too."

She put her phone down and finished off her pizza. "One more month."

"Yeah, and all that booty will be mine."

They both laughed.

"Anyway," Bria said, "please don't do like Chance did and forget to order your tux." She sighed. Chance was her best friend's husband. "He was so busy trying to make sure all his groomsmen remembered to order their tuxes that he forgot to order his own."

Spade was glad she reminded him, because with his packed schedule he easily could've forgotten too.

Bria gulped down her drink and let out a burp. "Excuse me," she laughed.

Spade laughed too. People wouldn't believe how silly and down-to-earth this intelligent, well-behaved, gorgeous woman could be, he thought. He attracted pretty women but most of the time they weren't that smart or were real flighty or didn't have good personalities. Bria, though, she was the complete package.

She looked at him. "Six Flags tomorrow?"

"Sure."

The movie started, and she snuggled up next to him. He felt like the luckiest man in the world, and nothing, certainly not some little ol' lump, was going to change that.

Two

Bria had gone to Six Flags enough to know how to dress for the occasion. She pulled her straight hair back into a long ponytail, put on a sun visor, tank top, shorts, sneakers, and slathered sunblock on every exposed area of her skin.

Spade picked her up in his Dodge Durango. During the ride they listened to the demo CD that landed Spade his contract. Bria enjoyed listening to him. His lyrics had depth, his flow was on point, and the beats were catchy.

"I love all these songs," she complimented him.

"Thanks, beautiful."

Every time he called her "beautiful" her insides quivered. She felt beautiful being with him.

"Are you excited?"

"I am, but it hasn't settled all the way in yet." He drove on I-20. "My manager has been inundating me with information and stuff to do. It's a lot to take in. I mean, I have to meet with an image consultant, a stylist, a producer to listen to beats, write new music, and on and on." He took a breath. "There's so much that goes into dropping a CD. The label liaison is responsible for getting a release date for my CD. I've been told we're going to have a CD release party and a full-fledged promotional tour. I didn't expect it to be this intense. I just wanted to make music, you feel me?"

"I understand," Bria said. He had a lot going on, but she could tell he was still happy and excited. "I guess it's true that stars aren't born, they're created." Regardless, her man was a star in her eyes.

They arrived at the park promptly at ten o'clock in the morning, and it was already starting to get hot. Bria tapped her phone to check the weather and discovered that the temperature was 78 degrees. She was glad that she had drunk plenty of water the night before and in the morning to keep herself hydrated.

So much for trying to get to the park early on a Saturday. They stood in line behind thirty-five people. Bria knew the exact number because she counted them. She had just a touch of obsessive compulsive disorder (OCD). Because of it, she kept an immaculate house, would occasionally find herself obsessing about whether she unplugged the iron, and counted random things. They made small talk as they inched their way to the front of the line and purchased their tickets.

Once inside, they acted like big kids trying to decide what roller coaster to ride first.

"We gotta do Batman," Spade insisted. No surprise there, considering he loved all things Batman. The same way talk-show host Wendy Williams adores Wonder Woman, Spade admired Batman. He even drank out of a Batman coffee mug every morning.

"It's your day," Bria relented.

So they headed to Gotham City. The line had a forty-five-minute wait posting, and they maneuvered their way through. Some of the areas smelled like urine. Bria imagined some drunken guy taking a leak in a corner, stinking up the spot.

When they reached the front of the line and it was their turn to get on the ride, Bria felt excited. As soon as they were secure and ready to go she closed her eyes and held on tight. She felt some type of sonic wave on her insides. She had this ribcage thing going on where her largest body cavity, her chest and stomach, resonated like a guitar body. She screamed during the entire ride and didn't open her eyes until they came back to the boarding dock.

Spade was so stoked that he wanted to ride again. Bria didn't like to ride the same ride back to back, but for Batman she'd make an exception. That ride was fun! Plus, she wanted to make Spade happy. They got back in line and did it all over again.

Next they rode Mindbender, and then Goliath. Bria didn't mind the long wait times, because the time passed by quickly. Especially the way she and Spade joked with each other and playfully touched each other. What she didn't like were the unpleasant odors, mainly the funk emitted after people got hot and started sweating.

Nearly four hours had passed and they had worked up an appetite. They sat down to eat smoked turkey drumsticks and drank Cokes. Those drumsticks were huge. They looked like something from the Flintstones, but they tasted like a piece of heaven on earth. All flavorful and juicy.

A group of teenage girls were gawking, pointing, and giggling in their direction.

"What's that about?" Bria said. She wasn't feeling the rudeness.

Spade shrugged. "Don't know, don't care." He patted her hand.

Two of the giddy teens came over to them. "Aren't you Spade?"

A smile wider than the moon appeared on Spade's face. He licked his lips. "Yes, I am."

"Oh my God!" they squealed.

The light-skinned one with strawberry blond hair said, "We're your biggest fans. We met you when you came to our school for Career Day. And we have your mix tape. Can we get your autograph?"

"Of course you can." He looked around for something to write on and settled for a napkin. Bria handed him a pen from her fanny pack. "Who do you want me to make it out to?"

She looked over her shoulder at her friends who were cheesin' hard looking starstruck. She looked back at Spade. "You can make it out to me, Rasheeda," she pointed at her friend standing next to her, "Porsha, and my two friends over there, Jasmine and Ebonee."

"You got it." He wrote their names and *Thanks for your support. Love, Spade.* He handed the young girl the napkin.

Pressing the napkin next to her chest, she asked, "Can I please get a hug?"

Spade looked at Bria who gave him the go-ahead. Who was she to come between Spade and a fan? This was his life, and she needed to get used to it. What choice did she have? He was about to blow up even more. She was certain that after his CD dropped, his popularity would soar. Fans asking for autographs would become standard practice.

He briefly hugged the girl, and before he could sit back down, her friend spoke up, "Me too."

So, he gave her an innocent hug as well. One would've thought they had just met the king of the south the way they ran off all giddy.

Bria smirked at him. "Well, that was interesting, Mr. Superstar." She could tell that made his chest stick out a little further. "Oh, Spade," she teased, "may I please get your autograph?" She squeezed his bicep.

"Yeah, okay. But my girl is a little touched in the head." He made a circling motion with his index finger at the side of his head. "She doesn't take kindly to women touching on me."

That got a chuckle out of her. Slurping the last bit of her soda, she asked, "What's next?" Out of the corner of her eye she noticed a couple walking by pushing twins in a stroller. Her eyes followed them. That would be ideal for her, she thought. One pregnancy, two babies. A double blessing.

Spade studied his folded map of the park and said, "We still have to ride the Cyclone, Superman, and Ninja."

"Don't forget the Great American Scream Machine," Bria added as she pointed to it on the map. She wiped sweat from her brow with a napkin. "I need to go to the bathroom."

There were restrooms across from them, so they both went. A few minutes later they met back up and went on to the next fast, wild, gut-wrenching ride, leaving Bria feeling nauseated. The Superman ride proved to be too much for her, as she threw up at the end of the ride, grossing Spade out. Those turkey legs come up tasting nothing like going down. Lucky for her she always carried a travel toothbrush, toothpaste, and mouthwash in her bag. Those items came in handy today, so she didn't have to walk around with vomit breath.

At six o'clock in the evening they were winding down and rode a splashy water ride to cool off. No sooner than they got off the ride the clouds opened up and poured buckets of water on their heads. They tried to run for cover but there was no use. The raindrops stomped on them with a vengeance. They were completely soaked, so they just made a mad dash to the SUV. Spade had a couple of towels in his trunk. They spread the towels over the leather seats before sitting down. That didn't matter. Water still got on the seats.

"That was fun," Bria said, then burst out laughing.

"I prefer my showers in the privacy of my bathroom, thank you very much."

"Did you have fun?"

He leaned over the console and kissed her soft lips. "The best. What do you want to do about dinner?"

"We obviously can't go anywhere looking like this." With both hands she gestured from her head down. "Let's just go through a drive-thru somewhere."

"That'll work."

About ten minutes into their ride the rain subsided.

"I think you should move in with me and let your dad find a renter after we get married," Spade suggested.

Bria didn't say anything. She was trying to find a tactful way to say what was on her mind. She enjoyed living away from her parents during college. After she graduated her father insisted she move back into the family home until she got married. Her dad was old-fashioned like that. Spade had already proposed to her, so she could've easily married him just to get out of her parents' house. But, she didn't want to do that. Yes, she loved Spade with all her heart, but she wanted to accomplish more before she got married. So, she enrolled in an accelerated graduate program where she could complete her MBA in one year. And she did.

Recently, one of her family's rental properties became vacant. Since the home was in a desirable neighborhood and had been well maintained, she convinced her father to let her move in.

"I can't do it," she said. "I've been in my house less than a year. It doesn't make sense for me to leave a house and move into a condo. I don't want to share walls with anyone. Plus, we'd have to move again anyway after we started having kids."

"I hear you, but I'm a grown man. How does that look for me to move into my girl's house?" He was resolute and unswerving.

"It's not all that uncommon. Besides, why do you care what anyone thinks?"

"I don't. I'm just sayin'." He gripped the steering wheel a little tighter.

"When is your lease up again?"

"In June."

"We'd have more space at my house, and you could have a home gym and studio." She tried to make the offer sound enticing.

He seemed to ponder the idea. "That could work. I don't even know why I'm trippin'. At the end of the day it's not going to matter where we live right now anyway. When my checks start rolling in, I'm buying you a mansion." He showed her his teeth.

Bria loved the fact that Spade wanted to give her the world, but what mattered most to her was their love and happiness.

Three

Sunday morning rolled around, and Bria had a hard time getting out of bed. All those hours at the amusement park in the hot sun had worn her out. She would've loved to have stayed in the bed and hugged the pillow tighter just a little while longer, but she knew if she cancelled out on going to church, so would Nya—her best friend ever since the fifth grade—and Chance. She didn't want to give them an excuse.

She fixed herself a cup of hot coffee hoping it would help give her some "get-up-and-go." She cracked the blinds over her sink. Maple cabinetry with an antique white painted finish kept the kitchen light and airy.

As she sat at the breakfast bar reading the Sunday paper and sipping her Java, her cell phone rang. She perked up when she saw Spade's picture pop up and the caption "My Man" underneath. She immediately answered.

"When you get back from church I'm coming over. Put on something casual like jeans and flats. I have a surprise for you," he said.

She liked surprises as long as they were good. But she acted like a young child in the sense that she wanted to know what the surprise was in advance, and if no one told her, she'd spend a lot of time thinking about it, trying to figure it out.

"What is it?" she asked.

"Didn't I tell you it was a surprise?" He sounded like he wanted to add "duh" on the end.

"Fine." She pretended to pout. "Are you going to church today?"

Spade attended church on his side of town, which was about forty minutes away from Bria. "Yeah. I'll be headed out in a few. It's my Sunday to direct the youth choir."

She liked the fact that he was using his musical gift to give back to the kingdom as well. "Okay. I love you. Represent for the family."

He laughed. Whenever they had something important going on, they always told each other to represent for the family. In other words, do good.

"Love you too."

Bria got off the phone feeling more in love than ever. She looked forward to the day she could wake up next to Spade and cook him breakfast.

She drained her cup and called her mom to tell her not to expect her for Sunday dinner. As an only child Bria maintained a close relationship with her parents. She spoke to her mom every day whether she wanted to or not. That was her obligation as the dutiful daughter. And she usually reserved some time on Sunday to spend with her mom and dad.

Bria, Nya, and Chance met at their usual spot next to the enormous potted fern at the front entrance of the sanctuary. Chance stepped out first looking like the Jolly Green Giant with Nya nipping at his heels. Bria thought it was kind of corny but cute the way they wore coordinating outfits. As soon as they greeted each other with hugs and kisses on the cheek, Bria started cracking on Chance.

"Chance, the Jolly Green Giant called and he wants his outfit back."

"Here you go. Can a brotha get in the church good before you start?" he said. Being from Boston, Chance tended to act like the letter "r" wasn't a part of the English alphabet, and when he did use the letter it was often misplaced. It sounded like he said, "Heah ya go. Can a brotha get in the chuch good befah ya staht?"

They chuckled before going inside and taking their seats near the front. They preferred to arrive a few minutes early so that they could fellowship with some of the other members as well as get good seats.

Church opened with prayer; and then the choir sang three songs. Bria remained on her feet the entire time, clapping, singing, and praising the Lord. She could hear Chance singing off-key, but she wasn't about to joke. Oh, how badly she wanted to say, "Chance, your voice may not be best suited for singing." But she refrained, certain that to God he must've sounded like an angel. All that mattered was that he was in the house of the Lord praising His holy name, she reasoned.

One of the associate ministers led the responsive reading and the congregational hymn followed.

Finally able to sit down, announcements were made and they saw a PowerPoint presentation of the latest missionary trip to Africa. Bria felt inspired. Although she didn't feel being a missionary was her calling in life, she did want to help underdeveloped, underprivileged countries in any way that she could.

The pastor came out and gave a redemptive message about the power of forgiveness. Bria shouted many "amens," "preach pastor," and "hallelujahs." At the end of the sermon the pastor extended the gift of salvation and opened the church doors to anyone who needed a church home or wanted to accept Christ into their life. Young and old, men and women made their way to the front of the altar. Some were crying, and others were smiling. The congregation clapped and glorified God.

After service Chance offered to take them all out to Sunday brunch.

"I wish that I could," Bria explained, "but I can't. Spade said he has a surprise for me after church, so I need to get home." She made a pouty face.

Nya hugged her, and they were cheek to cheek. "Not a problem," Nya said in her usual Southern twang so sexy that any man born beneath the Mason-Dixon line couldn't resist.

They broke apart and looked in each other's faces. "You take your matron of honor duties seriously." Bria giggled. "I meant to thank you for e-mailing the guest list to the calligrapher, picking up the invitations when they were ready, and mailing them to the guests."

"Girl, please. That's what I do."

She looked into Nya's round face and for a split second she saw her as a little girl. A pleasant expression graced her face as she thought about the first time she and Nya met. She and her family had just moved into a subdivision in Stone Mountain, a suburb of Atlanta.

"Bria, come here," her mom had called to her. *"There's a cute little girl out there who I think you should meet."*

Bria was nervous and didn't want to do it.

"Don't be shy. Just go up to her and ask her if she wants to be your friend," her mom continued.

With her mother spying through the living-room window, Bria skipped to catch up with the brown-skinned, round-faced little girl wearing two pigtails and a plaid dress. Without making eye contact she said, "Do you want to be my friend?"

At the time it never occurred to Bria that Nya could've said no. Even though Nya responded favorably, that still did not stop her from occasionally poking fun at Bria about the proposal of friendship.

"Anyway," Nya said, interrupting Bria's thoughts, "let's talk about the grand opening of The Spa Factory in just one more week."

While an undergrad in college, Bria double majored in international business and marketing because she always wanted to be a businesswoman, a boss. During one of her core courses, she did a marketing analysis for a day spa in the Atlanta Metro area. Her professor was so impressed with her findings and well thought out, detailed business plan that he suggested she implement the plan. She agreed, because she had carefully researched the industry, the trends, the target audience, how to market to them, and so much more. She shared her ideas with her father, a prominent dentist, regarding her business. Her father loved her concept and agreed to help her secure the funding for her business.

After she graduated, she never lost sight of opening the spa. Halfway through graduate school she scouted out locations and found the ideal one. Her dad gave her the green light to proceed. She conducted more research to get the best products and establish relationships with the most credible vendors. When it came time to staff her organization, she immediately hired Nya to be her PR director. Nya had the gift of gab and a way with people that Bria admired. She was also the top sales rep at the company she worked for. She had no doubt Nya would be a good fit for the position.

Bria listened attentively as Nya went on and on about the outfit she was going to wear, the prominent people who were expected to be in attendance, and the media coverage that was guaranteed to make television, radio, and the local papers. When Nya finished rambling about the spa, she told Bria, "Have fun with Spade. Love you, girl."

Chance patted Bria on top of her head like a dog. "Run along," he teased.

She rolled her light brown eyes at him. "You're so not funny," she smirked.

He reached out and embraced her, patting her hard on the back like he was trying to burp a baby. "Be good."

"Ugh." She pressed against his five-month-pregnant-looking stomach. As a chef she figured that must be a part of his job description. How could anyone trust a skinny chef? she reasoned. She didn't think Chance was a sloppy kind of fat; he was more like the loveable, huggable teddy bear-type of guy. Not the type of guy she'd ever be interested in, but that didn't matter. He was Nya's man, and if Nya liked it, Bria loved it. "I'll call you." She directed her comment toward Nya and waved good-bye as she made her way to the Honda Accord her parents had given her the day she graduated from college with honors.

As soon as she entered her house she took off her shoes and trekked barefoot across the polished hardwood floors. Something about walking barefoot felt liberating to her.

She went upstairs into her bedroom and changed into a fitted baby tee, tight jeans, and flat thong sandals. She slicked her hair back into a long, flowing ponytail and touched up her makeup. Fifteen minutes later Spade rang her doorbell.

"Let me grab my purse and turn on the alarm," she told him after answering the door.

He grabbed her by the wrist and pulled her toward him. "Not before I get a kiss."

She slightly tilted her head to the left and kissed him.

"I'll wait for you at the car."

Her purse was waiting for her to pick it up on a bar stool in front of the island. She punched in her alarm code and locked the door behind her.

Spade opened the passenger door for her, and they drove toward Stone Mountain. She thought they were going to have brunch at one of her favorite spots, the Marriott Evergreen Hotel, but they didn't go that way.

Unable to take the suspense any longer, she said, "Please tell me where we're going."

Without taking his eyes off the road he said, "We're almost there."

Bria placed her hands in her lap and fiddled with her fingers. He pulled off the interstate onto a trail leading to a wooded area. She couldn't begin to imagine where they were going or what they were about to do. She wasn't the outdoorsy-type, and Spade knew that. What was he up to? The suspense was eating away at her like a flesh-eating disease.

The sound of the tires crushing the gravel and wood-chips underneath let her know they were in the boonies. She cut her eyes at him as Spade continued to follow the trail and stopped just before pulling up to a white wooden house.

"Where are we?" She tried not to sound annoyed.

He turned off the ignition. "You'll see. Come on."

They got out, and the rocks underneath Bria's feet made walking the trail leading to the house bumpy. She appreciated Spade holding her hand to help her keep her balance.

A blond guy came out and greeted them. Extending his hand he said, "You must be Spade."

Spade shook his hand and introduced Bria. "This is my fiancée."

"Terrific." Creases lined the guy's forehead. "Have either of you ever been up in a hot air balloon before?"

"A hot air balloon?" Bria repeated. Had Spade lost his mind? Why would he think she had any interest in riding in a hot air balloon? What if they got stuck in a tree? What if the heat thingy went out?

"No, we haven't," Spade told the guy. He wrapped his arm around Bria's shoulder. "Surprise!" He leaned over and kissed her on the temple.

She wanted to protest, but Spade looked so eager to do this. She just couldn't be Debbie Downer.

"You're in for an adventure," the guy said.

"I'll bet," Bria mumbled under her breath.

They went inside the gutted out house to sign some release forms and met two other people who worked there. The blond guy then took them out back where a huge multicolored hot air balloon was parked.

"You ready?" Spade asked her.

She took a deep breath and exhaled. She figured that if she was about to try something this daring, it may as well be with her life partner. This would be one of those stories they could share with their grandchildren, she figured.

"I'm ready."

The blond guy opened the door for them to enter and locked it behind them. That click sound made Bria feel trapped. She felt like hopping over the edge. Clutching Spade's hand she held on for dear life.

Blondie started up the hot air. Bria tried not to act nervous even though she couldn't have been more nervous.

"It's okay, baby," Spade assured her. "I've got you."

She looked up at him and relaxed somewhat. A rugged-looking guy assisted by untying the rope, and the balloon slowly ascended into the air.

Bria felt as light as the air they were ascending into. She couldn't believe they were floating on air. It felt surreal. Pretty soon they were flying above the trees.

"What do you think?" Spade asked, smiling as if he already knew the answer.

"I absolutely love it. The view is breathtaking, and the air feels right." She wrapped her arms around his neck and kissed him. "Thank you so much for this experience."

"You're always so supportive of me and my dreams. I just wanted to let you know that I'm proud of you too. You're about to open up a spa in less than a week. That's a big deal. I took you up here to show you that the sky's the limit." With her head resting on his chest he held her by the waist.

Bria's heart felt so full of love at that moment that if Spade did one more sweet thing, no matter how small, her heart would surely burst. She had been very vocal about her enthusiasm for starting her own company. Many nights she stayed up late sharing her business goals and long-term plans with him. He knew better than anyone how excited she was about this new venture.

Then she thought about the first time they met. Both were freshmen at Clark Atlanta University. They had an English class together, and he was such a clown, always cracking jokes and trying to make her laugh.

To her, he was the handsomest guy she had ever met. She had never seen eyes as sexy as his. His eyes had the same affect on her that kryptonite must have had on Superman. Coupled with his smooth bronze-colored skin, high cheekbones, full lips, and white, even teeth, he exceeded her wildest dreams.

His sense of humor attracted her even more than his good looks. They swiftly became friends and were insep-arable. Whenever they were out together and a female disrespected her by flirting with him, Bria never had to say a word. He would straighten the girl out by letting her know that Bria was his girl, and disrespecting her was not an option.

One of the many things she really liked about Spade was his street credibility. He was from Detroit and had never been stabbed or shot. When they went out, she felt safe and shielded from any peril that was common in big cities.

She enjoyed talking to him because he was easy to talk to. She felt as though she could tell him anything, and he seemed interested in whatever she had to say.

When she confided in him that she was a virgin and planned to stay that way until she got married, he ended up giving her a hug and kissing her on the forehead. Even though he went to church as a child, he admitted to her that he didn't fully understand what it meant to be saved. He had been told about God but didn't feel as though he knew Him for himself. He asked her to tell him more about Jesus, and she did. His thoughtfulness at that moment convinced her that he was the man for her. Not long afterward he got saved.

Bria could feel a breeze blowing against her skin as they slowly drifted in the sky looking at the grass, trees, and structures below. The blond guy made a few comments about where they were and what they were seeing. As Bria looked at the blue sky and cottony looking clouds next to her she could see her future in the clouds. She felt free and every fiber of her being came alive. To her, this was living life to the fullest.

She felt Spade's hand tighten around her waist. Being with him made her feel safe, protected, and cared for. She knew without a shadow of a doubt that she was marrying the man God had destined for her.

Just as the balloon wandered aimlessly in the sky without care or concern, Bria felt as though she too didn't have a care in the world.

Four

At nine o'clock Monday morning, Spade found himself sitting in the doctor's office getting examined.

The doctor touched the lump, and it moved readily with slight finger pressure. "Does that hurt?" the doctor asked.

"No."

"Okay. In regard to the lump," the doctor told him, "you have a lipoma."

Spade could've sworn the lump jumped from his back to his throat. He had to swallow hard. He tried not to panic, but his pounding heart let him know he wasn't doing a good job.

"Doc, if you're trying to scare me, you're doing a good job."

"No, no," the doctor said. "Lipomas are the most common noncancerous soft tissue growth." He scribbled some notes. "I'm going to remove it just to be sure the growth is noncancerous. I'll be right back."

Spade's leg shook nervously as he waited for the doctor to return. He didn't know the first thing about medicine, but he hoped and prayed the lump was as minor as the doctor made it seem.

The doctor knocked, and Spade told him to come in. He then explained the procedure. "I'm going to inject a local anesthetic around the lipoma, make an incision in the skin, remove the growth, and close the incision with sutures." He made it sound so simple, Spade thought. "You ready?"

"Sure."

His first instinct was to call Bria so that she could pray with him. They were prayer partners and prayed about everything. He was convinced that she had a direct line to God, because whenever they prayed together, miracles happened.

As badly as he wanted to tell her, he just couldn't bring himself to do it, though. She had enough on her plate with the opening of her business and planning the wedding. He didn't want to worry her needlessly, especially over some small outpatient surgery.

The doctor performed the procedure, and it turned out to be fairly simple, just like he described.

"We'll let you know when we hear back from the lab," was the physician's departing comment as Spade pulled his shirt back on and got ready to go home.

All Spade could do was pray for the best and wait.

Spade's week had been packed. Nonstop. Every day seemed like a new adventure. The A&R Department told him what producers they had gotten for him to work with as well as where the CD would be recorded. His CD recordings were going to be split between Atlanta, Georgia, and London, England. When he found out he was going to be spending time in London he felt like a true artist. William Shakespeare had moved to London, and the royal family still lived there. He imagined London as being a place of inspiration. He was going to wait to tell Bria and keep it a secret. The two of them had combined a list of every place they wanted to travel, and London was on the top of the list. He liked surprising her; her reactions never got old.

Since he already had an approved title for his CD, the art department had begun working on the CD cover art.

He knew they had the final say-so, but he was glad they asked for his input.

That early Friday afternoon was a day that changed the game for Spade. The doctor called to tell him his lab results were back and that Spade needed to come in right away so that he could go over the results with him. Nothing could've prepared him to hear the doctor tell him the dreaded words, "You have a form of cancer called lymphoma."

"What is that?" he asked. He didn't mean to sound so defensive, but this had taken him for a loop.

"Lymphoma is a type of cancer that begins in immune system cells. Not to sound like a textbook, but like other cancers, lymphoma occurs when cells are in a state of uncontrolled cell growth and multiplication."

Spade felt as if his mind was on overload. In the cascade of medical terms, the only thing he heard was the big C—Cancer—the same disease that killed his beloved grandmother.

"W-what?" Spade stammered, refusing to believe what he had just heard.

"I'm sorry, but—"

"No! Run the test again," Spade interjected, silently praying that he hadn't heard what he just thought he had. Spade's six foot two frame slumped over as tears welled in his eyes. He didn't consider himself to be sensitive by any means, but this broke him down like a fraction.

"I understand how you feel." The doctor sounded sympathetic.

"No, unless you've been diagnosed with cancer yourself, you *don't* understand how I feel," he snarled. Spade felt as if the air was being sucked from the room and right out of his lungs.

Oblivious to the suffocating effects, the surgeon let the other shoe drop. "We'll make an oncology appointment for you as soon as possible."

Spade didn't want to hear anymore. He slumped down in the chair and sobbed in his hands. All he could think about was dying young. He felt as if life had thrown him a major curve ball. This felt so unfair to him. He had so many hopes and dreams. Now this!

He looked up at the surgeon. "Why me?" Spade demanded. "Why now? This should be the happiest time of my life. I'm twenty-five years old, engaged to be married to an incredible woman, and, on top of everything, I just signed a recording contract with a major label."

Seizing the brief moment of silence during Spade's lament, the doctor said, "We'll call you with your oncology appointment."

"How serious is it?" Spade sniffled, wiped his now red eyes, and braced himself for the worst. "How long do I have to live?"

The doctor cleared his throat. "That depends on what stage you're in. I've known of people in the final stage to live as long as five years."

Spade couldn't take any more bad news. His hands began to tremble as he stared at the white wall behind the surgeon's head. "I just want to be alone for a few minutes."

The doctor nodded. "Take as much time as you need." He then left Spade to ponder his fate.

Spade stopped crying and started praying. "Father, I don't know what this is about. I want to trust you. I'm going to trust you." He sounded resolute. "I know that you will help me, but please help me until you help me."

He didn't know anything about the disease he had been diagnosed with. One thing he did know was that most cancers required some sort of treatment, most likely chemotherapy. He wasn't big on chemo because he and Bria often talked about having two or three kids. He knew that Bria wanted to be a mother someday, and he believed she'd make a great one. With this disease hanging over his head, how was that going to work? He could freeze his sperm in hopes that he'd beat the disease and still be able to become a dad. But the thing with cancer was that it was a beast within itself. It may or may not respond to treatment. Even if it responded to treatment, it was vengeful enough to sometimes come back. How could he live like that?

He was in a daze until his cell phone rang. It was his fiancée. He cleared his throat before answering.

"Baby, I want to see you," Bria said.

He wasn't in the right state of mind to see anyone, but Bria insisted. He had a hard time telling her no, especially when she sounded so sweet and upbeat. Against his better judgment he agreed to go over her house.

He sat in the doctor's office for five more minutes before composing himself enough to walk out. Whether real or imagined, he felt as though everyone in the doctor's office knew about his prognosis. He didn't want their sympathy. Not wanting to speak to anyone, he kept his eyes stayed on the ground and hurried to his car where he banged on the dashboard and hit the steering wheel.

He rode in silence to Bria's house. That was highly unusual for him. He would normally have music playing from the time he got in the car until he arrived at his destination. He'd even critique his own music during his drive time.

When Spade arrived at Bria's house he contemplated driving off. He just didn't have the nerve to face her. He sat in front of her house for nearly ten minutes trying to muster the courage to get out of his car.

"Man, stop," he told himself. "You're a man. You can handle anything that comes your way."

He took a deep breath and got out. As he walked up the driveway he swatted a bee buzzing around him. The pollen count was extremely high today. He felt some of that pollen tickle his nostrils and sneezed.

He stood outside Bria's door, and for a brief moment, he felt awkward. Like he didn't know what he was going to say. He rang the doorbell twice to let her know he was there. When she didn't answer quickly enough for him, he used the spare key she had given him for emergency purposes—which he never used—and walked in.

"I was just about to let you in," Bria said as she made her way into the foyer. She seemed happy to see him and kissed him on the lips. "My mom finally found her outfit! You wanna see it?"

He didn't answer. It took everything in him not to break down. Functioning on autopilot, he went into the family room and she followed.

"Are you all right?" she probed. "You're acting strange."

Spade felt uneasy as he sat down beside her on the light colored couch. He felt jittery, and the faint smile he did have disappeared almost instantly when he thought about the disease living in his body. For a moment he stared at a cobweb breezily dancing in the corner.

He couldn't do it. Them. The wedding. How could he marry her knowing he had been given a death sentence?

"I have something to tell you, and it's not easy for me," he said, holding her hand.

A nervous expression appeared on Bria's face. "You're scaring me."

He exhaled loudly. "I'm sorry." He felt like crying again. No—*screaming*. His emotions were a chaotic jumble of nerves and agony.

She sat quietly, studying his face.

"I can't marry you," he continued. Those were the most difficult words he had ever had to say. Cutting off his leg with a dull blade would probably have hurt less than this, he figured.

"What do you mean you can't marry me?" She snatched her hand away. Her eyes welled with tears. "We've been hanging out together just like we always do. We went on a hot air balloon ride together just this past weekend. How can you wake up today and decide, oh, I don't want to get married anymore? Was all of this a lie?" Her voice seemed to get louder with each word.

Unable to bear seeing the woman he loved so upset, Spade reached for her hand again. This time she didn't pull away. "Please," he pleaded.

"Please?" she repeated incredulously.

"Calm down." He thought it was ironic that he was telling her to calm down when deep down inside he was anything but calm.

She clasped her hands together. "I'm calm, now what?"

He lowered his head in frustration. Expressing himself through words was easy for him, but today, he couldn't think of anything to say. His mind couldn't formulate the thoughts to articulate what was going on with him. Bummer. Especially since he knew Bria deserved an explanation.

She gripped his dimpled chin with her thumb and first finger, tilted his head toward her, and said, "Why are you doing this?"

Unable to look her in the eyes, he turned his head away, forcing her hand to release its grip. "You deserve better." He didn't mean he wasn't good enough for her. Shoot, he was the only man for her. What he meant was that she didn't deserve to be with someone battling cancer. Further proof that his mind wasn't functioning properly. Why hadn't he just gone home? Stupid.

"Are you seeing someone else?" Her voice trembled. He could tell that she was trying to be strong and hold back the tears.

"No, no." He shook his head. Since they had been together he hadn't even entertained the idea of seeing anyone else. Bria was "it" for him.

"I thought you loved me." Her eyes begged for the explanation he desperately wanted to give her but couldn't.

"I do love you, more than anything else in this world," he said sincerely. His heart raced as he hugged her.

Her tears wet the left side of his cheek as her face pressed against his. "What's wrong?" she asked barely above a whisper.

"I know you deserve some answers, but I can't deal with this right now." He had too much going on at one time, and he felt himself getting angry. Not at her, just the situation. He needed time to sort through this thing. "It's over. Trust me, it's for the best." He looked her in the eyes. "I'm not doing this to hurt you. I'm doing this because I love you." He stood up, ready to leave.

He wanted to tell her the truth about his disease, but he didn't want to put that burden on her. One thing he knew about Bria was that she was loyal to a fault. When she committed herself to something, she went all in. He knew that she'd stay with him no matter what, but his heart wouldn't let him put her through that. She was young with so much to look forward to. She shouldn't have to worry about a terminally ill boyfriend.He didn't want her pity. What if he had to do chemotherapy? He wasn't about to let her see him all weak and busted like that. No way! He'd rather her not see him at all.

And so it was.

Five

Bria looked into Spade's eyes, hoping that the expression "the eyes are the windows to the soul" was true, because she needed answers. Spade's dazzling brown eyes that usually sparkled and made her fall in love with him time and time again seemed devoid of any happiness. In addition to the painful sadness they revealed, they were horribly bloodshot. She could see that he was upset. She wondered what could've happened.

She searched her mind trying to find a hint as to what could've caused Spade to behave this way, and she came up with nothing. None of this was making sense to her.

"Here." She took off her one-carat diamond and white gold engagement ring and handed it to him. As much as she loved her engagement ring it meant nothing if Spade didn't want her to be his wife.

Breaking eye contact with her, Spade looked down at the floor and said, "You can keep the ring."

Her jaw dropped. *That's it?* she thought. She felt angry. Her eyes narrowed, and giving him a scathing look, she hissed, "Why won't you talk to me? Something is wrong! I can feel it." She wiped her face.

He stood up, turned his back to her, and paused as if he had something else to say. She waited, hoping he would turn around and tell her he didn't mean it.

When he didn't say anything she said, "What am I supposed to tell my family and friends?"

Apparently at a loss, he raised his hands in the air and sighed. "I don't know." Then he dropped his head and headed toward the front door.

"Wait! Did I do something?"

"No. You didn't do anything. I never meant to hurt you."

She was tempted to beg him to stay, but she remembered hearing Oprah talk about the man she pleaded with God to bring back, and in the end she thanked God for letting him go. Although she doubted that she would ever be thankful for losing Spade, she didn't stop him from leaving.

She locked the door behind him and allowed the fresh tears that had been hovering around the borders of her eyes to escape. She pressed her back against the door and slid down to the floor. Knees bent and her arms wrapped around to hold them in place, she cried in her lap. She felt hurt, betrayed, angry, and confused. She thought she had done everything right when it came to her relationship with Spade. She was a virgin. And most important, she prayed about her relationship with him. She believed in her heart of hearts that he was The One! This was not supposed to happen.

So many questions resonated in her mind, and she wondered if he ever loved her at all. No, she refused to go there. Of course he loved her. Had he not he wouldn't have put a ring on her finger. And as Steve Harvey had often stated, "If a man loves you, he'll give you a title." Well, Spade had claimed her as his girlfriend, and then his fiancée. He made his intentions known that he planned for her to be his wife. His actions had always been consistent with his words . . . at least until now.

How could he be so insensitive? she wondered. Why did he tell her that the wedding was off the day before the grand opening of her day spa? Did he have such little regard for her that he didn't care about ruining her celebration? She didn't want to believe that, but thinking about his timing made her more furious. No, she couldn't in good conscience call Spade insensitive. Through the years he demonstrated to her on more occasions than she could count how in touch with her feelings he really was. Therefore, whatever "it" was that he was going through had to be of huge, gigantic—no—enormous proportions.

What if she were off base altogether? What if he had changed now that he was about to blow up? Was that possible? She thought about the young girls at Six Flags. What if he didn't want to get married because it didn't go with that whole rapper lifestyle? Everyone knows rappers are known to be promiscuous. Was she in denial?

She tried hard to silence the questions that plagued her mind as exasperation engulfed her. *The insanity of it all!* she fumed. She hated having more questions than answers. It made her feel vulnerable, which was something she tried not to do.

She wiped away her tears and continued to try to quell the questions that gnawed at her psyche. Spade's behavior today was totally inconsistent with the man she thought she knew and loved.

"Snap out of it," she said aloud. So many memories. She had to force herself to stop thinking about Spade, because she was making herself more depressed by the second.

Even though she felt like crawling into bed and never getting out, she knew that she couldn't do that. She needed a pep talk, and Nya was just the person to do it.

Without so much as a "hello" or "how are you doing?" as soon as she heard Nya's voice on the other end of the phone she blurted out, "The wedding is off."

"What? What happened?" Her voice went up an octave.

Bria could not even get the words out without bursting into tears.

"I'm on my way," Nya assured her before hanging up the phone.

Less than thirty minutes later, she was knocking on Bria's door with a bag filled with Butter Pecan ice cream and a box of Kleenex.

Bria looked at her five foot two inch, twenty pounds overweight friend through rheumy eyes. Nya seemed to carry most of her extra pounds in her butt. She brushed past Bria, and her scent could only be compared to the yellow puff flower balls on an acacia tree.

Bria put the ice cream in the freezer and carried the box of Kleenex into the living room where she cried and recapped her conversation with Spade.

"I'm in shock right now," Nya said. "In all the years I've known Spade, one thing I was always convinced of is that not only does he love himself some Bria, he really likes you. I don't know what's going on, but this is way out of character for Spade." She paused. "If you ask me, Spade's acting like a punk and a coward. What's his number? I'm about to call him!"

"Don't do that." Bria found herself trying to calm Nya down. "It won't do any good." The last thing she wanted was for anyone to try to guilt Spade into being with her.

"Somebody needs to talk some sense into that negro."

Bria flopped on the sofa simply broken.

"Do you want me to have Chance talk to him?"

Was she kidding? Although Chance and Spade were cool, even friends, Chance considered Bria to be like his little sister. His loyalty was to her. Knowing that Chance could be somewhat of a hothead, and Spade such an alpha male, she didn't think that was a good idea. Although Bria was highly upset with Spade, she didn't want to risk an altercation between the two of them. Besides, she wasn't fully convinced that she and Spade wouldn't reconcile. She didn't want Spade and Chance to have any issues between them later.

"No," she said.

"What about all the money you've spent on this wedding? Is he going to pay you back?"

"Correction . . . all the money my *parents* have spent on this wedding." She rested her head on Nya's lap. "No, I'm not going to ask him to."

Nya rolled her almond-shaped eyes and sighed. "That's crazy. Don't let him off the hook that easy."

Bria felt the need to explain herself. "If he doesn't want to be with me, then I'm not going to be vindictive."

Bria figured that her man must've be going through something pretty heavy and needed some time to pull himself together. So, rather than accept the cancellation of their wedding and move on with her life, she was going to contact everyone and let them know that the wedding had been postponed until further notice. And she was determined to stick by her man's side . . . whether he wanted her to or not.

"That's so you." Nya raised a brow and smirked. "But if it were me, I wouldn't let it go that easy."

Unable to take any more of Nya's lecturing, Bria went into the kitchen and fixed them each a bowl of ice cream. Knowing the severity of the situation, she ignored the dainty and appropriate dessert bowls and took out the mega-sized ones. They sat around the island, eating their emotions.

"I'm sorry this happened. I know how much Spade means to you."

Bria nodded in agreement and ate a spoonful of ice cream.

"This is one time that I wish I were a guy," Nya said, "because I'd kick his behind myself. How dare he hurt you like this!"

She knew that Nya was serious. "I appreciate that." Bria let out a nervous laugh, the kind from the throat and not the stomach. On the surface, she could make light of the threat, but deep inside the very core of her person, tiny bits of her heart kept being chipped away.

"Do you want me to spend the night?"

"No, you've only been married six months. I don't want to come between you and your husband." In spite of her recent situation, Bria still had the utmost respect for love and marriage.

Nya leapt up and strode around the island to embrace Bria affectionately, wrists jingling with bracelets and bangles. "You're my girl, and I knew you long before I ever had a man. You know that I love Chance to death, but true girlfriends are hard to find. If you want me to stay, just say the word."

Bria offered a faint smile and again declined the offer.

Nya snapped her fingers. "I just remembered that Chance and I are supposed to go out to dinner tonight. Let me call him and tell him I can't make it." She grabbed her cell phone.

It seemed to Bria that Chance's favorite pastime was eating. He was a big dude, and Nya had easily packed on fifteen pounds in the eighteen months since she'd known him. Before Nya could touch the screen Bria said, "No, but I do appreciate your willingness to cancel your plans for me. I want you to go and have a good time. No sense in both of us sitting around being miserable. Don't worry about me." She meant it.

"I can't help it. You're the closest thing I have to a sister. I love you, and I don't want you moping around acting all depressed."

Acting depressed? It wasn't an act, Bria resolved. She forced a smile and said, "I love you too. Honestly, I'll be fine. I'm starting to feel better already."

Nya kissed her on the cheek and said, "Liar. You don't have to put on a brave face for me."

"I know. I'll call you if I feel like slitting my wrists or popping pills," she teased. No matter how sad she felt, she knew that suicide wasn't an option. The very act of taking one's life went against her spiritual beliefs.

"Don't joke about stuff like that because I'd have to take you to the *Pet Sematary*."

They both laughed, because *Pet Sematary* was one of their favorite horror movie classics.

Bria walked Nya to the door. They hugged, and Nya said, "I'm praying for you."

Unlike so many people who lie and say they'll keep you in their prayers, Bria knew that when Nya said she was praying for her, she actually meant it. They prayed for each other all the time.

"Everything's going to be all right," Nya promised her.

Bria closed the door behind her and asked of no one, "Can you assure me of that?"

After calling off his engagement, Spade spent the rest of the night sulking. He just moped around his condo in a daze. He didn't eat. He didn't take a shower. He didn't even brush his teeth. All he did was lounge around in his bed. When he did get up, it was to go to the bathroom or sip some water. He didn't answer his phone or turn on the TV. No music either.

He knew that he couldn't avoid his mom longer than a day without her calling half of the town looking for him. He didn't want her to mess around and call Bria. He finally mustered up the courage to tell his mother that the wedding was off. Knowing his mother as well as he did, he needed some super-duper industrial-strength courage to deal with her. One would've thought she was an amateur detective the way she asked question after question.

When he called his mom and heard her voice, he felt like hanging up, but he didn't. "Hey, Mom. I have something to tell you."

"Oh, Lawd. That doesn't sound good at all. What's going on?"

He paused before answering, "Bria and I aren't getting married."

"What happened?" He had to pull the phone away from his ear. "Are you all right?" Her concern was evident.

He closed his eyes and squeezed the bridge of his nose. "I can't go into that right now."

She went from concerned to demanding. "Boy, what do you mean you can't go into it? You better tell me something. What have you done? I thought you loved that girl."

He felt like a steak—about to be grilled. "I do love her."

"Then talk to me." She paused for a moment, and when Spade didn't volunteer any information she continued, "I don't think you cheated because one, you love her, and two, I raised you better than that. I don't believe you caught her cheating because you're *my* child, and you'd be calling me from jail if you had. So the only other things that make sense are you're either running from the law or you're dying. Which is it?"

His mom was so logical, it drove him nuts! He hated when she played amateur detective. Why couldn't she just let this go? "Look, Mom, you know I love you, but I'm not ready to talk about this. I have to go." He hung up. He expected her to blow up his phone, but she didn't. And he was glad.

Six

Bria woke up early Saturday morning so that she could pray and meditate. "Geez, Louise," she said, looking into the mirror in her luxurious bathroom where Tocca candles burned and eau de parfumes adorned granite surfaces in pretty glass bottles. Bria loved beautiful things: a strutting peacock, hot toast and lashings of melting butter and honey, the ripple of a brook, birds chirping, sunlight warming her bare feet, white sandy beaches, and waterfalls. Most of all, Bria loved love, for nothing was more beautiful to her than that.

Her eyes were as billowy as marshmallows from all the crying she had done since her breakup yesterday. She pressed a chilly, wet washcloth over her eyes for a few minutes and brushed her teeth. Satisfied that only time would erase the vestiges of her sorrow, she went downstairs into the kitchen and cooked.

Over breakfast she read the *Atlanta Journal-Constitution*, or as it was more familiarly referred—AJC. Then the phone rang and interrupted her. She almost didn't answer when she saw Spade's mom's name pop up, because she didn't want to burst out crying. But, she answered anyway.

"Bria, sweetie, are you okay? My son told me what happened."

Bria hoped Spade had told his mom more than he had told her. Maybe she'd be able to shed some light on the situation. "I'm still in shock but hanging in there."

"I just wanted to call to let you know how sorry I am. If there's anything I can do, please don't hesitate to ask. Do your parents know?"

Bria dreaded having that conversation with her parents. Not wanting her parents to worry, she decided to postpone telling them about her broken engagement until after the grand opening. "No, I haven't told them yet. I want to wait until after the grand opening."

"Oh, I see." She sounded shocked herself. "Well, when you finally do tell 'em, please let them know how sorry I am about everything. You and my son belong together. I don't know all that happened, but I've been praying for y'all. You know you'll always be my daughter no matter what."

"Thanks. I appreciate that."

"Don't give up on my son."

She acted as if Bria had a choice. Spade had given up on her. She hadn't given up on him.

"Sometimes couples go through rough patches, but for the sake of love you work it out."

"That's just it," Bria whined. "We weren't going through any rough patches. We were happy and in love. At least that's what I thought. This came out of the blue. And I still don't know what happened."

"Whatever it is, he'll tell you when he's ready. Just let him work through it. I know my son; he'll be back. Don't think for a minute that he doesn't love you; he does."

Bria's heart ached hearing Spade's mom defend him. She sounded so confident that Bria wondered if she knew more than she was letting on.

When they finished talking, Bria put her food away. Her appetite was gone. She felt tense and stressed again. The only thing she knew to do was to run on the treadmill for forty-five minutes, so she put on some workout clothes. While in the guest bedroom she had a moment.

That was the same room she was going to let Spade turn into a gym. Spade had become such an integral part of her life that she didn't feel as though she could ever escape him. She dropped to the ground and did one hundred crunches. She touched her tight abs and felt a tinge of sadness. Spade loved to rub her flat stomach and would often pretend to talk to the baby he wanted to someday plant there. She bit her lower lip to stop it from quivering. Her face was kissed with sweat, so she blotted it with a towel.

Her phone was hot, she thought as it rang. This time it was her mother calling. She took a deep breath before answering.

"Hey, Mom." She hoped her mom wouldn't pick up on the sadness in her voice. "You and Dad are still coming to the grand opening, right?"

"Yes. I wanted to know where we're supposed to meet you."

She gave the information. "I just finished working out. I need to go take a shower."

"Okay. See you tonight. Love you."

"Love you too."

Although she did have to take a shower, that wasn't the complete truth. Knowing that the breakup had taken a toll on her she kept her conversation with her mom short. She wasn't good at faking and didn't want her mom to pick up on the emotional turmoil in her voice. She silently prayed that everything would go according to plan and that the grand opening would be a success.

Bria went into the master bathroom and took off her workout clothes. She stepped into the steamy shower and allowed the hot water to pulsate against her soft skin, slowly alleviating her stress.

After taking her shower, she moisturized her body before slipping into a long satin robe. She sprinkled a dab of fish food into the fifteen-gallon tank residing in her bathroom. There were roughly ten goldfish thriving in their Lucite home.

With a few hours before the grand opening she did not want to do much of anything except relax. Chamomile tea always seemed to calm her nerves, so she went downstairs, filled her favorite black-and-white bovine-motif teakettle with water, and placed it on the stove over a high open flame.

While she was waiting for the water to boil, the telephone and doorbell rang simultaneously. Since she wasn't expecting company, she contemplated not answering the door. The phone rang again, so she grabbed the cell phone and walked to the door to answer it too. It was Nya on the phone.

Holding the phone to her ear, she looked through the peephole and saw a man dressed in a baseball cap, Polo shirt, Windbreaker, and khakis pants carrying a huge bouquet of multicolored roses. After telling Nya to hold on, she held the phone in her left hand and opened the door with her right.

"May I help you?" she said as the teakettle whistled loudly from the kitchen.

"I have a delivery for Bria Murray."

She signed for the order and thanked him before taking the flowers into the crook of her arm and saying, "Hold on a sec. I'll be right back."

She placed the vase and telephone on the antique white colored island, turned off the stove, and went into the family room where her Michael Kors bag was sitting on a glass end table. She then grabbed a few dollars from her wallet and gave the delivery man a tip.

She went back into the kitchen and resumed her telephone conversation.

"Who sent *you* flowers?" Nya said, emphasizing the word you.

"Don't sound so shocked."

Bria removed the small card that was neatly tucked between the roses and read aloud.

Congratulations on your big day. I love you.
Spade

What in the world? Her head was reeling. She paused and felt confused to learn that the beautiful arrangement was from Spade. How could he send her flowers when she hadn't heard one word from him since he had broken her heart? Was he trying to torture her? Why would he do that?

"Don't let that get you down," Nya scoffed. "We have too much to look forward to today than to allow the enemy to get to us."

By enemy she knew that Nya meant evil forces and not Spade per se. Bria was glad that she had chosen Nya to be her PR director. That way, Nya could do most of the talking at the event. Because based on how Bria was feeling at that moment, she did not think she could handle it herself.

"I'm glad you're on my team. Thank God for you." She confirmed the time that Nya and Chance would be arriving at her house so that they could ride to the event together and hung up.

In a tiny spot below her shattered soul, Bria was also excited, she had to admit, because this was her dream come true. She poured hot water over two teabags in her cup. She liked it strong. She allowed the bags to steep for a minute or two before adding lots of lemon, honey, and sugar in the raw.

She stared at the bouquet and thought, *Were these ordered before or after you broke up with me?* It didn't matter anyway, she reasoned. "I'm not going to give you any more of my energy," she muttered aloud.

Inhaling, she took a nice long whiff of the roses. She wasn't about to toss them out, regardless of the situation. She loved the smell of fresh flowers. So much so that she faithfully purchased a bouquet every Tuesday and Friday. And Spade knew that. To her, fresh flowers were a luxury that she refused to live without. They brightened up a room and turned a house into a home.

Taking her tea cup and saucer into the family room, she decided to watch TV because she had time to catch a movie before getting ready. She was pleasantly surprised that the 1975 classic *Cooley High* was on. She loved that flick. At the end she dried her eyes because no matter how many times she watched it, she always cried when Cochise died.

Turning off the flat-screen TV, Bria went upstairs into the master bathroom and pulled her hair back into a long ponytail. She preferred wearing ponytails for numerous reasons. One, she thought she looked chic. Two, it showed off her oval face and delicate features. Three, her hair hung down her back past the bottom of her bra strap; therefore, slicking it back was convenient. And, of course, four, with it being so hot in Atlanta a ponytail was literally the coolest hairstyle she could rock.

Then she applied her makeup. She only wore MAC brand, because she loved the matte finish. Before putting on her lipstick, she brushed her teeth and gargled, again. According to Bria, fresh breath was a beauty essential. Then she dabbed J-Lo's perfume behind her ears, her neck, on her cleavage and inner thighs. She preferred to wear fragrances that weren't too strong, because she didn't like the scent to linger in the air. Like most people living in and around Atlanta, she suffered from sinus problems and allergies mostly due to the dangerously high pollen, grass, and weed count.

She was primped and preened, powdered and perfumed, and stuffed into a long black form-fitted backless lace and satin gown with a plunging neckline. She felt sexy and thought she looked elegant. Black open-toed shoes accented her French pedicure.

Not long afterward, the doorbell rang. She figured that it was Nya and Chance, so she grabbed her matching clutch purse and wrap. She greeted them at the door with their usual hugs and kisses on the cheek. Nya's sexy black glitter gown caught her eye.

"Work it!" Bria teased. "You look beautiful." With her hair pulled up she thought Nya's round face appeared more oval.

"Thanks. So do you." She adjusted the sheath around her meaty shoulders. "My shoes are already pinching my toes."

Bria chuckled. She glanced at Nya's open-toed rhinestone shoes, exposing her freshly painted red toenails. For those shoes, she would've endured some pain too.

Chance stood approximately six feet tall, complete with a spare tire around the middle, and dressed in a black tuxedo looking like a penguin. She couldn't decide whether his bald head reminded her of a Milk Dud or chocolate M&M. His goatee was neatly trimmed and full lips curled at the ends. He looked decent for thirty-two, she figured.

"We look like we're going to the Grammy's," Bria commented. As soon as she said it she regretted it. Her thoughts immediately went to Spade. They had often talked about attending the Grammy's together in hopes that Spade would one day be nominated for one.

"Almost," Nya said. "Wait until you see the limousine."

Bria liked riding in limos on special occasions and tonight was no exception. Outside waiting for them in the driveway was a Baby Bentley limo. Bria was impressed. She locked the door behind them. The driver opened the car door for them, and they sat in back on plush leather seats.

"I could get used to this," Bria said.

Nya gave her a dimpled smile, and Chance nodded in agreement. Bria enjoyed the smooth ride as she checked out the amenities. She noticed that there was a wet bar, TV, and DVD player. She wished that Spade could have been there with her. Then she made up in her mind that she was not going to go there.

She did not converse much during most of the ride, because Nya chatted enough for everyone.

They arrived at The Spa Factory an hour and a half early to ensure that everything was in place. Bria couldn't believe her place of business was about to be open for business.

The driver opened the door for them, exposing them to the red carpet that led to the entrance of the building and a huge red ribbon wrapping the front like a present. Photographers were positioned outside waiting to snap pictures of the guests. They stopped and posed for the cameras. Bria felt like a celebrity. She used to fantasize about walking red carpets with Spade.

When she went inside Bria met with her office manager, Dani, who oversaw the setup. Dani was in her late twenties, had an MBA, and five years of spa-related experience. She looked very stylish, yet professional.

"Were there any problems?" Bria queried as she took in her surroundings. Flickering candles strategically placed throughout the room emitted a very pleasing scent of cinnamon with a touch of vanilla.

"Not a one."

Bria felt confident that that was true because she compared Dani to a quiet storm. Dani appeared non-threatening and unassuming, but if you underestimated her, you were in for a rude awakening.

"Glad to hear it."

Bria left her alone and went to check on the food, catered by Justin's Restaurant & Bar. She was pleased with the display consisting of catfish fritters, baked crab cakes, chicken saté, and New Zealand BBQ lamb chops.

The feast smelled delicious and looked appetizing. Another table consisted of fresh fruit, raw vegetables, an assortment of cheeses, and a variety of dips. A chef dressed in traditional chef's attire stood behind a table prepared to carve a succulent-looking roast. The waitstaff and bartender wore traditional white tuxedo shirts and black bow ties with matching vests and slacks, which also met with her approval. Bria loved it when a plan came together.

A short while later Bria's parents arrived, and she greeted them with hugs. Her dad looked distinguished in his tuxedo with a black and gold designed vest to spruce it up. His salt-and-pepper hair, moustache, and laugh lines added character, Bria thought.

Bria didn't get many opportunities to see her parents dress up, so when they did she marveled in it. Her mom looked stunning too with her hair loosely pulled up into a bun, a perfect fit for the gold suit accentuated by rhinestone buttons on the jacket. Bria thought her mother looked sophisticated and classy. She represented women of a certain age well.

"Where's Spade?" her mom asked, looking around the room.

Bria's heart sank. She wanted to slink into the corner and disappear into the wall. Clearing her throat, she responded, "He, um, had a conflict, but he sent some gorgeous flowers."

"Oh." She sounded surprised and disappointed. "I guess this is what you'll have to look forward to being married to a musician."

Her mother's words felt like a stingray stabbing her in the chest and piercing her heart. Bria checked her dressy designer watch that her parents had given her for her twenty-first birthday. They told her that every woman should have some good pieces of jewelry, especially her timepiece.

"Time to meet the public," she said.

Bria and Nya stepped outside. As the invited guests started arriving, they greeted everyone with handshakes. The guests seemed excited and eager to enter. And Bria noticed a crowd was beginning to form.

"Are you ready?" Nya whispered in Bria's ear.

She drew a deep breath and slowly released it. "As ready as I'll ever be." Bria stood in front of the door and thought about how special this moment was for her. People showed up to support her vision. That meant a lot to her.

"Welcome to The Spa Factory!" Her voice projected confidence and enthusiasm. Thank goodness she didn't look like what she was going through. "I want to thank you all for coming out tonight to join us in celebrating our grand opening. I hope the traffic wasn't too bad."

There were some chuckles and rumblings before the crowd applauded. Bria flashed a warm smile. Next, she introduced the mayor who made a brief speech before assisting Bria with cutting the red ribbon in front of the spa.

"The doors are officially open," Bria announced. "Come on in and tour the facilities. We have food and drinks for everyone."

The stampeding crowd passed her like a herd of nimble gazelle. The dimly lit room smelled like vanilla as Bruno Mars's song "Treasure" played in the background. For the moment, Bria was out of her funk and felt like socializing. She mingled with the guests and made sure they were comfortable. The waitstaff walked around offering champagne and hors d'oeuvres. She was glad that the staff was attentive to the guests, and everyone appeared to be having a good time.

Mini massages were available. A robust lady had her eyes closed and appeared to be a head nod away from falling asleep as the massage therapist kneaded her shoulders like dough, Bria noticed.

"I've been looking for you all evening," a man whispered in Bria's ear, startling her.

She turned around and said, "Oh? Do I know you?"

"I'm Kerryngton. Kerryngton Kruse."

Bria guessed he was older than she was. Not because he looked old, just that he conducted himself like a more mature man. If she had to guess his age, she'd say somewhere around thirty.

Extending a hand to him, she said, "Nice to meet you."

He took her hand and gazed into her eyes. His stare sent a chill through her body. She almost shivered. Although she had never met him before in her life there was something oddly familiar about him, but what? She couldn't quite figure it out. She released his hand and said, "Are you having a nice time?"

"Better now that I've had an opportunity to speak with you."

She tried to figure out his game because she thought he was cooler than the actor Morris Chestnut in the movie *The Best Man,* or her mother's all-time favorite Denzel Washington in *Mo' Better Blues*. Regardless, he had swagger with a capital "s." He acted like he knew her, and that caught her off guard. At this point, she was not sure whether she should be suspicious or intrigued.

He smiled, revealing beautiful white teeth and congratulated her.

She thanked him and politely said, "It was a pleasure, Kerryngton."

Grabbing her hand he asked, "Will I see you again, Ms. Murray?"

His attention was like sunshine, and she basked in the delicious warmth of it. He had totally disarmed her. She was at a loss for words. Even though she was broken-hearted from her breakup with Spade, she wasn't blind and thought that Kerryngton was very good looking. She was tempted to give him a business card, but felt as though she was being unfaithful to Spade, so she did not. She pried her hand away from his, and before she could walk away, he handed her his card instead. She studied the black card with gold lettering and when she looked up, he was gone.

That was smooth, she thought, grinning from ear to ear. Her father had often schooled her on the ways of young men. If a guy had a way of making a woman eat out of the palm of his hands, her dad would say, "That joker's a smooth operator." From what little she could tell about Kerryngton, he certainly qualified. Now she was the one standing there thinking about him. She momentarily left the crowd and placed his card in her contemporary-styled office on top of her desk. Then it dawned on her. How did he know her last name? She hadn't told him that. She had a feeling that she would be seeing him again.

Seven

Spade needed to work to get his mind off of his cancer and Bria. He booked some studio time to work on his CD. He had a hard time focusing on work even though he spent most of his time in the studio hoping to get inspired. With everything going on he hadn't been able to eat, sleep, or concentrate. Bria had been on his mind even more than his condition. He tried to throw himself into his work, but he couldn't get into it. When he tried to write a song, everything sounded the same . . . like a country love song. He had it bad and couldn't stop pining away for Bria. Even when he tried to do freestyle raps he noticed that his timing wasn't right. His heart just wasn't in it.

"Man, what's up with you tonight?" his sound engineer asked.

Spade took off his headset and sulked. He thought going into the recording studio would help get his mind off Bria, but he was wrong. He kept wondering how the grand opening was going. Tempted to call Bria just to let her know he was thinking of her, he mentally reprimanded himself for being so selfish. Hearing her voice would make him feel better, but he knew hearing his would upset her. He didn't want to confuse the situation any more than he had already done. Tonight was a big deal for Bria, and he made the difficult decision to stay away. He just hoped and prayed she would be able to forgive him someday.

"I don't know. I'm just not feeling it," he finally admitted.

"I thought tonight was your girl's grand opening. Why are you here instead of there?"

Spade didn't think he could feel any worse than he already did, but this line of questioning made him sink to a lower level of low. At the time when he made the spur-of-the-moment decision to break up with Bria he had forgotten all about the opening of her spa. He thought he was making the ultimate sacrifice for the sake of love. He wanted to spare her, even if it meant breaking both their hearts. Instead, he realized that not only had he deeply hurt the woman he loved, he quite possibly ruined one of the most important nights of her life. He felt like a complete and utter jerk.

Although he wasn't surprised that Bria hadn't called him to acknowledge the flowers he had sent her, he still felt disappointed. He had ordered those flowers weeks ago just to make sure they'd arrive on time for Bria's big event the second weekend in May. At the time, he hadn't wanted to risk the chance of him forgetting or getting too busy to place the order. He wondered if he had made matters worse. *Since when did being thoughtful turn out to be a bad thing?* he thought. Right about now, Spade felt like if it wasn't for bad luck he wouldn't have any luck at all.

He shook his head and his muscular shoulders slumped just a bit. "Man, we broke up," he blurted out.

The sound engineer turned down the music. "What happened?" His New York accent was more evident than ever.

Spade could tell that what he was really asking was, "What did you do to mess this up, man? How did you blow it with one of the finest women in the A?"

Anyone who had ever seen Spade with Bria knew she was the best thing that ever happened to him. By nature, Spade could come off as straight to the point and hard core. Bria helped him to find the good out of life. She exposed him to art museums, plays, walks in the park, and sushi. She had him literally smelling flowers.

Before he could give a response, a big-name producer assigned to work on Spade's CD came into the studio with his entourage. They wore hoodies with baggy, saggy jeans, the latest kicks, and talked loudly. At first glance, they looked like a bunch of thugs ready to snatch and run. But in reality, they were rich and accomplished in the music industry.

The sound engineer gave him a look that let him know he didn't have to give an answer right then, but the conversation wasn't over.

The entourage had hot wings, french fries, sodas, bottles of booze, bags of the best marijuana money could buy, and the nefarious drug Molly.

As soon as Spade saw the weed he tensed up. Back in the day he used to be a bona fide "weed head." He smoked weed every day from the time he was fifteen to eighteen years old. Most of his teen years were spent in a haze. Like a lot of people he didn't see anything wrong with getting high. Nearly every guy he knew got high.

His grandmother had told him, "Smoking marijuana is just a momentary escape from life and doesn't solve your problems. Getting high only compounds your problems. Satan wants to keep you in bondage to marijuana; God wants to set you free."

He had justified it because it was a plant, grown from the earth. "How bad could it be?" he had told her.

"Baby, yes, God did create the plant marijuana comes from. However, God never ever intended for you to dry the plant out, go buy a pack of plastic Ziploc bags, crumble the dried plant in the rolling paper, roll it up, and smoke it. That's a perverted use of God's creation."

He wanted to laugh because he wondered how his grandmother knew so much about it. He knew she would've slapped the sound straight out of his mouth if he dared disrespect her by asking. Instead, he defended, "It's safer than cigarettes and alcohol."

"First of all, it's illegal. The only reason you smoke marijuana is to get that 'high' feeling. God wants us to have a sound mind, not an altered mind! When you're high you're not able to think clearly."

Spade still wasn't convinced.

"Listen to me, Spade. I'm not going to keep lecturing you. I'm going to pray for you, because what you do in your early years will have an effect on your later years. You may not care now, but one day when your short-term memory is gone you can think back to these times."

His grandmother's concerns weren't enough to stop him, though. It wasn't until he met Bria and she told him that she didn't date guys who smoked weed that he stopped. She meant so much to him that he willingly cleaned up his act. He hadn't lit up since. And then he realized that everything his grandmother tried to tell him was true. Whenever he had difficulty remembering something, he wondered if it was a side effect of his years of getting high.

"Hey, I'm not trying to be funny," Spade told the guys in the studio, "but I don't feel comfortable with y'all having drugs in here. If the cops roll up in here, I'm not trying to catch a case." The look on his face let everyone know that he was serious. He didn't have a criminal record, and he wasn't trying to get one. Plus, the police department seemed to have a special task force dedicated to busting rappers. He didn't want to give them any reason to bust him.

There were four things Spade didn't play with and that was his relationship with God, his freedom, his money, and his love for his woman.

The producer nodded in his direction and instructed the guy with the ganja to get it out of there.

One thing Spade hated about the industry was the acceptability and accessibility of drugs. Temptation was everywhere, and he refused to entertain her.

Spade spoke to everybody who spoke to him. The producer offered him some wings and the smell of hot sauce made his empty stomach growl. He accepted the wings and an individual basket full of crinkled fries with lots of ketchup. He didn't realize how hungry he was until he devoured the food.

While licking his fingers he noticed a female walking into the studio. He didn't like women in the studio because they were a distraction.

Dressed in provocative attire, she said, "Hey, I'm Kola. I'm supposed to be singing some of your hooks." Judging by her Coke-bottle shape, Spade figured that's how she must've gotten her name.

"Oh, okay."

Some of the guys made catcalls and nearly all of them were eyeing her big boobs and fatty.

Spade turned his attention to the producer and told him his vision for his CD and let him hear some of the new tracks he had already laid down. He knew he was fortunate to be able to give his creative input on his first CD. So many artists complained that the record labels created their sounds and crafted their images with little to no regard for who the artist really was or what the artist really wanted.

Spade knew that he needed to get his head in the game. He was a professional, and he needed to place his personal problems on the back burner and handle the business at hand. If he didn't, he risked losing everything he had worked so hard for. Asking the question, "What would Jesus do?" had become a mainstream slogan, more like a cliché, but his personal mantra when it came to business was, "What would Jay-Z do?" He figured Jay-Z would put his emotions in check and hustle harder, and that's what he was determined to do.

Eight

Bria perused the Sunday paper and felt a sense of accomplishment when she saw an article about The Spa Factory. She thought the picture of her and the mayor cutting the ribbon was a nice touch. She immediately called Nya to share the news.

"We made the Sunday paper," Bria boasted.

"That's exciting. I hardly slept a wink last night with Chance wanting a late-night rendezvous." She yawned, and then apologized.

Bria was so used to hearing about Nya and Chance's love life that she turned a deaf ear. She read the entire write-up to Nya, and they agreed to meet in front of their church at their regular time.

When Bria got off the phone she warmed up a bagel in the toaster and spread a generous amount of whipped strawberry cream cheese on top. She ate upstairs while getting dressed in a dark colored outfit as a TV evangelist sounded in the background, preaching about prosperity.

She laughed when she saw her reflection in the mirror because she had a flashback to her college days. While in college, she favored the color black so much that her wardrobe was exclusively black, and people started calling her Elvira. It did not matter the season. Even her nail polish and lipstick were variations of black. It was not that she was depressed or morbid; she simply loved the hue. Eventually, her mom and Nya took her shopping and convinced her to add some color to her wardrobe.

Hesitant at first, she eventually conceded. She stuck with it after Spade told her how vibrant she looked. His opinion meant a lot to her.

She felt a tinge of sadness thinking about Spade but quickly did a paradigm shift. She thought about the successful opening of the spa and felt somewhat better. She figured that if she and Spade were meant to be, they would be. And she was not going to stress about it anymore.

She grabbed her purse and keys and went to church. She prayed for a good parking spot because she didn't want to mess up her shoes by parking on the unfinished overflow lot filled with dirt and gravel. Sure enough, someone from an earlier service had parked close to the door and was backing out. She mouthed the words "Thank you, Jesus" and whipped her Honda into the spot.

An usher wearing a vest that read, "How may I serve you?" handed her a program at the door. She grabbed it and stood off to the side waiting for Nya and Chance. They arrived ten minutes later, both out of breath. They must've speed walked.

They entered the sanctuary through double doors and took three seats near the front. The services began with prayer, and the congregation stood on their feet. Then the choir gave their rendition of a few selections. The words to the songs appeared on a projector screen, and Bria sang along, raising her hands in praise. By the time the pastor came out to preach his sermon, Bria felt uplifted. When the pastor used the analogy between life and riding an elevator, Bria was not sure where he was going with the message until he broke it down and simplified the meaning.

He said, "When we ask God for something, it's like pushing the button on an elevator. You know it's coming, but you have to wait a moment. And when you're on an elevator that's going up, hallelujah! If you stop on different floors and people tell you they want to go down, let them. You stay on the elevator and keep going up." He used his handkerchief to dab sweat from his brow. "And there will be people who are on the elevator with you who will end up getting off before you reach your destination. Let them. Don't carry people with you who don't believe in where God is taking you."

The message resonated with Bria. She wondered if it applied to her and Spade. Was he not supposed to be a part of her lifelong journey? Had their season together really come to an end?

At the end of service they headed back to Bria's house to talk and watch a movie before it was time to go to her parents' house for dinner. Imagine Bria's surprise when she pulled up and noticed her parents' car parked outside on the left side of the driveway. They never came over unannounced. *What are they doing here?* she thought as she pressed the button on her remote to open the garage door. She hoped everything was okay. She drove in on the right side while Nya and Chance parked behind her outside. Together, they entered through the garage and Bria pressed the button on the wall to close the garage door.

Bria's mom was in the kitchen preparing another one of Bria's favorite dishes, meat lasagna. Her dad was in the family room half-asleep on the couch with the TV watching him. The gentle breeze from the open kitchen window permeated the smell of freshly cut flowers, which Bria loved, and a combination of meat, cheese, and sauce through the air.

"What are you doing here?" Bria asked.

Nya and Chance interjected with their greetings and sat on the love seat.

"Since you usually come to our house for Sunday dinner, we decided to bring it to you."

"That was sweet. Thanks, Mom." Bria hugged her. She offered to help, but Mrs. Murray told her that the meal was almost finished, so Bria joined everyone else in the family room.

"How was church?" her mom hollered from the kitchen.

Bria told her that it was good, as usual, and gave her an abbreviated version of the sermon. Since Mrs. Murray and her husband attended early morning services at a different church, Mrs. Murray reciprocated by telling them about the message she received regarding not being overwhelmed by your blessings.

When Bria's mom announced that dinner was ready, Bria and Nya set the formal dining-room table that seated six and Mr. Murray woke up from his nap. They gathered around as Mr. Murray blessed the food. At the end of the prayer, Chance said, "Eat now," and everyone laughed.

"Everything looks so good," Bria said, her mouth watering.

They each ate a side salad before filling up on thick pieces of lasagna and warm garlic bread, fresh from the oven.

"I'm so glad we finally found the perfect dress for me to wear to the wedding," Mrs. Murray said to Bria. "I was starting to get worried."

Nya choked on her sweet tea, and Bria's eyes got bigger than the gold hoop earrings dangling from her ears.

Swallowing hard, Bria admitted to her parents, "Mom, Dad, I have something to tell you." They stared at her, making her feel uncomfortable. "There isn't going to be a wedding . . . at least not right now."

Mrs. Murray covered her mouth as if someone had smacked her there, and Mr. Murray dropped his fork.

Removing her hand, Mrs. Murray could only mouth, "What?"

"Spade broke it off a couple of days ago."

As soon as Bria said that it happened a couple of days ago, she wanted to recant that statement. The surprised look on her mother's face said it all. Bria could tell that her mom was hurt and disappointed she had not told her about this as soon as it happened.

"Are you all right?" Mr. Murray asked.

Bria nodded her head in the affirmative.

Mrs. Murray got up and gave her a hug. "I don't understand," she said. "What happened? Were you having problems?"

Truth be told Bria didn't understand either. She had spent countless hours trying to figure out what went wrong and came up with nothing every time. "He really didn't say. Just that he wasn't ready to get married."

"Is he seeing somebody else?" Lines formed on Mrs. Murray's forehead.

"He told me he wasn't."

Mrs. Murray took a seat and continued. "Honey, I wouldn't worry too much if I were you. Sometimes men get cold feet." She looked at her husband. "Your dad and I went through a bump in the road before we got married."

"Really?" That was the first time Bria had heard that.

She chuckled. "Oh yes. Your daddy was quite the ladies' man. I went through a lot waiting for him to get his act together."

Bria had always thought her dad was the perfect guy. Hearing this was surprising, and if she was being honest, a bit disappointing.

Mr. Murray stood up from the table. "I'm going to talk to him."

Bria assured her parents that she was fine and they did not need to talk to Spade on her behalf. Mr. Murray wasn't hearing it. He excused himself and said he was going for a drive. Bria knew what that meant. A drive straight to Spade's condo. She hoped he wasn't at home. The last thing she wanted was to see her father on the news for jacking up her ex-fiancé. Not that her father was physically stronger than Spade. Just that Spade had so much respect for her dad that he wouldn't dare lift a finger to harm him.

Apparently everyone sitting at the table thought the same thing, because they finished their meal in silence.

Nine

Spade was headed to the studio, but Mr. Murray had thrown a monkey wrench in his plans. He had rededicated himself to his music. What choice did he have? He needed to take more tests to determine what stage his cancer was in. He couldn't sit around feeling sorry for himself anymore. In the meantime, he couldn't let his career suffer.

A conversation with his sound engineer reeled him back in and helped him remember why he needed to work around the clock writing and recording.

The engineer had told him, "A lot of artists work really hard recording music when they know they're going away for a while. Imagine what would happen if they had that same discipline day-to-day. Tomorrow isn't promised. If people treated every day like it could be their last, people would stop procrastinating. When you think about it, what are you waiting on anyway?"

That was all he needed to get back on track. He hoped and prayed that he would beat his condition, but just in case, he wanted his music to live on.

Judging by the sound of Mr. Murray's voice over the phone and the fact that he insisted on meeting, Spade figured he must have finally wanted to talk to him about his calling off the wedding. He suspected it was coming. He had the utmost respect for Mr. Murray and felt he owed him an explanation for breaking his only daughter's heart. That's why he adjusted his schedule and agreed to meet up.

After all, getting Mr. Murray to trust him enough to give his blessing for Spade to marry his daughter was not an easy feat. By the time Mr. Murray finished grilling Spade about his relationship with his family, his upbringing, his spiritual beliefs, his career goals, fiscal responsibility, and credit score, Spade felt like he should've been awarded a Top Secret government clearance and hired by the CIA. Later, Bria revealed to him that her dad had run a criminal background check and pulled a credit report on him. Spade wasn't upset about that. If he had a daughter, he felt certain he'd be just as protective, if not more.

He looked around his living room and picked up the clothes strewn on the couch and sneakers on the floor. Keeping a clean place hadn't been on his list of priorities lately. He threw the clothes in the dirty clothes hamper and lined his shoes up in his walk-in closet. He didn't want Mr. Murray to think he was a total slob. Then he sprayed the air with freshener to get rid of the musty tennis shoe smell.

Looking in his refrigerator he noticed that the only things inside were bottled water and cans of Red Bull, which he kept stocked to help keep his energy level up. He wasn't big on grocery shopping, so there was no surprise that he didn't have any food. Most of the time he either ate out or stopped by the grocery store to pick up what he wanted when he wanted. Shopping in advance didn't appeal to him, because he didn't know what he'd be in the mood to eat from day to day. He hoped that Mr. Murray had eaten, because he didn't have so much as a cube of cheese to offer him.

The doorbell rang, and Spade suddenly felt anxious. His palms turned blotchy with red spots. He took a moment to get his mind right before letting Mr. Murray in.

"Hey, Mr. Murray, how are you doing?" Spade shook his hand.

"I've been better, son." He made his way to the couch and sat down.

Spade was glad he had gone to church that morning and got prayed up. He didn't know what was about to jump off, but he could tell that Mr. Murray was about the business. He offered him some bottled water, but Mr. Murray declined. Spade sat down too, but he didn't get too comfortable.

Out of the corner of his eye he noticed a thin layer of dust on his wooden coffee table. On a regular day he couldn't have cared less. But the way Mr. Murray came across like he wanted to grind him in a meat grinder made him conscientious of minor details.

"I'm going to get straight to the point," Mr. Murray said in a serious tone. "What's this I hear about you calling off the wedding?"

His right leg started shaking, something that happened whenever he felt nervous. For a brief moment he considered telling Mr. Murray, in a respectable manner, to mind his own business, but he knew that wouldn't go over well. Knowing how close Bria was to her father, he knew that if he stood any chance of getting back with Bria in the future he couldn't alienate Mr. Murray. He needed him to be on his team, so he decided to confide in him.

He leaned forward and pressed his hands together in the praying position. "Mr. Murray, I love your daughter."

Mr. Murray cleared his throat as if to say, "That remains to be seen."

"I didn't used to believe in love at first sight, but I can honestly tell you that I felt something for your daughter the first time I laid eyes on her. Then after I got to know her, I knew in my heart that one day she'd be my wife." He put his hand over his heart, then placed it on his lap. "That was almost seven years ago and nothing has changed." He shook his head. "I love that girl so much that I'd willingly give up my life if it meant saving hers. If she needed a kidney, I'd be the first person in line volunteering to donate mine. That's how much she means to me."

Mr. Murray propped his elbow on the arm of the couch and used his index finger to prop up his head. "If what you're telling me is true, son, then I don't understand what could've happened between you and my daughter that the two of you can't work out."

Spade sighed. "What I'm about to tell you I need you to promise me you won't tell Bria or Mrs. Murray."

"Well," he hesitated, "I don't feel comfortable making a promise like that without knowing what I'm agreeing to."

"I understand that, but I need your word." Spade looked him in the eyes.

He clasped his hands together. "Just tell me this. Did you cheat on my daughter?"

He shook his head. "No, sir," Spade assured him.

"Did you break the law? Are you going to jail?"

"No." He shook his head.

Mr. Murray pressed his back against a sofa cushion. "I can't imagine what it could be, but in that case, you have my word. Now, lay it on me."

Spade told him about his prognosis.

Mr. Murray stood up and paced the stain-free beige carpet. He exhaled. "I'm sorry to hear that, son. Do you know what stage you're in?"

"No, they have to run more tests." He smoothed his fingers over his lips.

Raising a brow, Mr. Murray said, "Did you get a second opinion?"

"Not yet."

"I see." He squeezed the bridge of his nose. "If something happened to you, Bria would be devastated."

"I know."

He stopped pacing and sat back down in his previous spot. "Have you been feeling sick?"

"No. That's the tripped out part. I feel fine. None of this is making any sense to me."

He continued, "I'm glad to hear that you're feeling fine, and I'll be praying for you. Son, this is serious, but you're not giving Bria enough credit. I happen to know she adores you. She's in love with you. She would want to be there for you."

"I hear what you're saying, but I'm a man." He patted his chest. "It's my job to be strong. What if I have to get chemo, and I'm all broke down sick and stuff?" He shook his head. "I can't have Bria seeing me like that throwing up and poopin' on myself. She shouldn't have to be my nurse." That visual popped into his mind, and he shook his head again trying to shoo it away. "No." He sounded firm in his decision. "I'm going to wait it out."

"You're making decisions not just about your future but Bria's future too. I know my daughter, and she's not the type of person to leave you while you're down. You shouldn't deny yourself and her the chance to be together. Life is fleeting and isn't guaranteed to anyone. The fact that you have someone willing to go through the tough times with you is a blessing."

Spade scratched his head. "This isn't just a rough patch in my life. According to the doctor, I could be dead in five years."

"Don't talk like that. God has the final say-so. And even if God calls you home, you shouldn't rob Bria of precious time and memories with you. She would never get over it."

Spade held his head down.

"No matter what happens, you need to trust in the love you and Bria share. She's a lot stronger than you think." He chuckled. "I should know; I raised her."

Spade lowered his voice. "I miss her, but I have to focus on getting better and creating music. I can't give Bria what she needs right now."

Mr. Murray got up and patted him on the back. "I can tell she misses you too. Why don't you consider postponing the wedding but staying in a relationship with her?"

"Mr. Murray, I hear what you're saying, and I respect it. Just let me handle this my way. I'm praying to God that everything works out so that Bria and I can get back together. If I beat this, I'll pursue her with a vengeance." He looked away. "And if I don't, well, it won't really matter because I'll be dead anyway."

"Let me be blunt, you have a distorted view of reality. You've been diagnosed with cancer. If you survive, you'll still have to tell Bria eventually. Especially if you plan on getting back with her. On the other hand, if you don't beat this, Bria's heart would be forever broken. You would've robbed her of precious time that she can never get back. And what about the position you're putting me in? Because of a promise I made to you I have to stand by and watch my little girl suffer. And when she finds out that I knew she'll hate me. You may be willing to live with that, but I can't."

Spade rubbed his eyes. "Sorry."

"And here's some food for thought. What if while you're going through this you wait too long and she meets someone else?"

Spade stroked the lower half of his face. He knew that any man would be lucky to have Bria. Convinced that it was just a matter of time before the sharks smelled blood in the water and circled in for the kill, he became angry at the thought of Bria being with another man. Why did Mr. Murray have to bring that up? He hadn't even considered the possibility of Bria getting with someone else, and the thought of it made him sick to his stomach. What would he do if he lost Bria to some other joker?

Mr. Murray seemed reflective for a moment. "I'll give you six months to tell her."

"Huh?"

"That should be enough time for you to know exactly what's going on with your condition." He paused. "Son, I know you said a test confirmed your results, but don't take that as the gospel. Doctors and all the people working in their offices and labs are human beings. That means there's always room for error. Don't just take what they're telling you at face value. Do your due diligence and get a second or even a third opinion."

Mr. Murray saw himself out and left Spade to his private thoughts. And think he did. What if he had acted prematurely? What if his cancer wasn't in the advanced stages? Or what if the doctor had been wrong and he didn't have cancer at all? Spade owed it to himself and Bria to find out.

Ten

Bria and Nya met at The Spa Factory early Monday morning. They were still on an emotional high that the doors were officially open to the public. Nya loved herself some Bruno Mars and had turned Bria on to the artist. They popped his CD in the player. Nya fixed a fresh pot of chai tea and displayed the fruit trays and Krispy Kreme doughnuts.

In Bria's office, she noticed the business card Kerryngton had given her sitting on her desk. She picked it up and read aloud, "CEO/President, Up and Up Records." According to his card, he worked as a record label executive. *Great!* she thought. *Another person in the music industry.* That was the last thing she wanted or needed. She was tempted to toss his card in the trash, but the image of his radiant smile popped in her head.

She hadn't heard a word from Spade, and her heart broke a little more every day. She wanted to believe in Spade and wasn't ready to move on. She wasn't sure she could ever really move on. She wondered if Spade was even thinking about her.

Nya entered and startled her. Bria stuffed the card inside her desk drawer. She didn't want Nya to see the card and start making a bigger deal out of it than it really was. She knew Nya well enough to know that she'd want every detail of her brief encounter with Kerryngton.

Nya told her that the tea was ready, so they each poured themselves a cup and grabbed one glazed doughnut apiece.

"How're you feeling?" Nya said.

"I've been trying to stay busy and keep my mind off Spade, but it's hard. It's especially frustrating, knowing that he's going through something, and he doesn't feel he can share it with me."

"This is one of those 'Men Are From Mars, Women Are From Venus' situations. Spade has a problem, and rather than talk about it, he goes into a cave, figuratively speaking, of course."

"What am I supposed to do in the meantime?" She licked glaze off her lips.

"Wait and not pressure him. When he's ready to talk, he will. If you try to force it out of him, he'll just go deeper into the cave and take longer to come out."

"When did you become a relationship expert?"

"Girl, marriage is a full-time job. According to the books I've read, you should treat your relationship like a plant. Don't wait until it's withered and dying before watering it."

They laughed. Members of the staff started coming in and interrupting them. Bria told them to help themselves to the refreshments.

For the next few hours, Bria worked nonstop. She and Nya took an hour and a half lunch break and came right back to work. Bria was typing on her laptop when the intercom sounded. It was Dani, asking if she could speak with her. Dani entered the office and stood in front of Bria's desk.

Pushing her glasses farther back on her nose, Dani said, "A guy named Kerryngton Kruse called. He wants you to call him." Dani handed her a pink slip of paper. "I asked if anyone else could help him, and he said it was personal."

"Oh. How did I miss his call?" she wondered out loud.

"He called when you and Nya went out to lunch."

"Okay. Thanks." Bria looked at the paper, then back at Dani wondering why Dani was still standing there. "Please be sure to patch him through the next time he calls."

Dani agreed.

Bria could tell that Dani really wanted to probe deeper and find out what was going on, but when Bria refused to come up off any information, she went back to her workstation.

Bria was curious why Kerryngton had called her and a faint smile appeared across her face. She removed his card from the drawer and studied it again. She considered calling him back but changed her mind. What would she say? Then she placed it in her purse and decided to wait until he called back before speaking with him. *If it's important, he'll call again,* she thought.

A few hours later, Dani's voice flowed through the intercom speaker on Bria's desk. "Kerryngton Kruse is on the line."

"Patch him through please."

Bria took a swig from the bottled water on her desk before answering Kerryngton's waiting call.

"The grand opening was really nice," he said. "Congratulations." His voice sounded nice with just the right amount of bass. She could listen to him all day.

"Thanks. I'm glad you came out."

"For sure. I was just calling to see if you were okay, because I noticed a poignant sadness in your eyes, and you're way too beautiful a woman to have eyes so sad."

"Oh." Bria didn't know quite how to respond to that. "I'm okay."

"Glad to hear that. Well, I know you must be busy with a new business and all, so I won't keep you."

"Thanks for checking on me. That was really nice of you."

"My pleasure. I'll be in touch."

After getting off the call, Bria missed Spade even more. He used to be the person who would call or come by just to check on her. With a single look he could tell if something was bothering her. Why couldn't she figure out what was bothering him?

It was a few days shy of a week since Spade had called off the wedding, and Bria had been left with the daunting task of notifying the wedding guests and vendors. When it came time for her to contact her wedding guests, she wrote out a brief script that read: "I was just calling to let you know that my wedding has been postponed. I'd rather not go into the particulars, but I'll keep you posted." She needed that script to keep her on track and stop her from rambling or falling apart, because the earlier conversations went like this:

"Hey, Bria! You getting nervous about your wedding?"

"Well, uh, that's the reason for my call." Pregnant pause. "We aren't getting married. At least not yet."

"Oh, honey, no." Sadness mixed with pity topped with disappointment. Then the uncomfortable, "You two were so in love. What happened?"

Fighting back tears, "I'd rather not go into that right now. Sorry. I'll talk to you later." *Click.*

She seriously appreciated voice mail so much that day. Nya had warned her that making those phone calls would be difficult—that was an understatement—and to let her do it on her behalf, but Bria insisted. She felt she should be the one to notify everyone. By making the phone calls herself she was sending the message that there was still a chance she and Spade could get back together.

However, she did agree to let Nya contact the vendors. Overall, her family and friends had been so understanding and supportive when she notified them of her changed wedding plans, but that didn't take away the sting. People would still call her back just to see how she was holding up.

She had her good days and her bad.

Eleven

Spade had already started taking steps toward a healthier lifestyle. The first thing he changed was his diet. He started eating more organic and less processed foods. No more white foods—foods made from white flour or refined sugar—for him. And he replaced white rice with brown rice and white pasta with whole wheat pasta. He even enrolled in a yoga class. It helped Def Jam Founder/CEO Russell Simmons find his yen, he figured. Spade was determined to beat this cancer by focusing on his mind, body, and spirit.

He still worked hard, but not in a stressful way. Music became his release, his therapy.

A little over two weeks passed before Spade was able to see the oncologist. The oncologist sent him for blood work and a CT scan, both of which came back negative for any abnormalities. Spade thought that meant he didn't have cancer.

Rather than encouraging Spade, the oncologist discouraged him by insisting, "The previous lab work takes precedence over the lack of other evidence."

"What?" Spade sounded shocked. "If the other tests didn't back up the original findings, isn't it possible that either the first test was wrong, or I don't have cancer?"

"You should seriously begin chemo right away. If not, you'll be dead by the end of the year." The oncologist acted as though he hadn't heard anything Spade had said.

Hearing the oncologist say he'd be dead by the end of the year really pissed him off. Something just didn't seem right to Spade. He thought about what Mr. Murray had told him. "Look, you're not God. You can't say something like that to me. That's some bull—" He cut himself off and inhaled and exhaled loudly. "Is there a possibility that the original lab results could be wrong?" he challenged.

"No. Not a chance."

There was no way Spade was going to accept this as an answer. If this oncologist wouldn't work with him, then he'd find another one who would.

"Are you ready to begin chemo?" the oncologist asked.

"No."

"What are you waiting for?"

Spade wasn't feeling this guy at all. He had lost confidence in him and didn't like his attitude. "I want a second opinion," he stated matter-of-factly.

The oncologist's face flushed, but Spade wasn't the least bit concerned about offending this guy.

"You can, but you're just wasting precious time. You should be getting treatment."

Spade wanted to punch this cocky mofo in the face. This dude . . . All Spade could do was shake his head. Apparently this dude thought he was God with a big G. Well, somebody told him wrong.

In Spade's mind, this wasn't adding up. And before he started such an invasive treatment, he needed to be sure he had what they said he had. He wasn't about to go along with the flow just because this doctor said so.

Bria had spoken with Kerryngton a couple of times. During their first conversation, he'd asked her how business was going and gave her some insight into being an entrepreneur, totally impressing her with his business acumen.

When he called a second time she said, "I'm curious. How did you know my last name?"

"I'd rather not say."

Bria didn't like him trying to be all mysterious. She wondered what was up with that shroud of mystery. She felt like she was at a disadvantage. He knew about her, but she didn't know about him. "Why are you holding back information? It's not fair that you knew about me before we met."

"Honestly, I just think I heard somebody say your name," he assured her.

She wasn't sure whether she believed him. With a smirk she responded, "Uh-huh," and let it go.

Today, though, the conversation took a different turn. "Are you seeing anybody?" Kerryngton asked.

Bria hesitated for a second. She hadn't seen or spoken to Spade in three weeks. This would've been their wedding weekend, and she felt a bit depressed. She was trying to hang on in there, but she was starting to have her doubts about them getting back together. Maybe Spade really was serious about dumping her. They had never gone more than a day without speaking to each other. Every day she was tempted to call but fought the urge by working harder or calling Nya instead.

She hadn't expected it to take this long before Spade told her something—anything. But there had been no change, and she was even more disillusioned.

"No. My fiancé and I broke up," she finally answered.

"Wow. I'd be lying if I said I was sorry to hear that. I mean, I'm sorry if you got hurt, but not sorry that you're single."

"I know what you meant." Bria folded her lips.

"Can I take you out to dinner?"

Bria massaged her temple. She had gone on dates with guys before, but not since she and Spade had become exclusive. She felt conflicted. A part of her wanted to get to know Kerryngton better because he seemed nice enough. The other part of her wondered if she was giving up on Spade too soon.

Right now she needed to preserve herself since Spade had tossed her to the side like yesterday's newspaper. She remembered hearing that the best way to get over a man was with a new man. She reasoned that an innocent dinner wouldn't hurt. Besides, she didn't want to spend her wedding day alone, feeling rejected, eating ice cream.

Twelve

Kerryngton picked Bria up at the spa in his Mercedes-Benz SL-class convertible and treated her to a delicious pan-grilled mountain trout dinner at the upscale Vinings restaurant Blackstone Steaks & Seafood. She thought Vinings was quaint and upscale but felt weird being on a date in that area knowing Spade lived nearby. She prayed not to run into him.

Kerryngton opened doors for her and acted the perfect gentleman. They had reservations and were immediately seated in a cozy booth with soft, inviting lighting. Bria liked the warm wood décor, exposed brick walls, and colorful paintings on the walls.

"How did you end up at the grand opening for my spa?" Bria asked.

He chuckled. "Not trying to sound arrogant, but I'm a novelty in Atlanta. Nothing happens in this city without me knowing about it."

She laughed. "Duly noted."

"Seriously, though, I went because I work with a lot of women and all of them are into spa treatments. I like giving gift certificates as gifts. I wanted to check the spot out first."

She took a sip of her ice water. "How did you get into the music business?"

"When I was a senior in high school I got a job as an intern at a major radio station in New York. All kinds of artists used to come up through there. I became cool and even friends with most of them. I hung out in studios and saw how the artists and producers made the music. Behind the scenes I'd hear the artists complain about not getting paid what they should while the execs made all the money. So, I knew I wanted to be an exec. Like the Wu-Tang Clan said, 'Cash rules everything around me.'" He grinned.

His smile reminded Bria of Song of Solomon, chapter 4, verse 2: "Your teeth are as white as sheep, recently shorn and freshly washed. Your smile is flawless, each tooth matched with its twin" (New Living Translation).

"I was trying to get the money," he added.

Bria nodded. Although the restaurant was full and a local band performed, Bria felt as though they were the only two people in the room.

"After I graduated from high school, I lost my way." He clasped his hands together. "I found out that I was adopted and lost it. I joined a gang, more like a black Mafia. We rolled deep from L.A. to the 'A.' Made a lot of money drug trafficking. I started my label and made even more money. Produced some popular artists too."

At a loss for words, Bria's jaw dropped. Deep down inside she actually felt sorry for him.

"And then I got busted and went to jail for three years."

Suddenly, he wasn't looking so good to Bria anymore.

"While I was gone my label still ran successfully. Everything I had before, I still have it. I've been out of prison for three months."

Three months? "How's it possible that you still have everything? I thought when people got busted for drugs, all of their assets were seized." Bria felt confused.

"Depends." He stared into her eyes. "There are ways around that."

A part of Bria felt like ending the date, but there was something about Kerryngton that held her attention.

Maybe it was his dreamy eyes or rugged good looks, but whatever it was had a hold on her.

"That life is behind me now." He sounded sincere. "I no longer have those affiliations."

So, he's been punished for his crimes, and now he's reformed. Everyone deserves a second chance, right? Bria pondered.

"But you know what?" he said.

"What?"

"Having money isn't what makes me happy."

She gave him a curious look. She found that hard to believe.

"Money gives me options, but now it's all about helping people. To whom much is given much is required. My goal is to directly touch one million lives before I leave this earth."

"How do you plan to do that?" She hung on to his every word.

"I'm glad you asked that question." He seemed more than willing to share his intentions with her. "I started a foundation that helps disadvantaged youth and low-income families. You know how the churches give school supplies to kids in need?"

"Yes." She knew firsthand because she had personally donated items to her church.

"Well, my organization takes that a step further. We give $500 clothing vouchers to 10,000 kids every year for school clothes and uniforms."

Bria thought that was phenomenal. Not only was Kerryngton a shrewd businessman but a philanthropist too. Somehow he had managed to impress her again. "That's incredible."

His face seemed to light up as he talked about helping others. Bria could tell he had a heart for people. He didn't come across as bragging, just thankful to be of service.

"And you know how the recession has caused a lot of people to lose their homes?"

"Yes." Some of the people in her neighborhood had lost their homes due to foreclosures, and she felt sad for them.

"I know I can't help everyone—Lord knows I wish I could—but I do the best I can. Instead of just giving meals during the holidays and toys at Christmas, my foundation identifies 10,000 families with children and pays their mortgages during the months of November and December. That's my way of saying Happy Holidays."

Bria felt all warm and fuzzy inside. That was the sweetest, most generous thing she'd ever heard. "You're very generous, Kerryngton. Have you ever been married? Got any kids?"

"I was married for three years." He cut into his blue cheese lamb chops. "I was young and trying to make it. I thought I could build my career, make a whole lot of money, and then focus on my marriage." He cut a piece of meat and ate it. "Well, my wife had a different view. She wanted me to spend more time with her and stop spending so much time away from home. When I wouldn't, she found another guy who would. She cheated on me, and I found out about it. After that we tried to make it work for our daughter's sake but couldn't. She was only two years old when we got divorced. But you know what?"

"No, what?"

"I don't regret any of it, because I learned a lot. At least I know how *not* to treat a woman."

That got a chuckle out of Bria.

He ate another piece of tender lamb. "My daughter Alexis is the bright spot of my life." He showed her a picture of Alexis on his phone.

"Very pretty," Bria complimented. His daughter had light brown hair that went all the way to her waist. "Look at all that hair." She thought the little girl's hair was gorgeous, like the fairy-tale Princess Rapunzel.

"Her mom's Puerto Rican." He put the phone away. "She's eleven now. Really good kid. Honor roll student, plays the piano and violin, and speaks three languages fluently."

"That's impressive."

"I work hard so that she can have opportunities I didn't have."

Bria could tell that he was a devoted father and that impressed her even more. She had respect for men who actually raised and provided for their children. Never in a million years did she ever think she'd be interested in a guy with a kid, but now she understood why one should never say never.

"Does she live in Atlanta?"

"Yes. My ex and I have joint custody. Our relationship is pretty cool. I bought them a house in Alpharetta, about ten minutes away from mine."

No baby momma drama, Bria reasoned. "That's good." She ate some more of her fish. "So, how old are you?"

He chuckled. "I'm thirty." He stared into her eyes. "Is that too old for you?"

Even if she thought that was too old for her before, she didn't now. "Not at all."

"If I'm overstepping my bounds, just tell me." He paused. "What happened with your engagement?" He seemed genuinely interested.

She told him how abruptly her engagement ended about a month ago, surprising herself with how comfortable she felt talking to him.

"That's pretty recent." He took a sip of Hennessy. "But I'm a patient man. I can wait for you."

He had scored major points with that one. All night he kept her laughing with his wittiness. He held her interest by telling her fascinating stories about the many countries he'd visited and the famous artists he'd worked with. She found him intriguing and hung on to his every word.

As far as Bria was concerned, the time went by too quickly. It was 10:30 p.m. when Kerryngton dropped her off at her car.

"When can I see you again?" he asked.

"When do you want to see me again?"

"As soon as possible. I enjoyed your company."

That made Bria feel good. She felt desirable again. Being rejected by the man she loved had taken a toll on her psyche, no matter how hard she tried to act like it hadn't. She found herself wondering if Spade was still attracted to her. What if he no longer thought she was pretty? Perhaps he didn't find her sexy. When nothing else made sense, she questioned herself.

Bria said, "Maybe we can have lunch one day this week."

"I would like that. Just let me know."

She opened the car door. "Good night." She kissed him on the cheek.

"Call or text me to let me know you made it home safely," he requested.

"I will." She found his concern endearing. She got out and closed the door behind her. Kerryngton waited until she was in her car and pulling out before driving off. *Now that's a man,* she thought.

Bria decided to call instead of text Kerryngton when she got home, because she liked the sound of his voice. Apparently he liked the sound of hers too, because they spent two hours on the phone talking about Bria's love of flowers, the spa, her friendship with Nya, his job, and whatever else they chose to discuss. To Bria's surprise, by the time she got off the phone with Kerryngton she not only felt as though she knew him, but she could see herself dating him.

Thirteen

Rather than going into the office, Bria and Nya decided to work from Bria's house. Bria felt confident with her staff, because they all had previous years of industry experience. She loved working for herself. She enjoyed having the flexibility to work from home and set her own hours. It made her feel free. For Bria, success meant being able to do what she loved and make a decent living in the process. Working strictly for money had never appealed to her. She did not want to put a lot of effort or energy into doing anything that she was not passionate about.

Drinking an Uptown—a combination of freshly brewed ice tea and lemonade—Bria wiped the condensation from the side of the glass and took a swig.

"How was your date with Kerryngton?" Nya asked.

She closed her eyes and sniffed one of the long-stemmed roses—light pink with hot pink trim—Kerryngton had delivered to her doorstep that morning. He wanted to surprise her by having the flowers delivered to her place of business, but when she told him she would be working from home he asked for her address so that he could have something sent to her. Ordinarily, she would not have given her address to someone she didn't really know. However, she felt comfortable enough with Kerryngton to trust him with that information.

She opened her eyes, marveling at the sweet fragrance. The image of Kerryngton's smile flashed on the screen of her mind, leaving her with a warm feeling. "Our date went very well." She filled Nya in on all of the details of their dinner date, including his ex-wife, daughter, and oh, yes, criminal record. "And you better not tell Chance about Kerryngton's record," Bria warned.

"I'm not going to tell Chance, but I want to know, have you lost your mind?" Nya raised her voice.

"Am I detecting some attitude? What's up with that?" She cut her eyes at Nya.

"Yes, you're detecting *plenty* of attitude!" With a smirk, Nya said, "I don't know why you're gushing over this ex-con. I'm not feeling that."

Bria held up her finger. "Hold up, Nya; you're out of line."

"Humph!" Nya ate some of her fruit salad.

"I'm not gushing," Bria lied.

Nya pointed her fork at her. "I can't—and won't—support this. Besides, you're weaving a dangerous web. What happens when Spade comes back?"

She sighed. Why did Nya have to mention him? "I love Spade. Losing him took a chunk out of my heart. I felt like dying. I didn't think I'd ever smile again, let alone be happy. I understand how the original Sparkle felt after Stix left and she told him she was so miserable she didn't think she could get through another second."

Nya said, "I get it. That's some serious misery. But Kerryngton has got way too much going on." She popped a grape in her mouth. "It's bad enough you're acting like his criminal record isn't a big deal, but I can't believe you're okay with Kerryngton having a child. Thought you didn't want to date a guy who has kids."

"I know, right?" She grabbed one of the hot and spicy wings sitting on a plate in front of her and took a bite. "I used to feel like that. I didn't want to deal with anybody's baby momma. But he's such a great guy it doesn't even matter." Bria was taken aback by how much she was gushing over Kerryngton.

"I'm going on record saying that I think you're doing the most. He's not right for you." She looked up at the ceiling, then sighed. "You're going to do what you want to do anyway, but be careful. Rebound relationships can be a mess. They don't usually last."

"I'd hardly call what we have a relationship. We're just getting to know each other. That's it."

Nya grunted again. "When can I meet him?" She raised a brow.

Bria licked sauce from her fingers. "You can meet him tomorrow when he comes to pick me up for lunch."

"Have you told him that you're still a virgin?"

Where'd that come from? Bria eyed her like she had an extra head resting on her shoulders. "No, I have not. That's not the type of thing you just spring on somebody. I'll tell him when the time is right." She lowered her voice. "Who knows? The time may never be right."

Nya paused for a moment. She seemed reflective. "I never told you this before, so I'll tell you now." She looked Bria in the eyes. "When I found out about the covenant that you made as a little girl, I had never heard of anybody having a ceremony vowing to remain a virgin until marriage."

Bria held the purity ring hanging from a necklace around her neck that served as a reminder of her commitment to sexual purity and gave a faint smile. On her wedding night she was supposed to give the ring to Spade as a celebration of promises given and promises kept.

Nya continued, "Then I saw how serious and committed you were, and I wished I had done the same thing. I respect you for staying true to yourself and what you believe in regardless of what anyone else might say. That's why I think you deserve better than this guy."

Bria sighed. She wished Nya would stop with all the Kerryngton bashing. "I'll admit that it's not always easy.

I've been curious, but it's like the Apostle Paul said, 'For it is better to marry than to burn.'"

Nya nodded. "Let's get back to work."

Bria reviewed the numbers from the business. She studied the sales from body massages, body treatments, skin treatments, nail treatments, hair removal, airbrush tanning, injectables such as Botox, and gentleman's services. She would use this data to determine what services she needed to promote more, what services generated the most revenue, and what needed to be changed, if anything. She noticed that spa packages and gift certificates had done very well. She looked at Nya and saw her staring at her.

"What's wrong with you?" Bria rubbed her nose, wondering if she had a bat in the cave.

"Nothing."

She put down her ink pen. "I don't want to fight with you. I don't like it."

"I know. I don't like it either," Nya admitted. "Look at us handling professional business." She shuffled some papers. "You're one of the smartest people I've ever met." She laughed. "I remember when we were in high school and you were our class valedictorian I envied you, because I had to study hard just to get Bs and Cs. Same thing in college, you were cum laude, and I was praying, 'O Lord, just let me graduate.' Eventually, I finished on the five-year plan while you went on to graduate school."

"You're a mess!" Bria chortled. "So, if you're cracking jokes, does this mean we're good?"

"For now. I meant what I said, though."

Bria wasn't going to press the issue. She knew that Nya needed to process the information and work through it in her own time.

Nya checked her watch. "It's four o'clock." She shut down her laptop. "I'm going home to start dinner before Chance gets home."

"Look at how domesticated you've become," Bria teased. "I remember a time when you could barely warm up a microwave dinner. I guess being married to a chef has its perks."

Nya smirked and put her computer in the carrying case. "Don't work all night. Office tomorrow, right?"

"Yes, ma'am."

Bria felt as though she had put in a full day's work and decided to call it a day. She prepared a relaxing bath. Lighting white candles around the edge of the tub, she put on Tamar Braxton's *Love and War* CD and filled up the Jacuzzi tub with warm water and Tahitian milk bath.

While the water was running she went into the kitchen, poured herself a nonalcoholic strawberry daiquiri into a large cocktail glass, and topped it with whipped cream. Then she grabbed her cell phone just in case anyone, namely Kerryngton, called.

Stepping into the tub, she turned on the jets, which heated up the water just the way she liked it.

She found her mind staying on Spade, how much she loved him and wanted to marry him. The moment she laid eyes on him in her freshman year she was attracted to him. He was popular in college, and so many girls wanted him. She remembered playing it cool whenever they attended study group sessions together. It was not until their senior year when he invited her to a movie, without their friends, that she realized he was interested in her personally. She went, and he took her to Piedmont Park afterward where they talked for hours. That night he asked her to be his girl, and she gladly accepted.

She had plans, and her plans included graduating from college, then grad school, marriage, and children. In that order. Spade knew that and said he was cool with it. It wasn't easy for them to abstain, because their flesh would often rise up. They were sexually attracted to each other, but they countered it by going on group dates and staying out of intimate settings, staying busy, and working out at the gym. They wouldn't watch movies containing nudity or sexual scenes. They even joined a "support group" with like-minded Christians to help keep them on their path. That's why they set their wedding date within three months of her finishing up grad school. She never envisioned being twenty-four, thriving . . . and alone.

Then, there was Kerryngton. She couldn't say enough positive things about him. He had the intellect, business acumen, maturity, and humor she liked. The fact that he was easy on the eyes didn't hurt either.

Tears rolled down her cheeks. Her heart still ached for Spade. As much as she tried to fight it, she was slowly coming to accept that she and Spade might not get back together.

An hour later her fingers and toes were wrinkled like newly born Shar-Pei pups, a sign that she had been in the water too long. She did not mind because she preferred taking lengthy baths.

Before drying off, she splashed baby oil all over her body. Slipping into a yellow satin nightgown that complemented her cinnamon skin, she began reading the book *When the Fairytale Ends*. She felt as though her fairy tale with Spade had ended, but Kerryngton definitely seemed to be a knight riding in on a white horse.

Then the phone rang, interrupting her. Remembering that she left it on the side of the tub, she ran into the bathroom to get it. Picking it up, she checked the caller ID and was glad to see that it was Kerryngton. *He must've been feeling my vibes,* she thought.

Fourteen

Every morning Spade started his day reading healing scriptures and praying. His favorite was Psalm 103:1–5 which read: "Bless the LORD, O my soul: and all that is within me, bless his holy name. Bless the LORD, O my soul, and forget not all his benefits: Who forgiveth all thine iniquities; who healeth all thy diseases; Who redeemeth thy life from destruction; who crowneth thee with lovingkindness and tender mercies; Who satisfieth thy mouth with good things; so that thy youth is renewed like the eagle's."

He believed that God was going to perform a miracle and give him a new testimony. He had finally gotten a referral for a different oncologist and felt as though things were starting to look up. As soon as he got an appointment scheduled, he contacted his original oncologist for copies of his medical records to take with him.

Before his appointment, records in hand, Spade began to search the Internet for explanations of every word in his medical records that he didn't understand to see if he could learn more about his condition. To his surprise, after carefully examining his records, Spade noticed a word that he had a difficult time making out. The writing was so bad it was nearly impossible to figure out what it said.

"Well, I'll be . . ." he said in a barely audible tone. All sorts of bells were going off in his head.

To top it off, the lab report stated that the lump biopsy was being sent for another test called "clonality"—yet no results of that test had been included in the records Spade had received. He wondered what clonality was and why those results hadn't been included in his records.

He double-checked the records thoroughly to be certain. Sure enough, no clonality test was there. He immediately contacted his former oncologist's office to find out what was up.

"Sorry, Mr. Spencer, but we have no record of the clonality test," the physician's assistant told him.

"It's in my records," Spade said.

"Let us check into it and get back with you." He verified Spade's contact number and ended the call.

So, while he waited for them to frantically search for the results, Spade looked up exactly what that test was. It turns out clonality determines if all abnormal cells are coming from a single clone. In other words, if the results are positive, the test is strongly suggestive of cancer, such as lymphoma.

He threw up a quick prayer and called Bria's dad to give him an update, which he did after every doctor's appointment and test. Since Mr. Murray was the only person who knew about his condition, he became Spade's confidant by default. Who else could he tell?

"How's it going, son?" Mr. Murray said, sounding as encouraging as he usually did.

"I believe God is getting ready to work something out."

"What's going on?" He sounded curious.

"I got copies of my medical records and stuff looks real shady."

"What do you mean?"

"My oncologist was all convinced that my lab test was the end-all be-all, but no test says outright that I have cancer."

"Son, that's great news."

"I think it is." He thought about Bria and how much he missed her. He studied the framed 5x7 photo of her on the nightstand next to his bed and stretched out on his bed. Putting his phone on speaker, he asked, "How's Bria?"

"She's making it. Even though she doesn't say so, I know she's throwing herself into her work to cope with the breakup." He coughed. "My wife mentioned that Bria went out on a date."

Spade rolled his head on a pillow so soft he thought it could've been a cloud. That was the last thing he wanted to hear, especially since his manager told him he had to take a trip to Europe in just one week and that he'd be gone for fourteen days. Between his health and career obligations he wouldn't have time to get with Bria until he got back.

"I know this isn't what you want to hear, son, but as soon as you get your results one way or the other, you need to call her."

That's exactly what he planned to do. He hadn't spoken to Bria in several weeks and missed hearing her voice. There wasn't a day that went by that he didn't want to call her, but he didn't want to complicate the situation. He needed to get a clean bill of health from his doctor before dragging Bria back into his world. The fact that their wedding date had come and gone didn't make things any easier.

"I will; I'll call her."

They disconnected the call. Spade figured that even if she was seeing somebody else he refused to believe some random guy could be a serious threat to what he and Bria share. He knew Bria better than anybody, and she would not get over him that quickly. He had let her go for the sake of love, and he held on to the belief that same love would bring them back together again. They belonged together and as soon as he was able, he'd tell her.

Fifteen

Kerryngton arrived at The Spa Factory looking casket sharp. From her office window Bria saw him pull up in yet a different Mercedes than the other three he had driven on their previous dates. They had gone to the movies, enjoyed expensive dinners, had a private art showing, went to a movie premiere, and he had even taught Bria how to play golf at the exclusive country club to which he belonged. Bria could tell Kerryngton lived the life of a sybarite, driving his expensive fleet of cars and traveling the world.

The women at the spa, including Dani, came out of their various rooms to the front waiting area just to get a look at him. Bria could hear women making comments like, "I'd like to take a bite out of that piece of chocolate" and "Mmmm, dark chocolate really is good for the body." She just laughed to herself.

Bria and Nya emerged from their offices in the back. Nya's eyes grew wide when she saw him. Bria made the introductions, and Nya extended her hand to him. A true gentleman, he kissed the back of her hand and Nya burst into giggles. She took her hand back and smoothed her relaxed hair behind her ear.

Kerryngton handed Nya a box of Godiva chocolates, her favorite! "Bria told me you like milk chocolate."

Nya took the gold box. "Yes, I do. Thanks so much. That was very sweet of you."

He kissed Bria on the cheek and his gentle, unobtrusive fragrance wafted in the air. "This is for you." He handed her a cube-sized box.

"For me?" She opened the box and pulled out a rhinestone monogram personalized red mug. "Fancy. I like it." She held up the cup for Nya to see.

"Glad you like it. I know you drink coffee or tea almost every day, so . . ."

"That's so thoughtful!" the dark haired front-desk receptionist interrupted as she held her hand over her heart.

Bria had no idea the young lady had been so engrossed in their conversation. "Thanks, Meagan."

Kerryngton simply smiled at Meagan before turning his attention back to Bria. "Ready to go?" He looked Bria up and down in an admiring sort of way.

"I'm ready." She adjusted her purse strap.

"It was nice meeting you," Nya told him.

"Don't go. Please join us," he offered.

Her grin widening, Nya said, "I don't want to intrude."

Bria knew she was only trying to be nice and would not pass up an opportunity to get a free lunch. Not to mention the fact that she could interrogate Kerryngton, which she fully expected Nya to do.

"Nonsense. I insist," he said.

Nya looked at Bria for approval, and Bria shrugged. "If you want to go, come on."

She held up her index finger. "Just a second. Let me get my purse." Quickly, she turned on the balls of her feet.

"Wait," Bria said. "Please take my mug with you and set it on my desk."

"Sure." Nya grabbed the box containing the mug and went to get her purse.

When she returned, Kerryngton escorted the women to his shiny S-Class and personally opened the doors for them. The interior was immaculate without so much as a gum wrapper out of place and smelled like baby powder. A stark contrast to Bria's ride. She used her car as a mobile office.

They made small talk as they drove the short ride to the CNN Center to dine at McCormick & Schmick's. Kerryngton parked in the parking garage across the street. They waited for several cars to pass before Kerryngton grabbed Bria's hand and led them to the other side of the street.

Once inside the stone-walled restaurant, they were taken to their table. Kerryngton pulled out Bria's chair, and the waiter did the same for Nya. After scanning their menus, the waiter took their orders. Bria ordered the lobster Cobb salad, Kerryngton selected salmon rigatoni, and Nya blackened chicken linguine.

Nya scooted her striped chair closer to the table. "Bria tells me you have a daughter."

Kerryngton nodded his head and beamed with pride. He talked about his daughter's academic achievements, musical talents, and foreign language fluency.

"She sounds lovely," Nya complimented.

"I think so," Kerryngton agreed. He looked at Bria. "I'm going out of the country for a month."

Bria's heart sank. "Really? When are you leaving?"

"Tomorrow."

"Oh," was all she could say.

"I'll miss you." She could see the sincerity in his eyes.

Nya pretended to have a coughing fit and drank some water. They both looked at her.

"Sorry," Nya said. "I thought y'all forgot I was at the table."

Bria kicked Nya under the table, and Nya rubbed her shin. "Don't mind her," Bria scolded.

"Don't mind me?" Nya repeated. "You're the one who sought me out to be your friend, remember?"

Bria cut her eyes at her. *Oh here we go. Not this again.*

Nya went on to tell Kerryngton the story about how she and Bria became friends. He seemed amused by the colorful way Nya told the story. She made it seem like Bria was some little stray puppy looking for a home and Nya took her in.

Bria exhaled and looked at Kerryngton. "So, is this a business trip?"

"Yes. My company is already global, but we're expanding into more countries. I'm going over there to oversee some of the operations and while I'm there I'll be working on some music with an up-and-coming artist. I'll be hemmed up in meetings all day. Definitely not a pleasure trip." He went on to explain what goes into global expansion: different cultures, different customs, different rules, regulations, and laws, to name just a few.

"A black Tommy Mottola," Nya quipped.

"I work hard so that the people closest to me don't have to struggle or want for anything. I want my daughter to have every advantage and opportunity that life has to offer." He tapped his finger on the table. "Probably the happiest day of my life was when I bought my mom her dream house in Florida and told her she could retire from her job as an educator. My mom gets whatever she wants from me. I spoil her rotten, because she deserves it."

Bria and Nya both said, "Awww . . ."

"What about your dad?" Bria asked.

"My dad is cool. He just goes with the flow. As long as my mom is happy, he's happy. He's old school; if Momma ain't happy, ain't nobody happy."

They laughed.

"He doesn't ask me for anything," Kerryngton explained.

"Do you want any more kids?" Nya asked.

He appeared to ponder the thought for a moment and stroked his chin. "No doubt." He looked directly at Bria. "I would love to get married again and have as many kids as I can afford . . . or as many as my wife is willing to carry." He winked at her.

Good answer, Bria thought.

Nya said, "Okay. I can appreciate that."

The waiter brought out their food. They said grace and ate. For the remainder of their lunch they talked about the spa and the unpredictable weather they had been having.

Lunch lasted for two hours. Kerryngton picked up the tab and took them back to the spa. He opened the doors for them and walked them to the entrance of the business.

Nya told him, "Thanks for lunch. I had a great time. Safe travels." She gave him a friendly hug.

"Thank you. We'll have to do this again when I get back."

"I'd like that." Nya went inside and gave Bria and Kerryngton some privacy.

"I like your friend," he said.

"I think she likes you too."

He welcomed her into his strong arms and held her tight. They stood there hugging for what felt like several minutes until Bria broke free.

"I'll be praying for you while you're out of the country."

"By all means, please do." He bent over to kiss her, but she turned her face to the side.

"I'm sorry." Her eyes pleaded for him to understand. "I really like you. It's just that it's too soon for me," she explained.

He touched her hand. "That's fine. Can I at least get another hug?"

"Of course you can."

They hugged again, and he rubbed her back. "You feel so good."

And he smelled so good. Very fresh, clean, soapy, and unique, she thought. Not to mention sexy. She gently nudged him. "What fragrance are you wearing?"

"Burberry Touch."

"I like it."

"Thanks. Since I'm going to be away for a while, may I take a picture of you before I go? I want to have something nice to look at."

She smiled at him and touched her hair. "Let me freshen myself up real quick first." She dug around in the bottom of her purse looking for her pressed powder compact and tube of lip gloss. She located the compact and powdered her nose. She then applied a coat of gloss to her full lips.

"You're a stunning woman." He held up his cell phone.

She thanked him and smiled pretty for the camera. He counted to three and snapped the picture. He looked at it, and then showed it to her. They both approved.

"I'll call you."

Be sure you do, she wanted to say. Instead, she waved good-bye to him as he got in his ride and drove off.

As soon as she entered the spa she could hear whispers about the fine man outside.

Meagan said, "How was your date?" She curled her lips.

Bria seemed to be in la-la land. "Terrific!" she sang out. She made her way to her office, and Dani followed her.

"Nice to see you smiling again. Didn't think I'd ever see that again knowing how hard you took your breakup." Dani paused. "No offense, but you and Spade restored my belief in black love. I'm not so sure about this guy. Rich guys tend to be controlling or sneaky."

"Kerryngton and I are just friends," Bria explained. "We're getting to know each other."

Dani said, "Friends, huh? Maybe someone should tell him that. That man is feeling you. He's trying to be way more than friends. I could see the lust in his eyes halfway across the room."

Bria stuffed her purse in her desk drawer. "You're funny."

Nya came out of the ladies' room tucking her blouse in her pants. She met Bria's stare and said a long, slow, "G-i-r-l . . . We need to talk."

Laughter filled the room.

"On that note, I'm going back to work," Dani said and left.

Nya continued, "I can see why you'd be attracted to him . . ." She smirked. "Yeah, he's fine, and he's rich. And he's in a power position. Lethal combination. Men like that have hoes in different area codes."

"Look, I'm not trying to marry him. He's just helping me keep my mind off of Spade."

"As long as that's all it is," Nya warned.

Sixteen

Spade used to hear people say, "God is still in the blessing business," and now he knew firsthand that it was true. He had witnessed the hand of God working miracles in his life, but this was some different stuff. The doctor's office finally located his "missing" last lab report, and the results were negative. Spade held on to that paperwork like a winning lottery ticket.

Things seemed to be looking up, and Spade's faith was stronger than ever. He believed that God was doing a mighty thing in his life, and he refused to be moved. He continued to read healing scriptures morning and night. He prayed throughout the day. And he thanked God in advance for the healing or the updated healthy prognosis.

By the time Spade went for his doctor's visit, he was empowered and fired up. He felt quite certain of his results.

The new oncologist examined him and carefully examined his medical records. "Mr. Spencer, I think I know what happened." He rubbed his temple.

"Please, tell me." He wanted to know.

"Mr. Spencer, I'm certain you have a lipoma, not lymphoma."

Spade searched his brain to figure out where he had heard that term before. "That's what my doctor said I had when he removed the lump from my torso."

"Yes, a lipoma is a fatty, slow-growing tumor that develops under the skin. They are usually harmless and not cancerous."

Spade trusted this doctor more than the previous oncologist. This doctor seemed to know what he was talking about, and that made Spade feel better by the minute.

"In my professional opinion, I think someone mistyped your prognosis." He pointed to the same hard-to-read word Spade stumbled upon. "That says lipoma, but someone at a glance could easily mistake it for lymphoma." He closed the records. "And once they put that in the system, everyone just went with it."

"My God." Spade closed his eyes and dropped his head. His emotions overtook him and he covered his face with his hands.

"I recommend that we send your biopsy to a specialist to confirm."

Spade uncovered his face and the doctor gave him a tight smile. "Yes, let's do that."

"Mr. Spencer, I'm sorry this happened to you. I can only imagine what you must've been going through," he said sincerely.

Finally, a doctor who understood that medicine wasn't an exact science and mistakes could be made. Spade couldn't describe how relieved he felt. The color had come back into his black-and-white existence. For the first time in a long time Spade felt like he was in a tunnel and the light he was seeing wasn't from an oncoming train. Could he finally be getting out of the tunnel?

Two weeks had passed since Kerryngton left the country. He would call and text Bria every single day. The time differences made it nearly impossible for them to speak. They had only spoken once, but that didn't stop Kerryngton from leaving her the most thoughtful phone messages. Plus, he'd send weekly lavish floral arrangements to her job, making all the women in the office envious.

While in her office she checked her e-mail and came across a message from Kerryngton with the word "Important" typed in the subject line. She clicked on the message and couldn't believe what she was reading.

"Oh my gosh. Nya, come here!"

"Where's the fire? This better be important. I'm right in the middle of reviewing our advertising budget and campaign."

"Pull up a seat. I just got this e-mail from Kerryngton." She read the e-mail aloud to Nya. "Bria, I know it's spur of the moment, but I hope you'll be open-minded. I'm in London, England, right now. I'd like to experience this city with you. My company owns a private jet, and I can send for you. I want to see you. Pack a bag and come on. You don't have to worry about anything else. I got you. Let me know if you can leave in the next day or two. Miss you. Love, Kerryngton."

Bria threw a hand over her mouth. "Am I dreaming?" She stood up and dropped her hand. "I've never been out of the country before. This is a once-in-a-lifetime opportunity."

"Are you seriously considering going?" Nya sounded shocked.

"You're the main one always talking about staying ready so that you don't have to get ready. I remember you telling me to get a passport because . . . What were your words?" She tapped her finger on her temple. "Oh yeah. You never know when an opportunity might present itself."

"I know, but—"

"The spa manager is perfectly capable of running the day-to-day operations in my absence." She had a dreamy look on her face. "A private plane. London . . ." She shook her head to help herself come back to her senses. "It's such short notice. I don't want him to think I'm hard up." She rested in her chair.

"You don't know that man like that." Nya sounded defensive.

She snapped her finger. "I know. I'll tell him that the only way I'll go to London is if you and Chance can go with me."

"Child, boo," Nya said. "Ain't nobody gonna go for that."

Bria smirked. "We'll see." She then crafted an e-mail that read: I got your invitation, and I'm flattered. I appreciate you thinking of me. I would be glad to visit you, but I have one request . . . I want Nya and her husband to come with me. That's the only way I'd be willing to come.

She pressed the send button and hoped for the best.

Seventeen

The next morning when Bria came to work she made a beeline for her office. She had been tired the night before and went to bed without checking her e-mail. She couldn't wait to see Kerryngton's response. Sure enough, he had responded. She opened the e-mail and read silently: Bria, I want to see you and share this experience with you. I can't lie; I'm not thrilled about you bringing your friends. But if that's the only way I can get you over here, then so be it. You can bring them. ~K.

She saved the e-mail, and as soon as Nya walked in carrying a cup of coffee in one hand and biting on the jelly donut in her other hand, she told her, "He said yes!"

Nya almost spilled her coffee. She set her drink on the desk and used the donut as a lid. "I'm not crazy about Kerryngton, but if he's willing to let me go with you to London, then, hey, I'm game."

"And what about Chance?" Bria tilted her head to the side.

"What about him?" She acted like she had forgotten she had a husband.

"What if he doesn't want to go or can't go?"

Nya made the deuces sign. "See him when we get back. I can't let you go over there by yourself. Your momma would kill me. And I need to play my position as the blocker. There will be no panty jackin' on my watch."

"Really!" Bria scrunched up her face.

"Now type back and tell him we're coming," Nya instructed.

"You haven't even told Chance that you're going."

Nya looked at her sideways. "Let me worry about my husband, okay? I got this." She widened her eyes. "Anyway, let's leave in two days so that we'll have time to go shopping. I want to look nice." She used a finger to touch her fingertips and count off all the stuff she needed to do. "I've got to get my hair done, eyebrows threaded, individual lashes, fill-in, pedicure, and a Brazilian." She threw her hands in the air in exasperation. "Yes, we need two days."

Bria typed back: I'm at work right now, but I told Nya. She's excited and wants to go. We can leave in two days. We haven't asked Chance yet, so I don't know whether he'll be joining us. I'll let you know as soon as I find out. Thanks so much. She hit the send button.

"How long should we stay?" Bria asked.

"We definitely need to factor in travel time. We could easily lose two days just on travel and jet lag. We'll need about five days for sightseeing and shopping. One week should suffice."

The reality that she was leaving her brand-new business set in. "I feel guilty being away from the business that long. Especially since we just opened the doors."

Nya pulled up the master spa schedule on the computer. She pointed at the screen. "You see that?"

Bria nodded.

"We are booked two months out. We're fully staffed, insured, and licenses are up to date. What's the problem?"

"I guess there isn't one." Bria smiled, feeling more secure about her decision. "We're going to London!"

They moved into a free space, clutched hands, and jumped up and down. Then they hugged.

"I've got to call Chance," Nya said. She grabbed her cell phone and called her husband.

Bria could overhear Nya telling Chance about the impromptu trip.

When she got off the phone she filled Bria in. "Chance has to check with one of his coworkers. There's a guy who wanted to be off the week of Labor Day but couldn't. Since Chance has that week off he thinks the guy would be interested in swapping. He's going to call me back after he speaks with him."

"Okay. I've got to tell my mom," Bria said as she pulled her name up in her directory and pressed the call button.

Mrs. Murray answered, "You all right? You don't normally call me in the middle of the day."

"I'm fine, Mom. I just wanted to tell you that Nya and I are going to London for a week." She sounded enthused.

"What? When? What about Chance? Is he going too?"

"We're leaving in two days. We're waiting to see if Chance will be able to go."

"Oh. You haven't mentioned anything about a trip. What brought this on?"

Bria scratched her scalp and put her mom on speaker. "Remember my friend Kerryngton that I told you about?"

"Yes. The record executive?"

"Right. Well, he's in London right now and invited me, Nya, and Chance to visit." She felt the need to stretch the truth just a little. She didn't want her mom jumping to conclusions. "His company owns a private jet, and he's sending it for us."

"Oh my goodness. Don't you think it's a bit soon to be going on a trip, especially out of the country with someone you haven't known very long?"

She knew that her mom meant well, but Bria trusted him and that was enough. "Kerryngton's not going to do anything foul to me or Nya." She tried to make her mom understand that Kerryngton was a successful business-man. "He's got deep ties in the community. He's even got his own Wikipedia page."

"I don't care if he owns the Internet." Mrs. Murray's attitude was evident; she obviously wasn't impressed. "You're my daughter, and I worry about you. I'd feel better if Chance was going for sure."

"Mom, you know how much I love you. I have the utmost respect for you and your opinion, so please don't take this the wrong way. I didn't call you to get permission to go. I was just calling to tell you where we'll be." Bria tried to sound respectful.

"I see," she snapped. Mrs. Murray paused for a moment. "I love you. I hope you and Nya have a nice time. Please be careful and call me with your itinerary."

"You know I will. Love you too." Bria pressed the end button.

"Ma not happy about you going out of the country to be with some man she's never met," Nya said.

"Not really, but she'll get over it." Bria knew that her mother meant well, but as a grown woman, her mother needed to respect her decisions.

Bria called an impromptu staff meeting to let everyone know that she and Nya would be out of the country. Meagan jokingly asked if they could pack her in the suitcase. And Dani gave fifty million reasons why she should go with them. Although she gave some compelling arguments Bria still refused to bring her along.

The following day Bria received an e-mail confirmation from Kerryngton letting her know that he had arranged for their private flight and provided her with their itinerary, which included the chauffer contact number and exact address of the accommodations. She e-mailed a copy to her mom and printed out copies for her, Nya, and Dani. Then she and Nya took the day off from work to get ready for the trip.

Chance's shift swap came through, and he was able to travel with them. Thank goodness!

Bria verified that her passport was valid for the dates she'd be out of the country, and it was. As a precautionary measure she made copies of her passport. That way, if her passport was lost or stolen, it would be easier to get a replacement with a Xerox copy as backup.

She then notified her bank and two credit card companies that she'd be travelling out of the country so that they would not question her charges in Europe. While at the bank she requested to convert some of her money into pounds. Not too much, 250 pounds. The teller informed her that the money would be ready the following day. She then requested $500 USD in small bills.

Knowing that her mom would be worried sick about her, she made arrangements with her cell phone provider to make sure she'd have use of her phone while in England.

As she packed for the trip she remembered that Kerryngton told her to pack a rain slick with a hood. He explained that no matter what time of year in Europe one could expect rain showers. She found a small, lightweight black roll up convenient enough to carry in her purse. He also advised her not to bring any new shoes—blisters from all the walking—or flip-flops because of the possibility of getting sunburned. She packed walking shoes and dress shoes that had already been broken in.

She checked and double-checked to make sure she hadn't forgotten anything like her laptop with the cord, cell phone and charger, camera and batteries, passport, driver's license, and London contact numbers. She left contact numbers, as well as copies of Nya, Chance, and her passports, with Dani and Mrs. Murray in case of an emergency.

Finally, she called Nya on the phone to go over the checklist with her, making sure that she and Chance were all set. When she finished talking to Nya she said a prayer for safe travels. Even still, an uneasy feeling settled in the pit of her stomach.

Eighteen

Kerryngton sent a car and driver to pick up Bria and her friends to catch their four o'clock in the morning flight to London. On any given day, Bria would've been just turning over in bed. Today, though, she felt so excited about her trip that she hardly slept a wink and still didn't feel the least bit tired.

"I can't believe we're going to London!" Nya said, unable to hide her enthusiasm.

"I'm beyond excited," Bria confirmed.

Chance just closed his eyes and slept the entire ride.

They arrived at the airport, and Bria felt like royalty not having to stand in line at the check-in counter and go through security . . . her least favorite part of traveling since 9/11. She didn't like having to take off her shoes. Something about standing barefoot in a public place seemed unsanitary to her.

They went straight to the large Boeing 727.

"Oh my God," Bria said when she saw the plane. "I can't believe that's us."

Nya stared in amazement.

The driver unloaded the luggage and assisted the baggage handler with loading the plane. Some things in life are just quintessentially perfect. One item on the list of perfect things for Bria was that unique scent that all aircraft emit and pervade while either sitting quietly or dancing through the skies. She loved the smell of burnt aviation kerosene in the morning.

The three of them walked a red carpet, boarded the jet, and a flight attendant greeted them. Once inside, Bria marveled at the plush interior decorated in cream, wood, and gold-framed art. The dining room could seat four and had fine china and crystal goblets for place settings.

"This is incredible," Nya said with her mouth agape.

"We're moving on up just like the Jeffersons," Chance smiled.

"Check this out," Bria said, pointing to the drop-down projector screen, DVD, and Blu-ray players.

"Impressive." Chance nodded.

Nya found the bathroom and shouted, "You've got to see this!"

The master bathroom boasted a bidet for ladies, deluxe vanity lighting, a circular shower, and a gold-plated sink. Bria took a moment to take it all in. They continued to tour the aircraft and ended with the master bedroom featuring a queen-size bed.

"The good life."Chance rubbed his bald head. "Must be nice."

The flight attendant came up behind them and asked, "Would you like to meet the pilot?"

"Sure," they all said.

They followed the flight attendant to the living-room area and met the captain sharply dressed in a captain's uniform.

"Welcome." The captain shook their hands. "I'm Captain Jordan Nussam."

"What made you become a pilot?" Bria asked.

"I always had a deep-seated passion to fly. There's no other feeling in the world like it."

Nya chimed in, "Have you ever flown any celebrity passengers? Come on, any juicy stories?"

He laughed. "As a private jet pilot, I've flown hundreds of celebs, but I'm afraid I'm sworn to secrecy. I can't give any details, but let's just say they lead colorful lives."

Everyone laughed.

"I had read that the pilot and the copilot can't eat the same meal. Is that true?" Chance asked.

"Yes, it's true. It's an unwritten standard operating procedure, but it's mainly due to the fact that we often travel to places where we could eat something and catch a stomach bug. For that reason, pilots will not order the same meals in restaurants either before flying."

Bria found that interesting.

"It was nice meeting all of you." He tilted his hat to them and went to the cockpit.

The flight attendant gave them safety instructions, demonstrated the air mask, and pointed to the emergency exits. "Please fasten your safety belts. We're getting ready for takeoff."

They clicked the gold-plated buckles in anticipation of takeoff. Chance said a quick prayer of protection.

The pilot's voice came over the intercom. "Ladies and gent, this is your captain speaking. We'd like to welcome you onboard this flight to London, England. The flight is nonstop and will take approximately eight and a half hours. We are expecting a fairly smooth flight today. Once again, we thank you for choosing to fly with us, and we hope you enjoy your flight."

Afterward, Bria looked out the window as the plane taxied the runway, ascended successfully into the air, and leveled off. Seeing the clouds reminded her of her hot air balloon ride with Spade. His words, "The sky's the limit," once inspired her and now they haunted her. She bit her lower lip and pulled down the shade.

The flight attendant gave them permission to take off their seat belts and move about freely. She brought them three bottles of sparkling mineral water and a tray filled with delicious fresh fruits, imported cookies and candies, fresh gourmet cheese, crackers, and incredible-tasting golden pineapple.

"Let me know when you're ready for breakfast," the flight attendant said. "You can choose a continental style or a traditional, hot breakfast. We also have orange juice, apple juice, cranberry juice, and coffee or tea."

"Sounds good. I'm not hungry right now," Bria said. "Maybe in an hour or two."

She gave them a pleasant smile. "Help yourself to the refreshments. I'll be up front if you need me." She pointed to a phone encased in the wall. "You can use that to reach me. You don't have to dial anything, just pick it up and start talking."

When they thanked her and assured her they didn't need anything else, she left them alone.

The captain's voice came on the intercom again. He sounded jovial as he told them the weather en route and expected cruising altitude.

Chance stretched and yawned. "I'm 'bout to go take a nap."

Nya tapped him on the rear as he stood in front of her. He looked down at her. "Sleep easy," she said.

He bent over to kiss his wife, and Bria pretended to gag. She could hear their lips smack. Chance stood to his full height and told Bria, "I don't know what you did to ol' boy to have him flying us around on a private jet and an all-expense paid trip to Europe, but your big-head self better not do anything to jack this up before we get back on American soil." He tousled her hair, annoying her.

"Ewww, you make me sick." She made a face at him. "Are you trying to pimp me out?"

"Well . . ."

"Chance!" Nya scolded him.

He sucked air between his teeth. "I'm just playin', but I don't want to get stranded overseas with no way to get back." He turned his pants pockets inside out. "I'm not ballin' like that. I can't afford to spend thousands of dollars on airline tickets."

"Just don't break the bed," Bria teased as Chance smacked her on the leg and retreated to the bedroom.

Nya shook her head. She stood up and stretched. "So what do you want to do?" She ate a pineapple chunk.

Bria retrieved a pack of Uno cards from her purse and held them in the air. "Ready to get your butt whipped?"

Nya sat down. "In your dreams. I'm the Uno Queen."

Bria smirked. Somewhat competitive Nya tended to talk trash whenever they played games.

"That remains to be seen," Bria said as she dealt the cards.

She ended up winning the first hand. Several hands later they called it quits with Nya waving her hands in the air and singing, "I am the winner" over and over again.

"You're such a baby," Bria teased her. She left the cards on the table and browsed the selection of DVDs. She stumbled across the last romantic comedy that she and Spade had watched together and blurted out, "What am I doing?"

"What's the matter?" Nya sounded concerned.

Holding the DVD in the air, Bria told her, "This was the last movie Spade and I watched together." She held the case to her chest.

"Oh, I'm sorry." Nya joined her on the floor and rested her arm around her shoulders.

"How am I supposed to get over him when little things trigger memories of him?"

"It'll get easier with time. Trust me. I remember my first heartbreak. I didn't think I'd ever get over it. But I did. Three months later I had moved on. Three years later I wondered what I ever even saw in him in the first place."

They both laughed. Bria did indeed remember Nya's first heartbreak and helped nurse her back to mental health. Many late-night crying sessions, lots of talking, too much ice cream, and plenty of prayers. She didn't think Nya would ever get over the high school jock that cheated on her and broke her heart.

Bria tossed the DVD to the side and picked out a dramatic suspense movie. The friends watched the entire movie before eating a continental-style breakfast. Afterward, they dozed off and slept soundly for the remainder of the flight.

The sound of the flight attendant jolted Bria out of her sleep. She nudged Nya, who wiped drool from the side of her mouth and face.

Yawning, Nya said, "We're finally here. This is so exciting!" She stretched her arms over her head.

Bria scrunched up her face. "Make sure you brush your teeth."

Nya placed her right hand in front of her mouth and blew. "Ewww." She opened her oversized handbag and ruffled around for her toothbrush and toothpaste. Then she went into the bathroom to brush her teeth. When she returned, she placed her face two inches from Bria's and showed her teeth. Bria could smell the faint odor of mint toothpaste."Happy now?"

Bria blew her an air kiss. "Much better." She then took her purse into the bathroom and freshened up. She brushed her teeth, gargled, blotted the oil from her nose, and brushed her hair.

Chance came from the back rubbing sleep from his eyes. He looked rested. "That was some good sleep," he said as he took a seat next to his wife and kissed her on the cheek.

The flight attendant instructed them to fasten their seat belts because they were getting ready to land. They did as they were told.

She checked her watch. "The time in London is . . ." she paused for a brief moment, ". . . six p.m." She glanced at them. "So, set your watches five hours ahead." Her friendly expression reassured Bria that she'd made the right decision to come on this trip. The attendant then took a seat and fastened her seat belt as well.

The captain's voice sounded across the intercom announcing they were cleared for landing at London Gatwick Airport. "The weather in London is sixty-seven degrees Fahrenheit with a slight chance of showers later in the evening," the captain said.

Bria rubbed her hands together. She felt like an inflated tire—ready to roll.

When they were safely on the ground the captain said, "Welcome to London, England." He told them to carry lightweight rain jackets with them everywhere because London is known for rain. "Enjoy your stay," he concluded.

They disembarked from the plane and a car and driver awaited them. Not just any car but a white-on-white Rolls-Royce! Bria's jaw dropped. Nya let out a squeal, and Chance coughed, covered his mouth with his fist, and mumbled something inaudible. They waited as the flight crew unloaded their luggage from the plane and into the car.

Nya turned to Bria and said, "That Kerryngton sure doesn't miss a beat."

The driver greeted them as he opened the car doors for them. Nya and Chance piled in the spacious backseat while Bria took her seat up front with the driver. The interior smelled like cigarette smoke. Bria could not stand that smell. She didn't want to be rude, but she couldn't take it. She pulled a small can of travel-size Lysol spray from her purse and sprayed the air. It immediately neutralized the odor.

"I have to call my mom," Bria announced. She placed a brief phone call to her mother just to let her know they had arrived safely.

"That's good," Mrs. Murray said. "I hope you all have a great time. Love you."

"Love you too." She put her phone away.

As the driver drove them to their hotel, Bria and Nya looked out the windows. London reminded Bria of an older New York. The driver took them to the heart of London where they would be staying at Hotel 41. Bria couldn't stop smiling when she saw the massive, neatly manicured green lawn with red flowers.

The driver looked into the rearview mirror and said in a British accent, "forty-one is a boutique five-star hotel · directly opposite the Royal Mews and just behind Buckingham Palace. It's about as close to the Royal Family as a visitor can get." He pointed. "Directly opposite Buckingham Palace are the green and leafy royal parks, St James's Park and Green Park. Not far beyond are Piccadilly Circus, Trafalgar Square, and London's West End theatreland."

"Wow," Bria and Nya said in awe.

"Your boy hooked us up," Chance said.

The driver parked the Rolls and unloaded the vehicle. He took care of the luggage while Bria, Nya, and Chance checked in. The moment they entered the ground-floor reception area they were given a friendly welcome. From there, they were whisked away to the fifth floor and taken to their suites. They reached Bria's black-and-white luxuriously decorated Conservatory Master Suite first. Bria marveled at the view. She looked forward to sleeping in such opulent luxury underneath the twinkling stars.

"If you tire of the view," the staff member demonstrated, "electric blinds turn your split-level suite into a private paradise."

"Impressive," Bria said.

Bria and Nya walked around the suite admiring the décor. Bria fell in love with the marbled bathroom and whirlpool tub. She couldn't wait to unpack and enjoy the stunning views. The open fireplace and soft furnishings set the mood of carefree glamour.

They left Bria's luggage in her room and headed to Nya and Chance's Junior Suite. A split-level Junior Suite gave the couple room to spread out. On the upper level, there was a luxuriously seductive bedroom; on the lower level, a spacious lounge for eating, relaxing, and entertaining. The eye-catching black-and-white suite had a homely yet thrilling feel. Bria detected a hint of romantic mystery about the room. Thoughtful touches such as fresh fruit and flowers, delicious snacks and treats, scented candles, rich mahogany furniture, and an open fireplace added to the luxury.

The staff member told them, "If you get hungry, you can enjoy round-the-clock informal and personalized dining. Choose between the stunning Executive Lounge, the Mezzanine level overlooking the lounge, or alternatively, the ultimate in-room dining experience. The glass roof of the Executive Lounge also makes for the brightest sunlit breakfasts and the most reviving afternoon teas. We also invite you to Plunder the Pantry." She used air quotes around the words *Plunder the Pantry,* then continued. "Each evening from 8:30 p.m. onward, you can take your pick of complimentary snacks and light bites in the well-stocked fridges of the Executive Lounge."

Bria loved her British accent! She sounded so prim and proper.

"There are plenty of grand restaurants nearby; two of them are right next door," she continued. "The award-winning Library at our neighboring hotel, The Rubens, is renowned for its roast beef and Yorkshire pudding, while the cool and relaxed BBar restaurant offers inventive cocktails and exciting South African-themed cuisine."

Bria and Nya exchanged glances. They had never eaten South African food before.

"Our guests can add bills from The Rubens and BBar to their forty-one Hotel account," she explained. "You can also enjoy our finest selection of champagnes with light dishes, including Sevruga caviar in the intimate, safari-chic Leopard Champagne Bar at The Rubens."

Just then Bria's cell phone rang. She saw that it was Kerryngton and answered.

"How was the flight?" he asked.

"Smooth. That plane was all that. You're spoiling me. I don't think I can ever view a commercial flight the same ever again."

He chuckled. "Stick with me, baby, and you won't have to. You checked into the hotel yet?"

"We're checked in." She smiled at Nya who was sprawled across the bed. She noticed Chance plucking a couple of grapes and tossing them into his mouth. "The rooms are . . ." She paused momentarily to think of the right word. "Exquisite," she said with an exhale. "This place is everything."

"Glad you like it."

"How could I not?" She gestured with her hand. "It's elegant, luxurious, and," she looked in the face of the staff member, "the staff is so caring. Thank you so much."

"Yeah, man," Chance yelled loud enough for Kerryngton to hear him. "Thanks."

"Don't mention it," Kerryngton said. "Once you all get settled in I'll send the driver over to pick you up for dinner."

When he mentioned the driver Bria remembered the Rolls. "Oh yeah, I can't believe I almost forgot about the Rolls-Royce. What in the world?"

"What, baby?" He sounded amused.

"I'm just sayin'. We weren't expecting all that."

"Well, get used to it. That's how I get down, and when you're down with me, that's how you'll get down too."

Bria's stomach fluttered. Kerryngton's take-charge attitude mixed with confidence but not arrogance turned her on. She couldn't deny that she was feeling him. His good looks, charm, larger-than-life personality, and alpha male characteristics were winning Bria over. Quick, fast, and in a hurry.

"You think you can be ready by eight?" he said. "I want to see you."

She wanted to see him too. She checked her watch. That gave her an hour to get ready. "Sure. How should we dress? Casual, dressy, what?"

"You can wear whatever makes you comfortable. You could wear a potato sack and still look good."

Bria tried not to blush. Kerryngton always knew exactly what to say.

"Okay. See you in a bit," she said and hung up.

What a man, she thought. Yes, what a man. But was he *her* man? She felt her stomach flutter again. Spade was supposed to be her man. What was she doing? She chastised herself. Was it too soon for her to be in a relationship with Kerryngton? Did the fact that she was on this trip mean they were seeing each other by default? She paced the floor, wondering if she was even ready to move on. Kerryngton was a great distraction—and she was feeling him—but she couldn't deny that her heart still belonged to Spade.

Nineteen

Bria was glad she opted to wear a sheath dress, because she, along with Nya and Chance, met up with Kerryngton at the upscale Pollen Street Social for a private dining experience. When Bria's eyes landed on Kerryngton looking all good in his designer duds she couldn't wait to melt into his arms. And melt she did. He held her nice and tight, squeezing her just right. She felt like a roll of Charmin toilet paper, squeezably soft. She closed her eyes and engulfed his masculine scent. She hadn't realized it before, but she missed him.

Kerryngton cupped her face in his hands and planted a wet kiss on Bria's glossy lips. Her lips responded naturally. Without so much as a second thought she kissed him back.

Chance cleared his throat. "Remember us?"

Bria licked her lips, feeling a little embarrassed by that public display of affection. She and Kerryngton had never kissed like that before, and she liked it . . . a lot. She wiped the corners of her mouth with her thumb and index finger.

Kerryngton pecked her lips one more time before extending his right hand to Chance. "Nice to finally meet you," he said. They shook hands.

"Same here," Chance told him.

He then turned to Nya and hugged her. "It's good to see you again."

Nya giggled. "It's nice to be seen."

They sat at the wooden table with place settings for six and the waitstaff immediately began serving them an appetizer of Cornish crab vinaigrette, Nashi pear, cauliflower sweet 'n' sour dressing, and frozen peanut powder. The food tasted delicious.

A waiter filled Kerryngton's glass with wine first. Kerryngton, an obvious wine connoisseur, swirled the fermented grape juice in his glass before taking a sip, savoring the flavor, swallowing, and then nodding his approval. The waiter then filled everyone else's glasses with the wine selection.

Bria hardly ever drank alcoholic beverages, but she didn't have a problem with an occasional social drink over dinner. "All things in moderation," her father would always say.

Kerryngton whispered in Bria's ear, "I would've offered to let you stay with me at Corinthia Hotel in the penthouse, but I didn't want to put you in a compromising position. Having you that close would've been too much of a temptation."

She smiled at him. Admittedly, she felt strong. However, she didn't readily place herself in positions to be tempted. She had sense enough to know that if she placed her hand atop a hot stove, she just might get burned.

"I hope you don't mind, but one of my up-and-coming artists and a music producer will be joining us for dinner," Kerryngton announced to everyone. "They are finishing up a track in the studio and should be here shortly."

"That's fine," Bria said.

They talked about how excited they were to be in London and all the places they wanted to visit. While laughing at one of Chance's corny knock-knock jokes Bria's laughter came to an abrupt halt when she saw Spade and another guy walk through the door.

Spade appeared stunned. He looked from Bria to Chance to Nya and stopped dead in his tracks. "What are y'all doing here?" He sounded surprised.

Kerryngton said, "What do you mean what are they doing here?" He pushed his chair back and stood up. "What's that about? I told you my lady and her friends would be joining us."

Bria was taken aback. She didn't quite know how to process being called Kerryngton's lady. They had never discussed that. He hadn't even asked her if she wanted to be his lady. He couldn't just assume they were in a relationship.

The guy who came in with Spade interrupted. He shook everyone's hands and introduced himself before taking a seat. Bria could tell he was trying to diffuse the situation. The way Kerryngton stood to his feet and took a power position one had no way of knowing if a fight was about to jump off.

"Your lady?" Spade repeated. His eyes never left Bria.

"Yes," Kerryngton told him. "This is—"

Spade held up his hands, palms facing outward. He then punched his right fist in the palm of his left hand. "No introductions needed. I already know them."

The hurt and disappointed look in Spade's eyes was more than Bria could bear. She ran out and stood in an area near the noisy kitchen. Nya followed.

With her hands resting on Bria's shoulders Nya looked her in the eyes and said, "This is some straight-up foolishness. How did you not know Spade was in London?"

Bria felt like a child being chastised by a parent. "I haven't spoken to Spade, and Kerryngton didn't mention it. I didn't even know they knew each other."

Nya removed her hands from Bria's shoulders and started turning her neck from side to side.

"What are you looking for?" Bria asked.

"I'm looking for the cameras. This is too crazy for us not to be on TV."

Bria agreed with her and found herself laughing out loud. "I don't know what I'm going to do. This is so awkward." Her voice sounded like she was pleading for answers.

"Follow your heart. You've got to be true to yourself. I get that you love Spade, but he hurt you. Now you've got this dream guy Kerryngton who seems like he would do anything for you. Don't jeopardize that. Tell him the truth about you and Spade. He'll understand."

Bria sighed. She knew Nya was on point, but that wasn't the point. Her concern was for Spade. She didn't want to flaunt her new "relationship" in his face. That wasn't her.

Kerryngton came around the corner and asked, "What just happened? Are you okay?"

Nya raised a brow and gave Bria a look that said, "Tell him." She then said, "I'll leave you two alone." She gave Bria's arm a light squeeze before heading back to the table.

The sound of metal clanking annoyed them.

"Let's go someplace quieter," Kerryngton suggested. He summoned a nearby staff member and told him he needed a room to talk. The staff member directed him to an office. The space wasn't very big, but it was neat and offered some privacy. Kerryngton licked his luscious lips. "What's going on, baby?"

Bria did not want to have this conversation, but she knew she needed to. In a low voice she revealed, "That's him."

His lips parted, but no words came out. He rubbed his face. "You were engaged to Spade?" He seemed to be asking for clarification.

Bria let out a deep breath and nodded her head.

"Okay, baby. That's in the past. Everybody's got a past."
He sounded so understanding. "Spade is an artist on one
of my labels, and I'm helping him with his debut CD.
That's why he's in London. We're working on his music."

"I see." Bria had heard many times that the world is
small, but right now it felt suffocating. She appreciated
him for clearing up why Spade was in Europe, but there
was one more thing that needed clearing up. She bit the
corner of her lip. "So, what's up with you calling me your
lady?"

He grinned, showing off his polished teeth. "You have a
problem with that?" His dark eyes searched her face.

"You never asked me." She stood her ground, trying
hard not to turn into putty in his strong hands.

He inched in closer to her and eased his hand around
the back of her neck. Getting within an inch of her lips
Bria thought he was going to kiss her. Instead, he said,
"I adore you, Bria Murray. I want to be with you. Do you
want to be with me?"

Adrenaline seemed to rush through her body causing
her to arch her back. She couldn't put into words the way
Kerryngton made her feel. His touch made every fiber
of her being come alive. "I-I . . ." She touched his pecs
and dug her fingernails in. She realized that she had no
reason not to pursue a relationship with him. Spade had
hurt her—and she still didn't know why, but she wasn't
bitter. She believed in love. Her parents had taught her to
judge people according to their merits, not based on what
someone else had done.

She remembered her mom telling her, "Trust your
heart. You may not always get it right, but you'll never get
it wrong."

She stopped denying the obvious. "Yes, I want to be
with you too." He then gave her exactly what she yearned
for . . . a long, lingering kiss.

Twenty

Bria felt somewhat relieved that when she and Kerryngton returned to the table Spade had already left. She didn't want to deal with a possible confrontation and was thankful she didn't have to.

After dinner, the driver took Bria, Nya, and Chance on a scenic tour back to the hotel. The busy streets reminded Bria of the crowded streets of New York.

During the ride Nya told Bria everything she missed at the table. "Girl, Spade was tore up! He tried to play it off, but I could tell seeing you with Kerryngton messed him up."

"Yeah, it was obvious," Chance cosigned.

"He had the nerve to blame me for you seeing someone else," Nya said and sucked air between her teeth.

"What?" Bria said.

"You already know I nipped that in the bud," Nya pronounced. "He comes asking me why I *let* you start dating Kerryngton so soon after your breakup. I read him his rights. I told him you're a grown woman, and I can't *let* you do anything. Then I told him if he hadn't broken up with you in the first place Kerryngton wouldn't be an issue. I let him know straight-up that if he wanted to blame someone, he needed to blame himself." She paused for a moment. "But then he said something I can't shake."

"What did he say?" Bria sat on the edge of her seat.

"That he didn't break up with you because he wanted to. He broke up with you because he had to."

Bria didn't know how to take that. What was that supposed to mean? Why did he have to break up with her? That sounded so mysterious, like Spade was a federal agent and had to protect Bria from danger. She had no clue what he meant by that.

"Well, he asked if he could come over once we got back to the hotel, and I told him he could," Chance added.

Bria reached over Nya's lap and pinched Chance. "Are you crazy?"

"Ouch!" He massaged the spot on his thigh she had assaulted. "Big-head girl, what's the matter with you?"

"Why would you do that? I don't want to see Spade," Bria insisted. She didn't really mean it. She wanted to see Spade to find out what he meant by having to break up with her. In spite of that, she still felt disappointed, hurt, and angry.

"Stop lying. You looked as helpless as Bambi standing in front of a hunter when you saw that man. The two of you need to talk and get closure."

Bria didn't want to give Chance the satisfaction of knowing she agreed with him, so she rolled her eyes and pressed her back against the soft leather. Folding her arms across her bosom she said, "What's the point? I'm in a relationship with Kerryngton now. There's no need to go backward." She tried to sound tough to conceal the vulnerability she felt. She didn't want to risk giving Spade any kind of opening for fear he'd break her heart again. She didn't believe she could handle that kind of heartbreak twice in one lifetime. No thank you, she resigned.

"Did you really just say that?" Chance eyed her suspiciously. "I don't know who you think you're foolin', but I didn't just meet you fifteen minutes ago. Save that for somebody stupid."

"I did," Bria fired back. "That's why I saved it for you."

Nya giggled and tapped both of them on the thighs, her way of telling them to calm down. They arrived at the hotel and as soon as they got out of the Rolls-Royce the muggy night air enveloped them like a blanket. They went to their rooms to shower and change. Bria's cell phone rang. When she saw Kerryngton's number pop up, she hurried up and answered.

"Just checking on you," he said.

She loved the way he cared about her. "I'm fine. Getting ready for bed."

"I miss you already."

His words warmed her heart. "I miss you too," she said and meant it.

He invited her to breakfast in the morning and she accepted. They ended the call, and Bria slipped into a tank top and shorts. Her phone rang again. This time Spade's name appeared; something she hadn't seen in a long time. Bria pressed her eyes shut, took a deep breath, released it, opened her eyes, and answered.

"Hey," Spade said. "I'm outside your hotel. Come on down," he insisted.

She had expected to hear from him after what Chance had told her. That's why she put on clothes instead of pajamas. "I'm on my way," she told him. She put on a pair of ankle socks with her sneakers and went to meet him.

As soon as Spade saw her he hugged her. She wasn't expecting that and hesitantly hugged him back. Her eyes immediately filled with tears. He smelled so good, and his body felt as fit as she had remembered, except for maybe a few pounds lighter.

He told her, "You look amazing."

She felt something she hadn't felt in a while: the stirring of tiny bees' wings in her stomach. She shook her head and looked away, disarmed by the intimacy of his gaze.

"I owe you an apology," he spoke into her loose hair.

She pulled away from him, remembering that he not only owed her an apology but an explanation. She stared at him, waiting for him to continue.

"Let's go for a walk," he suggested, grabbing her left hand.

She allowed him to take her hand, because no matter what had happened between them she couldn't hate him. They took a stroll in St. James Park. The park appeared well cared for. Bria admired the serene collection of gardens filled with colorful blooms, manicured lawns, and groves of trees.

They sat down on a park bench in front of a pond. Bria saw some squirrels running around and wished she had brought some monkey nuts with her to feed them. She had never seen so much wildlife freely roaming a park before. Some of the ducks and geese were swimming while others walked around. For the first time in her life Bria saw some swans. Those long elegant necks and white feathers immediately added the bird to her list of beautiful things. She almost wished she hadn't seen the swans at that moment, because forever more her first memory of seeing a swan would be attached to Spade.

"Bria," Spade began, "this isn't easy for me. You've got me all twisted right now." He made a gesture with his hands.

She placed a manicured hand on her chest. "I've got *you* twisted?"

"Yeah. The last thing I expected to see was you all booed up with some other nicca. I'm just curious, how did you meet Mr. Kruse anyway?"

"Noneya."

"Don't get smart. Tell me," he demanded.

No, he didn't just snap at me, Bria thought. "As if that's really any of your business—why do you want to know?"

"I just do. And for the record, I'm a little surprised to see you hanging out with him." He sounded serious.

"Interesting, I could say the same thing about you."

"Touché," he chuckled.

"If you must know, we met at the spa grand opening." She raised a brow.

He seemed reflective for a moment. "I see." His eyes penetrated hers. "Why haven't you called me?" The expression on his face softened.

Bria could not believe his nerve. If her feet weren't throbbing like a toothache from all the walking around she had been doing all day, she would've left him sitting there looking as stupid as his question sounded. *Is this negro trippin'?* she thought. She wasn't violent, but she felt like the lyrics from the LL Cool J song "Mama Said Knock You Out." She frowned and said, "*Excuse* me?" She wished he had the nerve to repeat himself so that she could go off and give him a real tongue-lashing.

He sounded angry. "I expected more loyalty than that from you."

"Hold up, Spade." She wagged her finger at him. "You *dumped* me, remember? I don't *owe* you anything." She felt herself becoming upset. *What kind of foolishness?* she thought. Was he serious?

He shook his head. "You know what? I'm wrong. I just never thought . . . Never mind."

"Never mind? How dare you do this to me again! Forget you, Spade!" She stood up, and he grabbed her arm.

"I didn't break up with you because I didn't want to be with you. I broke up with you because I was diagnosed with cancer," he blurted out.

Bria didn't realize that her knees had gotten weak until she found herself sitting back on the bench. Tears escaped her eyes. "What did you say?" she asked barely above a whisper.

He repeated what he had said.

Bria buried her freshly washed face in his chest and cried. *Cancer?* The thought frightened her. She wanted to hold him in her arms and never let him go. If she could take away his infliction and give it to herself instead, she would. That's how much she loved that man.

He rubbed her back. "Please don't cry. That's exactly why I didn't tell you at the time."

If Bria could have stopped the world from turning and got off, she would have. "My God, Spade, are you going to die?" She felt her heart skip a beat. "Are you okay?"

"Come to find out it was a misdiagnosis. I literally found out right before I had to come here."

She shook her head vehemently. "Why didn't you just tell me? We could've gotten through this together. I never would've left your side."

"I know, but I wasn't in my right mind. All I could think about was the death sentence I had received. I couldn't think about getting married."

Oh God! Bria thought. She had made an even bigger mess of things. Why didn't she just go with her first mind and wait instead of getting involved with someone else? Why hadn't she trusted the love she and Spade shared? Or is it share? Did they still have that connection? She wanted to believe in their love, but how could she when Spade hadn't communicated with her in weeks? She felt so confused.

No matter how many questions popped up in her mind, Bria could not deny the fact that Kerryngton was a real factor. She cared about him . . . a lot.

"I know I was wrong not to tell you, and I'm sorry." He touched her shoulders. "I know I messed up, and I don't blame you for how you feel. Just know that I never stopped loving you."

Until now she had avoided looking into his eyes. He had weakened her defenses by saying that he never stopped loving her, which caused her to lose her train of thought. She felt as though she had just looked into the eyes of Medusa and turned into stone. No matter how badly she wanted to, she could not move. He leaned toward her and she could feel his cool breath on her skin, smelling of peppermint.

"I'll do whatever it takes to make things right between us. I just know I don't want to be without you, and I still love you. I won't stop until I get you back," he whispered in her ear.

Bria tasted her salty tears and wiped her eyes. Through her blurry vision she noticed a pelican in the water. Then out of nowhere, a squirrel ran up Spade's leg and onto his shoulder. Bria almost ran out of the park, it scared her so bad. Spade simply shooed the creature away. He yelled behind her and caught up with her. They walked along the bridge to get a better view of Buckingham Palace.

"Exquisite," was all Bria could say about the breathtaking estate.

Spade wrapped his arm around Bria, and she flinched. She didn't even know why she flinched; she just did.

"Do you still love me?" he wanted to know.

His question halted her breathing for a second. She knew she needed to answer his question carefully. If she went all in and confessed her feelings for him, he'd expect her to break up with Kerryngton, and she wasn't ready or willing to do that. She looked at the ground and became nauseated by the sight of ants teeming all over a discarded hot dog bun.

She looked away and said, "Yes, I do love you. I always will. But I'm not ready to pick up where we left off."

He removed his arm. "It's like that?" He sounded so dejected.

"Spade, please." She felt herself getting choked up again. "As much as I loved you and still love you, you broke my heart. I had to change my way of thinking about you and us. I had no idea why you left me. That devastated me. When I didn't hear from you, I thought that was the end of us. Kerryngton has helped me through a difficult time in my life. He gave me a reason to smile again."

"I don't want to hear about how the next man made you smile. You're my girl." He patted his chest, then sighed. "You haven't slept with him, have you?"

"Of course not." She sounded offended. How could he ask her that? He knew how she felt about premarital sex. He was acting brand-new. Like he really didn't know her at all.

"Thank God," he mumbled. "Do you plan to?" He eyed her incredulously.

"Stop it." She wasn't about to go there with him and entertain this conversation. "You're focusing on the wrong thing."

"I want to be with you. As soon as I get the final test confirming that my results were wrong I still want to marry you." He pulled a folded-up check from out of his back pocket and handed it to her. "None of that has changed for me."

"That's because you had all the information; I didn't. I had no idea what was going on with you or what you were going through. All I was trying to do was piece my life back together."

If he had been honest with her, she would've married him anyway. She would've stayed with him until he took his last breath and not regretted a single moment of being with him. She would never abandon him when he needed her the most. How could he not know that?

She unfolded the check. "What's this for?"

"I got an advance from my deal. Give that to your dad. I want to pay him back for the wedding."

That was too much for her. She broke down crying and dabbed at the corners of her eyes.

He wiped her tears away. "I'm not willing to give up on us. Ol' boy might have all the money right now, but I'ma get paid too. I have a plan, and I'm working it. You'll see."

"It's not about the money," she told him and meant it. "It's about how I felt when you left me and how Kerryngton has made me feel since then."

He bent down, grabbed the back of her head, and kissed her. "I love you so much." As he talked, his lips brushed against hers.

Bria had never been more conflicted in her life. When she kissed Kerryngton, she felt guilty, as if she were betraying Spade. And now she felt guilty kissing him, like she was betraying Kerryngton. But she couldn't deny that kissing Spade felt so right! She wanted to break away, but she found herself being drawn to him like a rock star to a supermodel.

"Don't give up on us," he pleaded. Spade kissed her again before saying something else that tugged, more like yanked, on all of Bria's heartstrings. "I remember you telling me that you prayed about me . . . us. And that I'm your kindred spirit." He held her oval-shaped face in his hands. "If you believe you've already found The One, why are you wasting time with another man?"

Bria turned her face away, not wanting him to see the guilt that panged her. She didn't know the answer to that question. All she knew was that now she found herself caught up in the middle of a love triangle. She wished she could talk to her dad. He was always so good at offering her advice and helping her straighten out her problems. But he wasn't there now, and even if he were, the ultimate decision rested solely on her shoulders. What was she going to do?

Twenty-one

Bria went back to the hotel and pounded on Nya's door.

"Why are you pounding on the door like a madwoman?" Chance asked when he opened the door to let her in. He rubbed his eyes. "Oh, you *are* a madwoman."

She cut her eyes at him and headed straight to the bed where she joined Nya who was underneath the black-and-white covers. She kicked off her sneakers and settled on the bed.

"What's the matter with you?" Nya asked as Bria lay next to her.

"I met with Spade, and we finally talked." She wrestled with a plush pillow until she found a comfortable position.

Nya propped herself up on her elbow. "What did he say? Tell me everything."

And that's exactly what Bria did. She told her everything. Bria talked for ten minutes straight without taking a break and without Nya or Chance interrupting her. When she finally did stop talking, she showed them the check. Nya and Chance just stared at her and the check.

"Say something," Bria insisted.

"I wanted to make sure you were done," Nya told her. She sat up on the bed. "I can't believe Spade was diagnosed with cancer." She had a sorrowful look on her face. "And that he paid you back. Are you sure he's all right now?"

"That's what he says." She lowered her eyes. "His doctor believes he was misdiagnosed; he's waiting for some test to confirm it."

"I'm sad this happened to him . . . and to you. I always thought the two of you were made for each other." She gave Bria a sympathetic look. "Spade is my boy. I love him like a brother, and it would break my heart if anything ever happened to him. I pray that he gets the clean bill of health he's hoping for." She sighed. "I just wish he would've told you what was going on with him."

"Me too." Bria felt tormented inside. A part of her wanted to tell Spade yes, they could try again. She wanted to announce that the wedding was back on and live happily ever after with the love of her life. But she knew she couldn't do that. Kerryngton was the type of guy any woman would be lucky to have, she thought. He could have any woman he wanted, and he wanted her. He made her feel special. Not that Spade didn't make her feel special too, because he definitely did—this was different.

Chance ran his hand over his bald head. Then he surprised both Bria and Nya when he broke out singing his own off-key version of the old-school song "Him or Me" by the group Today. "Tell me, Bria, what are you gon-na do? Do you really want Kerryngton, or do you really want Spade?"

Bria tossed a pillow at his head. "Zip it."

He started laughing. "I'm just playing. But for real, who's it going to be?"

In exasperation, Bria admitted, "I don't know."

"Well, let's see," Chance said. "You and Spade have history, and the love is deep. He hurt you, but there was a reason . . . a very good reason."

"That's just it," Bria interrupted. "He didn't *have* to hurt me. All he had to do was tell me." Anger festered from deep within and boiled to the top. "I shed so many tears over that man." She felt herself getting choked up. "Why did he have to wait so long? It's not fair."

Chance came over and gave her a hug. "No, it's not fair. You just need to pray about it. But if I had to give my two cents, I vote for love. You and Spade are like peanut butter and jelly; you just go together."

Bria sniffled and used his white T-shirt to wipe the snot from her nose.

Chance patted her hard on the back. "Thanks a lot." He eased his way up, pulling the shirt away from his body.

"Don't mention it," she said as she smiled sweetly at him.

Nya added, "You already prayed about Spade a long time ago. You know he's the guy for you. Don't play yourself. Kerryngton is all glitz and glamour, but everything that glitters isn't gold. Remember when actress LisaRaye went through a very public divorce from Turks and Caicos Prime Minister Michael Misick? Well, when she was planning their wedding she talked about him being platinum, baby. And that he was the real deal. She had women all over the world hating on her. He was supposed to be some great catch. See how *that* turned out." She cleared her throat. "I'm just sayin'."

Sulking, Bria said, "Why didn't Spade just tell me the truth?" She didn't really expect anyone to answer her.

"Pride," Chance said.

Bria and Nya both looked at him.

"A man doesn't want his woman to ever think he's weak or not in control," Chance continued. "He'd rather risk losing you than to have you look at him with pity or stay with him out of obligation."

"But he didn't give me a choice," Bria explained.

"I'm not saying he was right," Chance clarified. "I'm just saying that's how some men are."

"As long as I've known Spade, and as well as he knows me, he should've known I wouldn't have left him."

"That's the problem," Chance said. "He does know you. He knows you're loyal to a fault. You would've stood by him no matter what. Knowing Spade like I do, he didn't want you to do that. He was probably thinking about every scenario. He was diagnosed with a terminal condition. He had to worry about how that would affect you. He's young, and he had probably never thought about his mortality until he got that death sentence. That's a lot to deal with. And even if he could fight the disease, going through chemo would make him sick and weak. Can't you see why he made the decision he made, even if you don't agree with it?"

Bria nodded her head. She hadn't previously considered any of what Chance said. He helped her to stop focusing on herself and understand what Spade must've gone through.

Chance continued, "Li'l sis, I know you're caught up in this whirlwind romance with Kerryngton right now, but I'm going to keep it one hundred with you. Just a few months ago you were ready and willing to commit your life to Spade. I agree with my wife. Nobody could've told you he wasn't The One. I don't think you're really torn at all."

His words stunned Bria. Nya and Bria stared at him with baffled expressions and said in unison, "What?"

"No, I think you're in love with Spade, but I think the diamonds-and-platinum lifestyle that come along with Kerryngton excite you. It's new, different, and fun. Once that wears off you'll find your way back to Spade. Just don't wait too long," he warned.

She knew her friends made great points. What was she going to do?

Twenty-two

A private internal lift led Bria to Kerryngton's penthouse retreat. Bria looked around the penthouse in amazement. She thought the dark limed oak paneling and red-leather-paneled bookshelves gave the lounge and study the genteel elegance of a refined gentlemen's club, albeit with light contemporary touches. Her mouth opened in awe.

"Do you like it?" Kerryngton asked.

"It's all that *and* a bag of Doritos."

On the upper turreted floor, as soon as Bria saw the king-sized bed she thought the place was fit for a king. The huge bed stood on a sumptuous rug surrounded by a dark stained oak floor, tinted with a light lime wash. The luxurious bathroom featured a walk-in shower encased in Nero Marquina stone and a bespoke Apaiser stone bathtub. She had no idea what type of stones Kerryngton was talking about but judging by the look and feel of the stones she knew it had to be top of the line. Kerryngton pointed out that the flooring had been formed from three varieties of marble.

"Very nice," she said.

Outside, on the private terrace with breathtaking views toward Whitehall and Big Ben, there was a giant chess set. Bria had never seen a chess set so large. The pieces stood as tall as a one-year-old child. She touched one of the pieces and felt the smoothness.

"Do you play chess?"

She shook her head. "Not really. My mom tried to teach me, but I just never took to it."

Bria could've easily lived in that penthouse. She thought about an article she had read about smart women marrying for money instead of love. According to the article, heart-stopping, knee-weakening, "when-is-he-going-to-call" kind of love wanes in about eighteen to twenty-four months, but the kind that comes in dollars and cents lasts a lifetime. She had heard all of the catchy phrases: "It's just as easy to love a rich man as a poor man." Or, "No Romance without Finance." And, "Marry the one you can live with, not the one you can't live without."

Far from being a gold digger, Bria wondered if she was naïve in her thinking. She had never considered marrying for anything other than true love. Then she thought about something she heard Dr. Phil say on his show. He told one of the guests, "If you marry for money, you'll earn every penny."

A faint smile appeared on her face. She knew that by worldly standards everything boiled down to money. However, she knew in her heart that the world's way wasn't necessarily God's way. She believed what the Word said about love covering a multitude of sins. She also believed that love could motivate people to succeed and become their best selves. No matter what that article stated, Bria knew herself well enough to know that she'd choose love over money any day of the week. She decided to stay prayerful about what she should do and let God show her the way instead of leaning on her own understanding.

After the tour, they enjoyed a lavish breakfast of freshly squeezed fruit juices, coffees, teas, fresh seasonal fruits, eggs cooked to their preference, streaky bacon, honey roasted ham, grilled mushrooms, vine tomatoes, cereals, and yogurts with granola. Although tempting, Bria passed on the freshly baked croissants and home-baked bread

with English honey, strawberry jam, and thick cut marma-
lade.

Over breakfast they talked about their plans for the
day.

"I'm superexcited about the Changing of the Guard
ceremony at Buckingham Palace, taking a tour of the
State Rooms, and a guided tour of the garden," she said.
She was so glad Kerryngton had already purchased their
tickets online in advance.

When they finished eating, they relaxed for a few
before heading over to Buckingham Palace at 9:00 a.m.
to meet up with Nya and Chance. When they got there
a small crowd had already gathered, but at least there
weren't so many people they'd have to stare at the back of
people's heads.

"This is exciting!" Nya said, sounding like a young
child.

"Yeah, it is," Bria agreed.

Kerryngton mentioned the two of them taking future
trips together, and Bria's stomach flopped. She and
Spade used to talk about all the places they wanted to
go together: Dubai, Paris, France, Italy, Sweden. Even
though their plans weren't etched in stone, the fact that
they entertained the possibility gave them something to
look forward to and strive for. She felt herself become
a bit misty-eyed because London, England, was also on
their list. The thought that she and Spade were both in
London, but not together, caused a tinge of sadness for
her. Bria turned her attention to the guards. She liked
the red and black uniforms with bearskin hats that the
soldiers wore.

Promptly at 11:30 a.m., the Changing of the Guard took
place. Bria took out her phone to record the memorable
event. The handover was accompanied by a Guards band.
The music played ranged from traditional military marches

to songs from films and musicals, and to Bria's surprise, even familiar pop songs. Forty-five minutes later the ceremony ended.

"That was incredible," Bria said as she stopped recording and put her phone away.

Kerryngton grabbed her hand. "Let's head over to our tours."

"I can't wait!" Nya said, schmoozing up to Chance.

Their first stop was The Queen's Gallery. On arrival, the group and their belongings went through an airport-style security check. Bria was disappointed to learn that photography, video recording, and filming were not permitted inside of the palace. She'd just have to pay particular attention and create some good memories in her mind, she figured.

Once at The Queen's Gallery, they stood in the entrance hall along with the other visitors. They had to go through security yet again before making their way to the galleries and activity areas on the upper level. Bria found herself paying acute attention to the details of her surroundings. Gold lettering that read: "THE QUEEN'S GALLERY" was prominently displayed above the entrance. Above that sat a red lion. The monumental entrance doors were made of oak. Framing the stone-arched entrance to the exhibition areas were two free-standing winged figures. Bria noticed that the entrance hall's robust rusticated style contrasted with the interior of the stair hall beyond, which was polychromatic and ornate. She looked up and observed that the ceiling was painted in fascinating red and green anthemion patterns above Ionic columns and pilasters in green scagliola.

Inside, both couples walked hand-in-hand. Bria saw the most unique reception desk made from curved pieces of Scottish elm with kilned glass and patinated copper. Dividing the reception from the main Gallery area was a patterned glass screen. The dramatic central stair of native timber led to the Gallery spaces above.

Bria thought the Leonardo da Vinci anatomist exhibit was fantastic! Very well organized, the staff was particularly friendly and happy to impart their knowledge.

To their dismay, they had to go through security again before going to the next exhibit. When they finished going through a full TSA scan of their bags, they proceeded to a forty-five-minute guided tour of the Royal Mews.

A warden, dressed in his striking red and navy livery, guided them on their tour. The tour itself introduced the work of the Royal Mews, whose staff was responsible for all the road travel by the queen and members of the royal family. Bria admired the coaches and carriages on display.

The guide talked about how the Mews serve the queen in the performance of her official duties and prepares for major State and ceremonial occasions. *Interesting,* Bria thought.

During their visit, they got to see some of the queen's horses that draw the coaches and carriages in the Mews. Even the horses looked regal—white, spectacularly large, and adorned in red, black, and gold.

They saw the bridle room, which displayed the gift from President Barack Obama to the queen—a set of horseshoes from a race horse and some bridle pieces. Bria felt proud to be an American. However, she did find it humorous that she had to go halfway across the world to occupy the same space her president once had.

In the stable area, they saw the carriage used in the recent royal wedding. They also got to see some of the fine livery worn by the queen's coachmen. Bria liked all the fine details. At the end of the informative tour, they purchased a few souvenirs and went to their last tour of the day.

Finally, an audio tour of the nineteen lavishly furnished State Rooms. *They saved the best for last,* Bria thought. The tour started out with an introduction by the Prince of Wales, chairman of the Royal Collection Trust, and took them through all the State Rooms and the special exhibition.

Bria pinched herself to make sure she wasn't dreaming. The sting of the pinch let her know she was very much awake and walking around an actual palace lived in by the royal family. The rooms were furnished with many of the greatest treasures from the Royal Collection, including paintings by Van Dyck and Canaletto, sculpture by Canova, exquisite pieces of Sèvres porcelain, and some of the finest English and French furniture in the world. Bria really liked the White Room with the ebony-veneered cabinets that held a concealed door!

The commentary provided a lively guide to royal history and the works of art from the Royal Collection. They heard about the palace's transformation over the last 300 years, from its early beginnings as Buckingham House to the world-famous palace. Along the route, staff of the Royal Household explained the role of the palace as an official residence of the queen and talked about their work, from arranging State Banquets and Garden Parties to cleaning the sparkling chandeliers.

Next, Bria got a better understanding of why diamonds are a girl's best friend. Her eyes grew huge as they witnessed the spectacular exhibition Diamonds: A Jubilee Celebration. The exhibition showed the many ways in which diamonds have been used by British monarchs over the last 200 years, including a number of the queen's personal jewels. They started out standing in line until Nya suggested they go around the back of the cases and peek over people's heads. They tried it, and Nya was right. They could see just as much and spent far less time waiting that way.

"Impressive," Bria said of a jeweled crown. The queen sure had it going on in the jewelry department, Bria thought.

When they finished, they took a guided tour of the most remarkable features of the famous garden.

The gray-haired tour guide told them, "The thirty-nine-acre garden is the setting for the queen's Garden Parties."

Hearing that sparked Bria's imagination. She imagined having tea with the queen in the garden.

She heard the guide say, "Described as 'a walled oasis in the middle of London,' the garden boasts more than 350 types of wildflowers, over 200 trees, and a three-acre lake."

The tour included the beautiful Herbaceous Border, the wisteria-clad summer house and Rose Garden, the enormous Waterloo Vase and the palace tennis court, where King George VI and Fred Perry played in the 1930s.

At the end of their tour they enjoyed a moment of downtime in the Garden Café on the palace's West Terrace while they took in the panoramic view of the lawn. They drank tea and ate sandwiches and delicious pastries specially created for Buckingham Palace. Bria felt like a princess.

Chance nibbled on a sandwich. "Man, I can't even imagine what it would be like to be a part of the royal family and live in a palace."

"I know, right?" Nya's eyes lit up like she was trying to imagine what being royalty must feel like.

Bria shrugged her shoulders. "I don't know, but I feel like royalty right now," she admitted with a huge smile on her face.

"Well, you're a queen to me, baby." Kerryngton took a napkin and dabbed a little shine off Bria's nose.

"Awww, how sweet was that?" Nya poked Chance in the rib with her elbow.

Chance shook his head. "See what you started?" He playfully directed his comment to Kerryngton and finished his sandwich. He licked his lips.

They finished eating their refreshments and Bria and Nya stuffed their empty pale blue cups with Garden Café Buckingham Palace scribbled on them into their purses. The guys just looked at them.

"What?" Nya said. "It's a souvenir."

"You know they have a gift shop, right?" Chance said. "We *can* get some souvenirs."

They made their way to the gift shop and had a hard time deciding on what to get because they wanted everything.

"How about this?" Kerryngton suggested. "Let's just get it all and have it shipped home."

Never in her life had Bria gone into a store and purchased absolutely everything that she wanted. She quickly tallied the numbers in her brain and determined that was way out of her price range. She had a budget for souvenirs, but she was thinking along the lines of postcards and maybe a piece of china.

"That's too rich for my blood," Chance said.

"Dude, I got you," Kerryngton assured him. "When you all are out with me you don't have to reach for your wallet."

"That's real generous of you," Chance acknowledged, "but I can't let you do that."

"Don't mention it. I want to. It's not every day you get to come to London," he insisted.

After a brief moment of hesitation, Chance agreed to let Kerryngton buy the souvenirs. Kerryngton spoke to the salesclerk and asked her to give them three—one for Bria, another for Nya and Chance, and a third for Kerryngton—of everything in the store. The clerk's eyes lit up like a Las Vegas slot machine. The clerk went around the shop gathering the merchandise. She rang up the items and Kerryngton paid with his black card. He then provided the clerk with a shipping address. He took his receipt, and they left the store.

"I'm exhausted," Nya said, trying to stifle a yawn.

"I'm with you, babe," Chance added. "It's been a long day."

"What about you?" Kerryngton asked Bria.

"I'm good."

"In that case, we can drop them off at the hotel and find something else for us to do," he suggested. "That is, if you're up for it."

"That works for me. I didn't come all the way to London to spend time in a hotel room," she smirked.

Kerryngton dropped Nya and Chance off and took Bria back to his hotel while he handled some business before taking her shopping. He told her he had to make a business call back to the States. Bria tried not to listen, but it was hard considering Kerryngton was yelling from the other room.

"I don't have time for incompetence!" he yelled. "Either make it happen or you're fired!"

Bria's heart jumped. She had never seen him upset before, and it made her uncomfortable. He came into the living room where she was switching TV stations trying to find something to watch. Funny thing was, when he joined her he didn't seem upset at all.

"Sorry about that." He shook his head. "I can't stand when people make excuses. To me, if somebody tells you no, that just means you're not asking the right person. Anybody who has ever worked with me knows I don't accept no for an answer."

Bria could tell that Kerryngton ruled with an iron fist. She was glad she didn't work for him, because she didn't like seeing that side of him. She would've hated to have been on the receiving end of that call. She had heard that some of the most successful, powerful people were the most difficult to work for. Apparently, Kerryngton wasn't an exception.

Twenty-three

The week had gone by too quickly for Bria. She had a magnificent time in London and hated to leave. She had gotten a taste of international travel and wanted to put some more stamps on her passport.

To her surprise, Spade would be flying back to Atlanta with the three of them. Kerryngton had made those arrangements prior to finding out about the two of them.

She didn't know how she felt about that. She hadn't seen Spade since that fateful night due to his demanding schedule, but he had texted her a few times just to say he was thinking of her. Kerryngton, on the other hand, would be back in one more week.

"Call me as soon as you land," Kerryngton requested as Bria was about to board the plane. He kissed her on the lips.

"I will," she promised.

Nya, Chance, and Spade were already onboard the private jet.

"You sure you're okay with Spade traveling with you?" He held her hands as he looked in her almond-shaped eyes.

She sighed. "I'm fine with it." Even if she wasn't, what difference would it make? she figured. Spade still needed to get back.

He kissed her on the forehead and hugged her. "I don't want you to go."

She nestled her face in his neck and inhaled his manly scent. She didn't really want to go either. "I'll miss you too, but we'll see each other in a few days."

"I know." He released her. "You'd better go before I don't let you go." He gave her a closed-mouth grin.

Bria waved good-bye to him and ascended the stairs to the aircraft. Cool air greeted her as soon as she boarded. Chance and Spade were cracking up over what she was sure was one of Chance's corny jokes. Seeing them together like that reminded her of old times.

She flung the Gucci purse Kerryngton had purchased for her during their shopping spree on the seat and sat down. Then she leaned her head back and stared at the blank projector screen.

"A wooden nickel for your thoughts," Chance said as he snapped his finger in front of her face.

Swatting his hand away like an annoying gnat, Bria told him, "I'm good."

Nya emerged from the bathroom wiping her hands on a paper towel. She crumpled it up and tossed it in a nearby trash receptacle.

Spade came over and said, "Tomorrow's the Fourth of July. We still hanging out?"

"Yeah, man," Chance told him.

Nya and Bria exchanged perplexed expressions. Although spending the Fourth together had become their tradition, Bria hadn't given any thought to the holiday and how that would've changed since she and Spade were no longer together. She did want to spend the holiday with her friends, but she didn't want to give Spade false hope. She wasn't sure where her relationship with him stood, and she needed time to sort things out.

Nya whispered in her ear, "Just go. It'll be fun."

Bria found it amusing how well Nya knew her. Nya could just look at her and know exactly what was going on inside. Giving Nya a reluctant smile, Bria agreed to attend the cookout.

Once they were in the air, they paired up into guys versus girls teams and played different card games for a couple of hours. They seemed to take turns winning and losing, and each team talked more trash than a little bit. Bria thought this truly felt like old times. They then watched a slasher film which Nya and Chance fell asleep on. With Chance snoring and Nya's head bobbing, Spade and Bria were left alone to discuss their issues. For a long while they just stared at each other in silence.

"Where's your engagement ring?" he asked, pointing at her hand.

She touched her naked hand as if she had forgotten her ring wasn't there. "No point in wearing an engagement ring when I'm not engaged."

His eyes dropped to the floor. "I guess I deserved that." He looked back up at her. "How long are you going to make me suffer for my mistake?"

"I'm not trying to make you suffer. It's complicated."

"You've changed."

She frowned. "What do you mean?"

"There was a time when I knew how much you loved me. I had a connection with you that I've never had with anybody else. I thought you had my back, and I had yours. I'm not gonna lie. I'm pissed off that you fell for the first guy that came your way. The Bria I knew never would've done that." He sounded so absolute.

Bria felt tears sting the back of her eyes. His words cut her like a steak knife. "You have no right to judge me."

He pointed his finger. "Let me tell you something. If the situation had been reversed, I wouldn't have given up on you. Even if I was remotely interested in somebody else, she would've gotten dropped for you. Hands down, end of discussion."

Whoever said words can never hurt lied. They obviously had never been in love. His words killed her like a stingray's poisonous venom to the heart. She could tell that underneath his hard-core veneer there was genuine hurt. His voice trembled, but she knew his ego wouldn't allow him to shed any tears. At least not in front of her.

She didn't appreciate him attacking her as if she had never loved him or didn't love him still. Why couldn't he understand that she was human? He cut her, and she bled, figuratively speaking. She couldn't turn her feelings off and on like a faucet. If she had never met Kerryngton, she could not have, nor would she have wanted to, imagine being with anyone other than Spade. She feared that if she dropped Kerryngton and ran back to Spade, she would always wonder what could've been. She didn't want to take the chance of resenting Spade one day. It's not like she had a whole bunch of dating experience to begin with. She simply wanted to explore her options before making a lifetime commitment now.

She wiped her face. "You can try to downplay it, but you know exactly how I feel about you." She softened her tone. "And I know how you feel about me too. Aside from Nya, you are my best friend. All I'm asking you to do is to give me some time. It's easy for you to tell me what you think I should do and what you would do. You've dated plenty of girls. That's how you can be so sure about me. You know what's out there. Well, I haven't had that much experience."

"But, Bria—"

"No, let me finish." She sniffled. "If we're meant to be together, we will be. I probably would've married you and never looked back. I'm certain I would not have regretted that decision a day of my life. But since that didn't happen, I came to realize that everything happens for a reason. Maybe I needed to live some more before getting married."

"So what are you trying to say? You want me to wait around while you play the field?" Frown lines etched his forehead.

As difficult as it was for Bria to say this, she said, "First of all, I'm not *playing the field*. Let's get that straight. Second, I'm not asking you to wait."

Spade clenched his jaw and grinded his teeth. "If that's how you want it . . ." He stood up. "There's nothing left to say. I'm going to lie down." He touched his temple.

"Is your head hurting?"

"Don't worry about it." He walked out, leaving her to unleash a new flood of tears.

The plane touched down in Atlanta at nine o'clock in the evening. The conversation with Spade had left Bria mentally drained. She couldn't wait to get home and sleep in her bed.

They disembarked from the plane and a very pretty brown-skinned woman dressed in a skintight outfit that showed off all her assets and tattoos waved Spade over. Bria and Nya exchanged curious glances while their driver and Chance loaded the luggage in the car.

The mystery woman told Spade, "Welcome back! How was your trip?"

"It was cool," he said as he stuffed his suitcase in the backseat of her Hummer.

The woman hugged him, and Bria felt an unfamiliar pang of jealousy.

"Aren't you going to introduce us to your friend?" Nya asked.

Spade scratched his head. "This is Kola. She's a singer. She performed a few of the hooks on some of my tracks." He pointed at Nya. "This is my homegirl Nya." He gestured toward Bria. "That's Bria."

Bria's face dropped. She was offended that everyone except her received some sort of special introduction.

Kola extended her hand to Nya first, then Bria. "Nice to meet you." She spoke with a Southern accent. She sounded like she'd been born and raised in Decatur, Georgia.

Chance came over and said to Spade, "Don't forget about tomorrow, man. Make sure you bring the Dominos."

"I got you," Spade said.

"Sounds like fun," Kola said. "I'm from Trinidad, and we used to play a lot of Dominos."

"If you want to come and get smoked, come on," Chance said. "The more the merrier."

What? Bria thought. She felt like kicking Chance in the shin. He didn't know this chick, yet he was inviting her to be a part of their Fourth of July tradition. The flight must've deprived his brain of oxygen.

"We'll see," she said. "It's a holiday, but for an artist that doesn't mean anything." She smiled at Spade, revealing her porcelain veneers. "Isn't that right, Spade?"

"That's right," he said. "We work all the time."

"We'd better get going," Bria said. "Have a good night," she spoke directly to Kola.

"You too." Kola dangled her key ring from her finger. "You want to drive?" she said to Spade.

Bria walked off; she didn't wait for Spade to respond. Chance and Nya followed behind her. The driver was waiting for them and closed the doors when they got inside the car.

"What's the matter with you?" Bria berated Chance.

"What are you talking about now?" He sounded exasperated.

"How are you going to invite someone you just met to spend the holiday with us?"

"I was being polite. What's the big deal?"

"There isn't one," Nya interjected. "It's not like Spade and Kola are dating. If they were, then you would've been out of line and insensitive."

"Hold up," Chance said. "You're jealous." He must've had an *aha!* moment. "Ol' girl does have that Coke-bottle shape going on. I see how she got her name."

"Shut your piehole," Bria told him. And she wasn't kidding.

"Just like a woman. You don't want him, but you sure don't want to see him with somebody else."

They didn't talk much after that during the rest of the ride. Bria sulked and couldn't stop thinking about Spade. The driver dropped Bria off first. As soon as she got inside her house she inhaled the familiar potpourri scent that perfumed the air. She unpacked first, and then made a round of phone calls to Dani, her mom, and Kerryngton to let them know she had arrived home safely.

She then showered and put on her nightclothes. She contemplated whether she should even go over to Nya and Chance's house tomorrow. She hadn't gotten over feeling a certain kind of way toward Spade.

"Why should I stay home?" she said to herself. "Nya and Chance are my friends. Spade inherited them by default. Forget that. I'm going."

Twenty-four

Bria showed up at Nya and Chance's house with six bottles of Jamaican ginger beer, a nonalcoholic ginger-flavored soda.

Nya kissed her on the cheek. "Chance is in the backyard grilling," she said as she ushered Bria inside.

Bria smirked. She set the bottles on the table. "Hold up. Why is Chance grilling? You know we get," she counted off on her fingers, "slabs of ribs, rum-baked beans, potato salad, Brunswick stew, and lemonade from Fat Matt's every Fourth." Bria was about to get an attitude if they were breaking their tradition. They had gotten turned on to Fat Matt's off Piedmont Road in Atlanta while in college. There would be a line of people standing outside waiting for the fall-off-the-bone tangy ribs. And the side items were always on point.

Nya laughed. "Now you know better. Chance already picked up the food. He just wanted to throw some salmon and barbecue chicken in the mix."

"Oh, okay." Bria calmed down.

The women decorated the dining-room table with a patriotic tablecloth and matching paper plates, cups, napkins, and plastic cutlery. When they finished, they went into the living room. The room appealed to all the senses. The space was dimly lit, just the way Bria and Nya preferred it. They both liked natural lighting. The room, while wildly eclectic for Bria's taste, had a very strict color palette—white, black/charcoal, brown, rust, and blue. There was plenty going on, but not overwhelmingly. Somehow, it all came together.

Nya put on a Ken Ford CD that played in the background, and she lit some lavender incense. The sweet smell of lavender filled the air. Nya swore by lavender. She claimed it helped her relax and calm her nerves. At bedtime she put a few drops on her pillow to help her get a good night's sleep. She even went as far as to put a few drops in a warm bath mixed with sea salts for a delicious spa bath. Lavender meant to Nya what fresh flowers meant to Bria.

"Spade called before you got here," Nya told Bria. "He should be here any minute. He had to stop off and get the dessert." She set out a deck of cards and stacked some board games on top of each other. "He's bringing Kola. Not because he wanted to but because Chance offered and she accepted. He told me he didn't want to be rude."

"That's fine. You want me to put out some potato chips and nuts?"

"Sure, but before Spade gets here, I need to know how you're feeling about everything."

"I'm okay. There's a part of me that wants to get back together with Spade and act like none of this ever happened. I feel sad that he went through the cancer ordeal by himself. I wish I could've been there for him. And if he's not out of the woods, I will be there for him. But he seems to be doing fine. I've been lifting him up in prayer, praying that he really was misdiagnosed and that he's healthy."

"Me too," Nya added.

"Now that I've had time to think about it, I do understand why Spade kept his condition from me. I don't agree, but that's life. I'm sure we could move past it. It's just that I like Kerryngton . . . a lot."

"I know you do, but you can't keep Spade dangling on a string. You know I've always been Team Spade. Even when he broke your heart, I didn't say it, but I was hoping and praying the two of you would get back together. Then when I saw you catching feelings for Kerryngton . . ." Her voice trailed off. She held up a finger. "But I'll tell you this. I saw the way you looked at Spade when you saw him with Kola. You couldn't hide your feelings. That's when I realized you needed to be with Spade, because your heart belongs to him."

"I can't do that to Kerryngton. He doesn't deserve it."

Nya looked her in the eyes. "And Spade does?"

Bria turned her head away. "Neither one of them deserves it."

Nya rested her chin on Bria's shoulder and spoke to the side of her face. "Kerryngton has a lot going for him, professionally speaking. But Spade is *your* man. I don't need to sell you on him because you already know what a jewel he is. He's young, but he's got his head on straight. Plus, he's got skills that will definitely pay the bills." She paused. "While you're around here playin', don't mess around and let some other woman scoop up your man."

The doorbell rang. Nya headed to the door while Bria went in the kitchen to wash her hands and prepare bowls of chips and nuts. She could hear Spade's voice as soon as Nya let him in. She exhaled and carried the bowls into the living room where she set them on the coffee table.

"Hey," Bria said to Spade and Kola, trying to sound chipper.

Spade eyed her up and down. "Hey. You look nice."

She knew she looked good, because she took extra time to get ready. She wore her hair parted on the side and curled at the ends, just the way Spade liked it. She also wore a turquoise halter-style sundress that showed off her square shoulders, impressive cleavage, and smooth back. She wasn't about to let Kola show her up. "Thanks. So do you."

Nya took the store-bought red velvet cake he was carrying out of his hands and went into the kitchen.

"Glad you could make it," Bria directed her comment to Kola. She caught a glimpse of Kola's enormous booty. It looked big in the dark, but in the light, it took on a whole new dimension.

"Same here. You need help with anything?"

Bria shook her head. "No, we're good. Chance is outside grilling some fish and chicken. Make yourself comfortable."

"Fish and chicken?" Spade said. His expression revealed his surprise.

"Calm down," she laughed. "Fat Matt's is in the kitchen."

"You already know what's up," he chuckled. "I was about to say."

"I reacted the same way earlier." She touched him and felt a slight static shock. As he looked down at her, she deliberately turned her face away.

Nya yelled from the kitchen, "Can I get anybody anything?"

Everyone declined.

Kola sat down, and Bria could've sworn she heard the couch ask for help. "I like this house."

Bria thanked her on behalf of Nya who joined them in the living room.

"I'll go see if my man Chance needs any help," Spade said.

As soon as Spade walked out, the ladies started talking about reality TV shows and all the drama they entailed. They were laughing when the guys came back inside with aluminum pans filled with meat.

Chance wiped the dripping sweat from his brow. "I need to take a shower."

"Yes, you do." Bria pretended to fan away funk that she didn't smell. "You're assaulting my nostrils."

"Shut it up before I cover your nose with my armpit." He raised his arm and Bria got out of the way.

"You'd better not, stink boy." She crinkled her nose.

Spade scooped a handful of mixed nuts and stuffed them in his mouth. "Bria, let me holla at you for a minute."

"Okay." She wondered what he wanted to talk about now. Hadn't they already said everything? Bria got up and followed him outside. "What's up?" she asked as she slowly closed the door behind them.

"We finished picking out the songs that are gonna make it onto my CD."

She smiled at him. She knew how much this meant to him. "Congratulations. I'm happy for you."

"Thanks." He pulled his CD cover from his pocket and showed it to her. "Here's my cover artwork."

She studied it for a moment. She thought Spade looked extremely handsome and sexy in a wifebeater, showing his impressive pecs, abs, and biceps on the cover. "I really like it. This is hot." She could tell her approval meant a lot to him.

"I'm having a CD release party, and I want you to come."

Since she had been there with Spade since the beginning she wanted to be there to support him. He might not be her man right now, but she would always consider him to be her friend. She figured this could be their first step toward mending their broken relationship. A baby step, but nonetheless, it was still a step. If he was willing to extend her an olive branch, she was mature enough to accept it.

"That should be fine," she told him. "We'd better go back inside before Nya puts out an APB on us."

When they returned, Chance had freshened up and changed clothes. They were right on time for one of his corny jokes.

"Knock, knock," Chance said.

"Who's there?" Nya and Kola asked in unison.

"Doris."

"Doris who?" they continued to indulge him.

"Doris locked; that's why I'm knocking."

As lame as Bria thought that was, Chance's joke actually got a chuckle out of her.

"Ready to grub?" he asked.

"Yeah," Bria answered, patting Chance's oversized belly. "I can see that you've been doing a little bit too much grubbin'."

"As long as my pookie butt likes it, it's all good." He gave Nya a hug and kiss on the cheek.

"Negro, please! Your plump behind better go to the gym before you run, I mean walk, around here looking as fat and bloated as the Goodyear Blimp," Bria said.

"Are you going to let her talk to me like that?" he said to Nya. He turned his face up and stared at her.

"Just call me Switzerland. I'm neutral," she said.

"That's right, thickalicious." She acted like he was the Pillsbury Doughboy and poked his belly with her finger. "Now what?"

"Why don't you take the Tyson approach and bite me?"

"Too much grease and blubber is bad for my cholesterol. I'll have to pass on biting you today. Thank you just the same."

"Kids, kids, *please*," Nya interjected.

Kola and Spade were busy cracking up laughing.

"Let's eat," Nya said.

They went in the kitchen and fixed their plates. The food smelled delectable. They said grace, and then ate until they got the "itis." The food was so good that the only sounds being made were chewing and finger licking.

When Chance finished eating, he said, "Now I got the black people syndrome." He rubbed his stomach.

They laughed and Spade added, "I feel ya."

"Anybody want dessert?" Nya offered while clearing the table. She and Bria usually ate a scoop of vanilla ice cream after dinner.

"Not right now," Chance said.

"None for me," Spade echoed that sentiment.

"Whatcha got?" Kola asked.

"Ice cream or cake?" Nya told her.

"I'll take a slice of cake, but I can get it." She pushed her chair back and got up.

The ladies went in the kitchen and fixed their desserts. They returned to the table already eating their sweet treats.

"I don't know how you all have the room," Chance said. "I feel like a stuffed pig."

"And you look like one too." Bria couldn't resist. She burst out laughing. In between laughs she managed to say, "I'm just kidding." Bria realized that in the presence of a stranger her teasing may seem a bit harsh, but that's just how she and Chance have always interacted.

Chance mean mugged her.

"You'll get used to these two," Nya said to Kola. "They act like a real brother and sister."

Chance said, "So, Spade, how's your CD coming along?"

"It's finished." He showed them the cover.

"That was fast," Nya said.

"It might seem that way, but the truth of the matter is that my CD was already recorded when I got the deal. We only had to record a few new songs and change out the music on some of the songs. That was it."

"Don't you write your own lyrics?" Chance asked.

"Definitely." He rubbed his hands together. "Matter of fact, I wrote a new song during our flight. Want to hear it?"

"Yeah," everyone said.

He cleared his throat and stood up. He started rapping about a lost love. Bria immediately knew he was talking about her, because he mentioned how he and the woman were best friends amongst other telling things like the way they used to just sit around and chill. He described Bria as his dream girl, but he messed up their almost perfect world. He broke her heart, and now he's the one crying. The lyrics moved Bria emotionally. By the end of the song, she felt exposed, and, in an odd way, flattered.

"Wow," Nya said. "That was deep." She eyed Bria.

"I like it," Kola said. "That was some LL Cool J 'I Need Love' stuff right there."

They all laughed.

Chance said, "I guess it's true . . . You can't become a great artist until you've gone through some pain. I felt that, my brother." He tapped two fingers over his heart.

"Let me know if you need me to sing the hook," Kola offered. "You know I got you." She batted her false eyelashes at him.

His gaze pierced Bria's soul. "Did you like it?"

"I did," Bria admitted. She scooped some ice cream in her mouth and licked her lips.

A loud pop sounded outdoors. People in the neighborhood were already setting off fireworks. They turned on the TV and tuned in to the Macy's at Lenox Mall celebration to watch the fireworks.

The lyrics to Spade's song stuck in Bria's mind like gum to the bottom of a shoe. He had poured his heart into that song, and she found that very romantic. He had professed his love for her for everyone to hear. If he recorded that song, their love would be forever immortalized. How could she not want to be with a guy like that?

Twenty-five

Bria appreciated the fact that Spade had respected her wishes and kept his distance. Translation: he wasn't calling her or demanding to see her. She attributed part of his ability to stay away to his demanding schedule. He had photo shoots and interviews. She knew this because he'd text her just to say hello or let her know what he was doing. Additionally, she had plenty of work of her own. She had to play catch-up at the spa. Neither of them had leisure time to spare, and that suited Bria just fine while she sorted out her feelings.

Bria was at the spa when Dani called her to the front asking her to bring her driver's license so that she could sign for a special delivery. Bria felt annoyed because anyone at the spa could sign for a delivery. Since when did she need to show her license to get a delivery? She didn't appreciate the interruption. She huffed to the front.

"Are you Bria Murray?" a well-dressed guy asked her.

"Yes."

He handed her a pen. "May I please see your driver's license?"

She gave it to him.

He verified her ID and wrote down her license number on an official-looking document. "Would you please sign here and here?" He pointed to two signature lines.

Bria scribbled her signature.

"Thanks." The guy handed Bria a set of keys and a keyless remote. "Congratulations on your new Mercedes-Benz."

"Wait. I didn't purchase a new car."

He scanned the papers. "No, you didn't. A Mr. Kerryngton Kruse purchased the car for you."

Bria's jaw dropped, and gasps could be heard throughout the spa.

"Have a nice day, ma'am."

Every spa employee that wasn't with a customer came out to see Bria's new ride. The shiny red convertible with gray interior stood out from every other car in the lot. People were ooh-ing and ahh-ing left and right.

Nya pulled Bria to the side and said, "He just upped the ante. Are you going to keep that car?"

Bria felt like her head was spinning. "I don't know."

"If you don't want it, can I have it?"

Bria smirked. "I'm about to call him." She went to her office to get her cell phone and call Kerryngton. She scrolled through her list of favorites and placed the call. When he answered, she could tell he had been expecting her call.

"Like your gift?" he asked.

"It's the most lavish gift I've ever received. It's too much. I can't accept it."

"Nonsense, baby. I want you to have it. Consider it my gift to you for opening up your own business."

"But it's so expensive. I don't feel right—"

"I know where you're going with this," he cut her off. "You don't have to worry. I'm not trying to make you feel indebted to me. I don't have to buy the snatch from any woman. It's a gift. No strings attached."

"Seriously?"

"Seriously," he repeated.

Bria mulled over what he said and came to the conclusion that she would accept the gift. "In that case, thank you."

"You're welcome. I'm back in the States, and I do want to see you, though."

"When?" She whipped out her iPad.

"I have my daughter this weekend. I'd like for you to meet her."

Bria's heart sank as if she was plunging down the dark freight elevator shaft of the once-glamorous Hollywood Tower Hotel in The Twilight Zone Tower of Terror, a thrill ride at Disney's Hollywood Studios theme park. "I-I wasn't expecting that. Are you sure you're ready for me to meet Alexis?" She really meant she wasn't sure she was ready to meet his child. She bit her lower lip as she pondered what this could mean for their relationship. If she and the little girl didn't click, that could be the end of them.

"I wouldn't have said it if I didn't mean it. Nothing too formal. You could come over to my house and meet her. Bring a swimsuit."

Bria swallowed the lump forming in her throat and reluctantly agreed. They settled on a date and time, and Bria added it to her electronic appointment calendar.

They ended the call, and Bria immediately summoned Nya into her office.

"So what's the verdict?" Nya asked as she closed the door behind her to give them some privacy.

"Oh." Bria had forgotten about the car just that quickly. "I'm keeping it."

"Yes!" Nya pumped her fist in the air like she had won a prize. "Why the long face then?"

"He wants me to meet his daughter."

"Oh." Nya slumped down in a chair, her facial expression matching Bria's. "Are you ready for that?"

"Honestly, I hadn't given it much thought."

"That's a big deal, girlie. He's probably introducing you to his daughter to see if there's potential for a future. If his daughter likes you, he can keep seeing you. If she doesn't, you're outta there."

Bria had never been a nail biter, but her thumb nail was looking mighty tempting right about now. She bit just a small piece off the tip.

"This is a good thing," Nya assured her. "This could either swing the pendulum in Spade's favor or bring you closer to Kerryngton. Either way, it'll help knock you off the fence. You know you've been straddling."

Now Bria chewed on her nail.

"I'm amazed at how fast you and Kerryngton are moving. You haven't even known each other that long, and you've already taken a vacation together, gotten a brand-new whip, and now he wants to introduce you to his daughter." She propped her elbows on Bria's desk and held her face in her hands. "You know what's next, right?"

Bria gave her a perplexed look. "No, what's next?"

"He's going to expect you to take him home and meet your parents."

Bria hadn't thought that far in advance. She hadn't given any consideration to letting Kerryngton meet her parents in spite of her mother's pleas to meet the guy who had taken her daughter out of the country. To Bria, taking a guy home meant the relationship was serious. Right now, she was having fun . . . or was she? He was supposed to be a distraction to help her get her mind off Spade. Instead, he had become her boyfriend. Nya was right about their relationship moving at lightning speed. Maybe she needed to pump the brakes.

Twenty-six

Bria drove her new Benz to Kerryngton's mansion. His estate looked like the houses people rented to use in music videos and movies. His property was gated with two huge lion statues at the entrance, so he had to buzz her in. Behind the gates was a European-inspired mansion complete with a circular driveway and an enormous fountain in the center. She could tell a professional landscaper was responsible for maintaining the upkeep of the pristine green lawn.

She parked her car and grabbed the gift she had gotten for Alexis off the seat and stuffed it in her Michael Kors bag. Kerryngton had previously told her that Alexis liked playing a handheld electronic video game, so she brought her two games. She took a quick second to mentally prepare herself for the encounter.

As soon as she got out of the car the front door opened up. She put on a smile and greeted Kerryngton's butler. She knew he had to be the butler because of his uniform.

When she saw the foyer, she took her heels off at the door and immediately felt like a midget. The butler handed her a pair of slippers, and she put them on. Kerryngton appeared from somewhere in the back and hugged her.

"Welcome to my humble abode," he said.

"This place is anything but humble," Bria said. She smiled at him.

"Please let me know if I can get you anything," the butler said as he excused himself.

"Alexis isn't here yet," Kerryngton told her. Since it was her first time at his house, he gave her the grand tour.

The home consisted of seven bedrooms, ten bathrooms, a grand double marble staircase, formal dining room, oval-shaped wood-paneled study, a two-story great room, gourmet kitchen, octagonal breakfast room, a two-story family room with a wet bar, a second-floor loft, billiards room with another wet bar, gym, home theater, patio with a swimming pool, and a six-car garage filled with expensive cars.

Kerryngton's home was a lot for Bria to take in. It was massive. "I can't believe you live here all by yourself," she told him.

"When we get married we can fill it up with babies."

Shut the front door! Did he really say what Bria thought she heard? Married? Babies? Was he serious? She had to know. "Are you serious?" she asked.

He eased his large hand around her trim waist. "I'm a businessman. There are two things I know: people and to trust my instincts. It doesn't take me long to make a decision. When I see something I want, I go after it."

"But we haven't known each other that long."

"Baby, let me tell you something." He scooted onto a bar stool, and Bria leaned against his thigh. "My parents knew each other for three months before they got married. And that was forty years ago. I know people who were together for years before they got married and couldn't make it to their first wedding anniversary. It's not about how long you've known someone; it's about the compatibility and your willingness to work on the relationship."

"I understand but—"

He placed a finger to her lips and shushed her. "You're overthinking this. We feel right together. There's no denying that." He removed his finger from her lips. "There aren't many people that I trust, but I trust you."

She could tell that he meant that, and she felt endeared to him. Knowing how torn she felt inside, though, she hoped she was worthy of all that trust he had bestowed upon her.

"I meet a lot of women, and most of them make it obvious that they want to give me the skins. I don't want a woman who comes to me too easy, because if she comes to me easy, then she comes to other men easily too. Not to mention Atlanta has got a high HIV/AIDS and herpes population. I'm disease-free with the paperwork to prove it, and I plan to stay that way. I need more than sex from my partner." He got up from his seat and rustled through some papers in a drawer. Then he sat back down and handed the paper to her.

"What's this?" She studied the paper but couldn't figure out what it was for.

"My paperwork showing I don't have any STDs."

Since he had brought up the subject of sex, she thought now would be the perfect time to tell him she was still a virgin. She turned to face him and looked him in the eyes. Placing the paper on the counter she didn't want to make her announcement seem dramatic, so she blurted out, "I'm still a virgin."

He raised a brow and started touching her.

"What are you doing?"

"Making sure you're not a figment of my imagination." She started laughing. "Stop."

He stopped groping her. "I didn't know virgins existed in this day and age, especially after high school. I thought they were as extinct as dinosaurs. You mean you and your fiancé never . . ."

"No." She then told him about her purity pledge.

"I can respect that." He wiped the corners of his mouth with his thumb and index finger. "I believe what you're telling me. It's just that . . ." he shook his head ". . . as fine as you are I know it had to be extra hard not to give it up. Pretty girls usually start having sex early because everybody wants them."

Bria appreciated the compliment. "When I was younger my parents kept me busy. I did a lot of after-school activities. Plus, my parents expected me to get good grades, so I really didn't have time to focus on boys. And when I did start dating, I was only allowed to go on chaperoned group dates."

"What about when you went off to college? Why didn't you go buck wild then?"

"I didn't because of the way my parents raised me. They taught me to respect myself. My dad also had a long talk with me before I left home. He told me that my parents may not know everything I do out in the streets, but God does. And I'd have to account for that. Then he reminded me that no matter where I was I still represented my family. I never wanted to do anything to embarrass my family, so I behaved myself." She laughed as she thought about her mom. "And my mom didn't play. She told me I better not even think about coming home with a baby out of wedlock. She told me abortion and adoption weren't options for me. Basically, she said I'd be stuck with whoever got me pregnant forever."

"I see." He had a seriously big grin on his face.

"Why are you cheesin' so hard?" She tried to soothe his cheeks.

"I'm just trippin' because you don't fit the typical church girl stereotype."

"I'm not a church girl," Bria clarified. "I went to church regularly and actively participated, yes, but my parents weren't ministers. We weren't in church 24/7. Although my parents raised me with biblical principles, they did not shelter me from life. I watched TV and movies according to my ages and stages in life. I listen to all types of music, but my dad told me to listen to the words and not just the beat. They taught me what I needed to know to be able to deal with all kinds of people and not just saved folks."

"I can't wait to meet your parents." He peck kissed her on the lips.

Ding, ding, ding, Nya was right! Was all of this just a setup so that he could meet her family? The more she thought about it, the more she realized Kerryngton probably should meet her parents. After all, she was about to meet his daughter, and they had already discussed marriage. What could it hurt?

"I'd like that."

His expression turned serious. "I believe people know not long after meeting someone if they could see themselves with that person. I knew after our first date that we had potential. I liked your personality. I could tell that you were easy to love." He held her hand. "I think about you all the time."

His words rang true to Bria. She did believe that people knew right away whether they were interested in someone. She didn't tell him this, but she had been raised to believe that the purpose of dating was to land a spouse. She didn't believe in wasting time on someone she knew didn't have the qualities she wanted in a mate.

"How do you feel about me?" He licked his lips.

Her heartbeat sped up. He was easy to love too, and she knew deep down inside that if she would only allow herself to let go, she could fall head over heels in love with him.

He blinked, and she noticed he had some long lashes fringing his bedroom eyes. This time when he looked at her she could see a softness in his eyes that hadn't been there before. He seemed vulnerable, and she liked it.

She exhaled and said, "I feel like I'm falling for you."

He closed his eyes again and opened them slowly. "You know I'ma marry you, right?" His words were deliberate, and he sounded absolute.

She paused to give herself a moment to process what he had said. She held his face in her hands. "I would like that." Her mind was all rainbows and butterflies at that moment.

"In that case, call your parents and see if they can come over for dinner tonight around six. I can send my driver to pick them up."

"Tonight?" What the what? Open mouth, insert foot.

"No point in delaying. Just let me know what they like to eat and my chef can prepare it."

He leaned in and kissed Bria with so much intensity she felt a stirring in the pit of her stomach. She imagined them in the throes of passion and quickly pulled away. She looked at him, and her lip gloss was all over his mouth. She grabbed a paper towel off the counter and wiped his mouth and hers. She then retrieved her lip gloss from her purse and reapplied it.

She felt like she was stuck between a wall and a car bumper. If she refused to call her parents, he'd most likely think she wasn't serious about him. If she called her parents, they'd probably think she had lost her ever-loving mind.

She sighed, silently praying that her mother wouldn't answer as she pulled out her cell phone and called her. She hadn't seen her parents since she'd gotten back from London and knew they'd jump at the chance to spend time with her.

Dang it! Her mom answered sounding like she had been sleeping.

"Did I wake you?" Bria asked.

"I was just taking a nap. How are you doing?"

"I'm at Kerryngton's house, and he wanted to know if you and Daddy would like to come over for dinner tonight."

"Such short notice."

"I know, but what do you and Daddy have planned?" She knew her parents were homebodies. Although her mom was only forty-eight and her dad fifty-two they liked staying in the house. They would go out to dinner or catch a movie, maybe twice a month. They took mini vacations every now and again as well, but she knew they didn't have any plans.

"*Excuse* me? What if me and my husband want to handle grown folks' business?"

"Oh my goodness, Mom! Don't nobody want to hear all that." She scrunched up her face.

She could hear her mom laughing. "I'm kidding. We'd love to attend. What time?"

Bria told her mom what time to be ready and informed her that Kerryngton's driver would be picking them up.

"A driver? We don't need a driver. We have a car."

"You can save on gas. Just go with it, Mom."

"Fine."

Sometimes her mom could be so feisty, she thought.

The intercom buzzed, and Bria hurried her mom off the phone.

"Dinner's a go. They'll be here," she said.

He had a pleasant expression on his face. "Terrific." He seemed genuinely glad. Kerryngton answered the intercom. Alexis and her mother were at the gate.

Showtime, Bria thought. She silently prayed. *Lord, please let this visit go well. If Kerryngton truly is the man for me, then let me and Alexis hit it off. And please, Lord, no baby momma drama. Amen.*

He opened the door and stepped outside while Bria stood in the middle of the enormous foyer feeling awkward and hoping she didn't look stupid. When he returned, Alexis and her mom accompanied him. Bria gave them her most gracious smile. She extended her hand to Alexis's mom.

"You must be Bria." She had the most pleasant-sounding voice with a slight Spanish accent. She shook Bria's hand. "Nice to meet you."

"You too."

Kerryngton then introduced her to Alexis.

"Hi, Alexis. You're even prettier than your pictures."

Alexis blushed. "Thank you."

Bria handed her the gift she had gotten for her. The little girl opened it up and her face lit up. "Thanks. How did you know I wanted these games?"

"Your dad told me the games you already had. I figured if I was your age I'd want these games in my collection too."

"Can I go play these? Please, Daddy?" she begged.

He tousled her hair. "Go for it."

"Yay!" She ran up the left staircase to her room.

"Have fun!" her mom called behind her. She directed her next comment to Kerryngton. "Call if you need to, but I know you won't need to." She lightly kissed Kerryngton on his lips before lifting her right hand and wiggling her fingers. "Tootles."

Bria couldn't believe she had been bold enough to kiss Kerryngton right in front of her face. What kind of mess? She didn't care how amicable their relationship was; that right there was not cool.

Kerryngton locked the door behind her. He acted like that wasn't awkward.

Bria wanted to say something, but she didn't want to come across as an angry black woman. And now wasn't the time. His daughter was in the house. Instead, she said, "Your daughter seems really sweet."

"That's my baby. She's a good kid."

They went into the family room where one of Kerryngton's housekeepers served them cold drinks and refreshments. Bria settled into the comfortable sofa. She plucked a grape from the vine and stuffed it in her mouth.

"Don't eat too much." He squeezed her slender thigh. "You've got to save some room for dinner. Speaking of dinner, do your parents eat seafood?"

"They're from Florida. Of course they eat seafood." She sounded so matter-of-fact.

"I'll let my chef know. You're in for a treat." He left her for a moment while he conferred with the chef. He came back and said, "I want to go swimming."

"I'm ready to go now." She pulled her hot pink bikini out of her purse.

"I see you teasing me." He grinned. "You can change wherever you want. I'll tell Alexis we're about to go swimming."

"Don't forget to put on your trunks. I'll meet you at the pool."

Bria went to the bathroom just off from the family room and changed. She applied sunblock on every area of exposed skin. She then removed the ponytail holder from her hair and allowed her locks to cascade down her back.

After she inspected herself in the mirror she placed her purse and clothes on the sofa in the family room and headed to the pool with her sunglasses in hand. She stretched out on a pool chair until Alexis and Kerryngton joined her. Alexis waved at her before jumping right in the water.

Kerryngton stood next to her and blocked the sun. "Looking good," he told her.

Her eyes landed on his bare chest. His pecs were looking right, and his stomach had enough ripples to grate cheese. She removed her sunglasses to get a better look. "So are you."

"You know how to swim, right?"

"Like a mermaid."

"Let's go." He grabbed her hand and helped her to her feet.

They got in the water and splashed around. Alexis floated on her floatie until her daddy tilted it over and caused her to plummet into the water. She started screaming and laughing. Bria swam a few laps and enjoyed watching Kerryngton play with his daughter. Their interactions seemed effortless and organic. Kerryngton grabbed three water guns and handed them out. The three of them took turns squirting each other in their faces. They laughed hysterically.

Three hours later they decided it was time to get ready for dinner. Bria showered in one of the guest bathrooms. The same hairstylist who had come over to do Alexis's hair washed and styled Bria's. She offered to do Bria's makeup too, and she let her. She had Bria's face looking like a glamour model. Her eyebrows were arched and shaped just right.

When she stepped into the bedroom she was prepared to put back on the casual outfit she had previously worn. To her surprise, Kerryngton had laid out a black Versace dress.

Bria held up the dress and the hem hit the middle of her thigh. She touched the delicate lace that formed the neckline, sleeves, and hem. She put on the dress and the form-fitting sheath accentuated her hourglass figure. A pair of golden Christian Louboutin pumps were perfect for accenting, not overtaking, the simple silhouette. He seemed to have a thing for labels. Everything he bought her was name brand and expensive. She wondered if he was trying to buy her. If so, she wasn't for sale.

Twenty-seven

Bria checked her watch and realized that her parents were set to arrive in half an hour. Kerryngton had already sent his driver to get them. She set her purse and clothes on a chair and went into the family room where Kerryngton had just inserted a CD into the CD player. Some seventies music started playing. Although she wasn't born in the seventies, she always thought that era had the best music.

"I love this song," she beamed as "Darlin', Darlin' Baby (Sweet, Tender, Love)" by the O'Jays piped through the surround sound system.

"I figured your parents would appreciate the musical selection. I have every seventies hit."

Her eyes got big. "Not just them. I appreciate it too. I'm going to have to borrow your collection."

He looked at her with admiring eyes. "You look so sexy and fine."

"Thank you so much for the dress and shoes. They're gorgeous." She modeled the outfit for him. "You're spoiling me."

"I enjoy spoiling you." He pulled out a small box from his pants pocket and placed it in her hand.

She opened the box, and her jaw dropped. She removed the teardrop diamond earrings. "They're beautiful."

"Just like you."

She thanked him and inserted the earrings in her pierced ears.

"Daddy," Alexis said as she entered the room, "there's a good movie coming on Disney. May I please eat my dinner in the theater?"

"You can, but you have to at least come down to meet Bria's parents. Got it?"

"Okay." She handed him a bottle of pink nail polish. "Please paint my toenails for me, Daddy."

He chuckled. "Sit," he told her as she took a seat and propped her small feet on his lap. Bria couldn't believe her eyes as Kerryngton applied two coats of polish to the little girl's feet. How sweet was that? she wondered. She liked seeing that side of him.

"Thanks, Daddy," she said as he tightened the cap on the bottle.

He leaned over and kissed her on the cheek and sniffed the air. "Something sure smells good." He followed the pleasant scent coming from the kitchen to see how dinner was coming along.

Alexis gave Bria a snotty look and whispered, "Don't think you're going to take my momma's place. He belongs to us."

Bria couldn't believe this child had turned on a dime. What happened to the sweet little girl she had been playing with all afternoon? The child looked like the devil's spawn with the distorted expression on her face.

"I'm not trying to take your mother's place," she spoke calmly.

"Good, because they're going to get back together, you know." She sounded matter-of-fact.

"Come on in here," Kerryngton called from the kitchen.

Bria had lost her appetite. She felt like calling her parents and telling them not to come over. Out of respect for Kerryngton she didn't go ham on his kid. She went into the kitchen as he requested. The chef had prepared steamed lobsters with garlic and melted butter on the side, salmon, broccoli, and baked potatoes.

The chef took a momentary break from his preparations to speak to them. "The sirloin steaks are still marinating. Mr. Kruse, I know you like your steaks medium-rare and Miss Alexis doesn't like steak at all." He looked at Bria. "How do you prefer your steak?"

She gritted her teeth. "Medium-rare for me too."

He nodded. "Thank you. I'll wait until the other guests arrive before grilling the steaks," he told Kerryngton. He removed two bottles of wine from the refrigerator. "I got a bottle of red and a bottle of white wine from the wine cellar. I thought it would be a good choice for the meal."

Kerryngton looked at the labels and gave the chef a thumbs-up. "I agree."

The chef also removed a large salad and chilled appetizer from the fridge.

Alexis said, "Daddy, may I fix my plate now, please? My movie's about to come on in five minutes."

The ultimate manipulator, Bria thought. Just then they received notification that Bria's parents had arrived.

"In a minute," Kerryngton told her.

The butler let Mr. and Mrs. Murray inside, and Kerryngton and Bria hurried to the foyer to greet them. Bria smiled when she saw how good her parents looked—fashionable and youthful. She gave them hugs and introduced them to Kerryngton. He shook her father's hand and kissed the back of her mother's hand.

"I see where Bria got her beauty," Kerryngton smiled.

Mrs. Murray chuckled and took her hand back. "Your home is spectacular," she said as she looked around the room.

"Thank you, ma'am."

Kerryngton gave them an abbreviated tour. Rather than taking them on the upper and lower levels, he only showed them the main level. They ended up in the kitchen with Alexis and the chef. Kerryngton introduced them to

Alexis who was well-mannered and pleasant. Nothing but the devil! Bria thought. She could tell the little demon had snowed her parents too.

Kerryngton explained, "Alexis won't be joining us for dinner. She wants to watch some Disney movie." He turned his attention to his daughter. "You have permission to take your plate to the theater."

"Thank you, Daddy."Alexis fixed her plate with a sample of everything except the steak and lobster.

The chef went over the menu with Mr. and Mrs. Murray and asked them how they preferred their steaks.

"Well done for me," Mr. Murray said. "I have to cut back on red meat, though."

"The salmon and lobster are plenty for me," Mrs. Murray answered.

The chef announced, "Fantastic. Dinner will be ready in five minutes."

Since it was only the four of them they ate in the breakfast room instead of the formal dining room. The chef placed the appetizers and salad plates on the table. He filled their water glasses and offered them wine. Kerryngton and Bria drank white wine while Mr. and Mrs. Murray drank sweet tea.

"I like your choice of music," Mrs. Murray said. "You're playing all of my favorites."

"Mine too," Kerryngton said.

Bria half expected her parents to get up and do the dance The Swing or start Chicago steppin' at any moment.

"Kerryngton, Kerryngton," Mr. Murray said. "I've been wanting to meet the fella who whisked my daughter out of the country."

Bria traced the brim of the crystal wineglass with her finger, hoping her dad wasn't about to say something to embarrass her. He wasn't usually embarrassing, but this was an unusual situation.

"You have a lovely daughter," Mr. Murray complimented.

"Thanks. She's my pride and joy."

"Just like Bria is my pride and joy." He looked him in the eyes. "My wife tells me you and Bria are dating."

"That's correct."

"She also tells me you're in the music business."

Kerryngton nodded his head.

"Then you're no stranger to fast women and fast living."

Kerryngton cleared his throat. "Afraid not. I have a past, and that's exactly what it is, the past."

"I'm sure that a man with your looks, wealth, and status has women throwing themselves at your feet."

"Yes, but—"

"What do you want with my daughter?"

Kerryngton stroked his moustache, then looked at Bria. "I want to marry your daughter."

Bria had to catch her breath. She wasn't expecting him to say that. She attempted to conceal the shocked look on her face.

Mrs. Murray spit out her tea and covered her mouth. Bria handed her some napkins.

"Are you all right?" Kerryngton asked.

"Yes. It just went down the wrong way." She dabbed her mouth, looked at Bria, then back at Kerryngton and said, "You two haven't known each other very long."

Kerryngton went on to tell them about his parents and their marriage. He said, "Bria is a special woman. She's too special to just date. She deserves to be a wife, my wife. I can date her when I'm married to her. I don't see the point in drawing things out to please other people when I know what I want and how I feel."

"How does your daughter feel about this?" Mrs. Murray asked.

"Truthfully, my daughter doesn't dictate my decisions. She's my child, and she knows her place. She trusts me not to place her in harm or danger. Alexis wants me to be happy, and if I tell her Bria makes me happy, she'll be happy for me, for us."

"Where's Alexis's mother?" Mrs. Murray wanted to know.

Kerryngton told them about his ex-wife, why they divorced, and their relationship now.

"I see." Mr. Murray furrowed a brow. "How old are you?"

Kerryngton chuckled. "I'm thirty."

Mr. Murray grunted.

"Bria's mature for her age, and I'm young for mine. We meet in the middle. Plus, I eat right and exercise. I'm in excellent health."

The questions ceased as everyone seemed to be thinking about the conversation. They finished off their salads, and the chef cleared their plates. He followed up by serving them the main course.

Mr. Murray dipped the succulent lobster meat in warm, melted butter and stuffed it in his mouth. "I've heard you tell me how you feel about my daughter. What I want to know is how does my daughter feel about you?"

Every eyeball at the table was stuck on Bria. She felt as though a spotlight had been cast upon her. She chewed a piece of the delicious salmon, savoring the soft textured meat with a mild distinct flavor. She refused to let her parents intimidate her. What her father was really asking was: What's up with Spade?

Twenty-eight

Bria put down her fork and said, "Ma, Dad, I know what you're thinking. It hasn't been that long since Spade and I broke up. You probably think this is some sort of rebound relationship, and everyone knows rebound relationships don't last."

Her parents nodded. "Keep going," her mother encouraged.

"Well, I had a chance to speak with Spade while I was in London. In fact, he was there too, working on his music. Kerryngton is the CEO of the label that signed Spade."

"Really?" Mr. Murray said, sounding shocked and amazed.

"Yes." She then told them about Spade's cancer diagnosis.

"I didn't even know that," Kerryngton said.

"Neither did I," Mrs. Murray chimed in. "How is he?"

Mr. Murray wiped his mouth with a napkin. "Pumpkin, I have something to tell you." He spoke up before Bria had a chance to tell her mother how Spade was doing.

"What is it?"

"Spade confided in me about his prognosis. He's been keeping me updated on his tests."

Bria felt a slow boil coming on. She steadied her breathing to take the lid off a full-blown explosion. "What?" She couldn't believe what she was hearing. If her father had just told her what was going on, she'd still be with Spade today.

"Pumpkin, I'm sorry. He swore me to secrecy. I thought the two of you would work things out once you knew the truth. I had no idea you'd jump headfirst into another relationship so quickly."

She heard her mother say she didn't know about Spade's condition, but after hearing her father's confession, she didn't know what to believe or who she could trust. She looked at her mother. Needing further reassurance, she asked, "Ma, did you know?"

"No, I didn't. Your father didn't tell me a thing."

"Calm down, baby," Kerryngton said in a soothing tone.

She wanted to tell Kerryngton where he could go with all that "calm down" mess. Her life had been turned upside down. She wasn't about to calm down. Rather than being rude to him she requested, "Would you please give us a moment alone?" All the while she glared at her father.

"Sure," Kerryngton said as he tossed his napkin on the table and left her alone with her parents.

She waited until he was out of earshot before saying, "Daddy, I know you said Spade swore you to secrecy, but you're *my* dad." She patted her chest. "Your loyalty is to me, not him. You know how devastated I was behind our breakup. You could've spared me a lot of heartache and confusion just by telling me what was up. How could you do this to me?" She tossed her hair out of her face. She could see the hurt look in her father's eyes.

"I don't have any defense." He sounded somber. "I'm sorry, pumpkin. I thought I was doing the right thing by keeping his confidence. He didn't have anyone else. It was never my intention to hurt you."

She could no longer look at her dad because her feelings were so hurt.

"Sweetheart, I can only imagine how you must be feeling," her mother said. "I pray that in time you'll be able to forgive your father. He didn't keep that secret to hurt you, I'm sure."

Mr. Murray nodded his head.

"Bria," Mrs. Murray continued, "I know you're feeling some kind of way right now, but you're going to have to trust me on this one. Slow down with that man in there. He's *not* the one for you."

"Yes, pumpkin," her dad chimed in. "I get that you're upset with me, but I agree with your mother. You don't know him well enough to make that type of decision. What's the rush?"

"There's no rush," she told him. Feeling broken, she said, "I don't feel like talking anymore. I want to go home." She excused herself from the table and found Kerryngton. "I'm sorry, but I have to go. Thanks for dinner."

He tried to stop her, but his attempt proved futile as she walked right out the door.

Bria's phone was hot after she left Kerryngton's house. Between her parents and Kerryngton blowing up her phone, her phone rang nonstop. What part of her "I don't feel like talking" didn't they understand? She needed time alone to sort through her feelings. She was tired of being in limbo.

When she got home she wrote out a list of pros and cons for Spade and Kerryngton. The pros for Spade far outweighed any cons. And the fact that he was her first love made their love more special and pure than anything she could ever hope to feel for Kerryngton. She finally admitted what she had been running away from all along—Spade is The One. He's the love of her life.

Once she had resigned in her spirit that she wanted to be with Spade, she called Kerryngton.

"Hey," she said. "Sorry I ran out like that. Things just got a little heavy, and I needed some air. I know you have Alexis with you tonight, so can we meet up tomorrow?"

"No, I can see you tonight. Alexis has a sitter."

"Oh, okay. In that case, come on over."

Less than an hour later Kerryngton showed up at Bria's doorstep looking as good as he usually did. "You okay, baby?" he said as he hugged her.

She broke the embrace and led him into the family room so that they could talk. "Before I get into what I called you over here for, there's something I need to get off my chest."

"Sure, baby. What is it?" He eyed her curiously.

Exhaling, she released, "What happened with your ex-wife wasn't cool. Her kissing you on the lips was very disrespectful."

"Oh." He sucked air between his teeth. "Don't pay her any attention. She just did that for effect. She was trying to get under your skin."

"Whatever," Bria continued. "The fact that you allowed it and didn't check her says a lot."

"It's not like that," he defended.

She halted her hand. "It doesn't even matter. Anyway, I've been thinking . . ."

And before she could finish her sentiment he dropped down on one knee and said, "I meant what I said earlier. I have real feelings for you, Bria." He pulled a ring out of his pocket. "Would you marry me?"

No no no! she screamed on the inside. This is not supposed to happen. She felt like the crud in her bathroom drain. There was no easy way to say this. She swallowed hard. "Kerryngton, please get up."

He had a confused expression on his face, but he slowly got up and sat next to her.

She looked him straight in the eyes and said, "I care about you . . . a lot. But if I'm being honest, I'm not in love with you."

He cracked a smile. "I'm not worried about that. Plenty of people get married first and fall in love later."

She took a deep breath and released it. "Not me. I'm not like that. I think you're terrific, but I can't marry you. I'm sorry."

He smirked. "I thought you were smarter than that. We could've been so good together. You obviously have no clue how lucky you are. I can't even count how many women would love to be in your shoes." He stood up. "I'm out."

Well . . . That was weird, Bria thought as she locked the door behind him. She hadn't expected that outburst, but she knew she needed to have seen it. Between his daughter and his erratic behavior, she was convinced he couldn't be the man for her.

Twenty-nine

Bria had too much on her mind to go to sleep so she called Spade.

"You up?" she asked.

"Yeah, I'm at home working. What's up?"

"Just needed to talk." Then she hesitated. She didn't want to tell him about her breakup over the phone. She wanted to see his face. "Never mind."

"Don't do that. What's the matter?"

"It's late, let's just talk tomorrow." She hung up and immediately regretted it. She didn't want to call him back and ask him to come over because he was working. She didn't want to disrupt his flow. However, she could drop by and momentarily distract him. He used to love when she did that. He called her a welcomed distraction.

She got in her car and trekked across town. The entire time driving Bria thought about what she was going to say to Spade. She hoped and prayed he still wanted to be with her in spite of everything that had happened.

When she pulled into his apartment complex she saw his car and knew he was still at home. She breathed a sigh of relief, because she knew she was taking a big chance just dropping by. Some habits die hard because she and Spade had the type of relationship where neither of them cared if the other stopped by unannounced.

She climbed the flight of stairs to his condo and knocked on the door. She waited a moment before knocking again. She placed her ear to the door and heard someone unlock the door. Bria almost tumbled down the stairs when she saw Kola standing there in a nightshirt.

"Hey, girl," Kola said, tossing her weave over her shoulder. "What are you doing here?"

All sorts of expletives went through Bria's mind, but she was too much of a lady to let them fly out of her mouth. She couldn't even fake a smile because she felt too pissed off. Suddenly she felt jealous and possessive, feelings she wasn't used to having when it came to Spade. She knew she didn't have any right to feel the way she felt, but she wanted to jack Kola and Spade up. Logically, she knew Spade wasn't cheating on her, but her emotions didn't get the memo. She composed herself as best she could and said, "Is Spade here?"

"He's in the shower."

More expletives.

She was about to turn and leave, but Spade walked out in a pair of boxer shorts. When his eyes landed on Bria and her "don't say nothing to me" expression, he sprinted across the room like a rabbit.

Bria started down the stairs but couldn't go as fast as she wanted to for fear of tripping in those Christian Louboutins and breaking her ankle.

"Bria, wait!" he yelled as he ran behind her barefoot and half naked.

"God forgive me," she mumbled before unleashing a string of cuss words at him. She was pretty sure she probably owed his momma an apology for calling him the son of a female dog and a person who didn't know who his father was. She was so thankful to hit that last step so that she could pick up the pace and get her stride.

Spade grabbed her by the arm and flung her around. She gave him the middle finger and in case he didn't know what that meant, she *said* it. She knew she wasn't acting very Christian-like, but her emotions had gotten the best of her.

"Baby, please!"

"Baby!" She acted like he had called her a female dog. "You trifling—"

He said in a stern tone, "Bria, you need to calm down." He threw his hands in the air. "There's nothing going on between me and Kola. We work together. It got late. I told her she could crash in my room while I stayed on the couch. I have not and would not sleep with her. You know I love you. It's always been you."

She wanted to believe him, but she couldn't see past her anger. What if she hadn't shown up? Would he have slept with her? Or worse yet, what if he had already slept with her? If he had slept with Kola, what right did she have to be angry?

She searched his face. At first she couldn't tell whether he was lying or telling the truth. It wasn't until she looked deep into his eyes that she could tell that he was telling the truth. She felt as though he had taken a soothing ointment and applied it on a cut, causing instant relief.

"You believe me, don't you?"

She hung her head. "I feel stupid. I never should've went off on you like that. I'm so sorry."

"It's cool. That just means you still love me." He grinned. "At least tell me why you came over."

"I came over to tell you that I'm not seeing Kerryngton anymore."

"Thank you, Jesus!" he shouted; then he kissed her.

She laughed at him. "Get back inside before the neighbors call the police on you for indecent exposure. We'll talk later."

He touched his bare chest as if he was just now realizing he didn't have any clothes on. "Tell me you love me," he demanded.

She waited a moment. "Fine, I love you." She felt good saying that.

"You know you're welcome to stay, right?"

"No, I'm good." That was the Spade she knew and loved. Always considerate of her.

She opened the car door and Spade took a step back. "Whose car is this?"

"Oh, um, Kerryngton got it for me."

He stood there looking dejected. He tried to conceal his feelings. "It's nice." He made sure she was safe in her car and driving away before going back inside.

She couldn't believe how she had shown her tail that night. She knew Nya was going to have a field day with that one.

Thirty

Spade replayed the previous night's events in his mind and laughed his butt off. Kola had already left. He had never seen Bria act like that in all the years he had known her. She went straight ham when she thought he was bangin' Kola. At least now he knows his girl is capable of getting jealous. He felt flattered. But he didn't know she even knew all those cuss words. It sounded strange hearing her talk like that.

Thank goodness she had come to her senses and gotten rid of Daddy Warbucks. He was about to call her, but an incoming call came from his doctor's office.

"Your test results are back. We need you to come in right away." The woman on the other end had a professional demeanor, expressionless. Her voice gave no indication as to whether his results were good or bad.

His heart plummeted. He knew she couldn't tell him anything over the phone, but that didn't sound good. "I'll be there as soon as I get dressed."

He had waited weeks for those results, and he didn't know what he'd do if the results weren't favorable. The thought hadn't even crossed his mind. He hurried up and got dressed in record time. He drove to the doctor's office at a speed that would've made one think he had a brick on the gas pedal.

He said a quick prayer before entering the doctor's office. There was only one other person in the lobby. When he checked in at the front desk someone immediately came out to escort him back. He waited a couple of minutes in one of the exam rooms before his oncologist met with him.

The oncologist shook his hand. "Let me be the first to tell you that you do not have cancer."

Spade took a moment to process what the doctor had just said. He clutched the cross around his neck, dropped to his knees, and thanked the Lord! He felt as if a huge weight had been lifted off his shoulders. It was official! His emotions broke through like the levees in the Ninth Ward during Hurricane Katrina. He couldn't stop it. He felt relieved, but that relief quickly turned to anger.

"Doc, had I undergone chemo and survived, they would've told me I had been cured of a disease I never had."

"Yes, what you're saying is true, and that's frightening. Thankfully, you declined the chemo." He offered a faint smile. "What you actually have is a lipoma, just as I told you before."

"Thank God!" He let out a sigh of relief. "And thank you for listening to me and going the extra mile."

Spade was certain he could handle anything now. God had worked it out for him. He didn't have cancer and for that he was extremely grateful. Now that his death sentence had been overturned, he was ready to make things right with his woman.

Spade didn't take his second chance for granted. He knew he needed to make a grand gesture, and he knew just the person to help him pull it off. He called Mr. Murray.

"Pops, I just wanted to tell you. It's official . . . I don't have cancer."

"Praise God, son! I knew He'd do it."

"Yes, He did." He cleared his throat. "I need your help, though."

"Name it."

"I have a surprise planned for Bria. Do you think you can get her to come over to your house tonight?"

He exhaled into the phone. "She's upset with me right now. I don't know if she'd be willing to come over."

"Why is she upset with you?" He sounded surprised.

"She found out that I knew about your condition and didn't tell her."

"Oh." He didn't like coming between Bria and her dad. "Sorry about that. You want me to talk to her."

"It's all right. I'll reach out to her. I can handle it." He sounded confident.

"Let me know if you need my help. You know I got you," he said sincerely.

Mr. Murray said, "Thanks, son. Getting back to tonight, did you have a particular time in mind?"

"How about six o'clock?"

"That should be fine. I'm sure my wife will have some dinner cooked."

He missed Mrs. Murray's delicious home cooking. He licked his lips just thinking about it.

"I'm going to call Bria now. I'll call you back if there's a problem. Otherwise, see you this evening," Mr. Murray said.

Spade got off the phone feeling pretty good. One thing he knew about Bria was that she loved her parents. She couldn't stay mad at them for long even if she tried. He threw up a prayer anyway. He had come too far to stop praying now.

Thirty-one

Thank goodness it's Friday! And thank God Bria worked for herself. Getting out of bed had been a struggle that morning. She had tossed and turned all night thinking about Spade, and she couldn't get Kerryngton's arrogant comments out of her head. She didn't show up at the spa until almost lunchtime. Even then she wore dark glasses to hide the bags underneath her eyes.

"Girl, you look beat," Nya told her as soon as she entered the office. "And not in the good way either."

She removed her glasses and placed them on the desk. "You wouldn't believe the night I had."

Nya held up her index finger. "Just one moment, child. I can tell you have some tea to spill." She popped a bag of microwaveable popcorn and pulled up a seat. "Okay, now you can spill it." She opened the bag and the aroma of freshly popped corn scented the room.

Bria's mouth ran a marathon as she gave Nya the rundown of the previous night's events. She told her everything from meeting Kerryngton's ex and daughter to the disastrous dinner to the marriage proposal to going over to Spade's house.

Nya munched on the popcorn like she was watching a movie. Judging by the many different expressions she made as each story was being told she found the drama just as entertaining.

"Girl, you had quite the night." Then she started laughing. "Now you know you didn't have any business going over to Spade's house unannounced. And then you had the nerve to get angry because he had a girl there. Honey child, news flash—he could've been doing the booty on the balcony and you still wouldn't have had a right to get upset. He was not your man."

"I know."

"You just happened to luck up on that one. Any other dude would've been doing exactly what you originally thought Spade was doing." She laughed harder. "I'm glad he wasn't though. You looked crazy enough copping an attitude. You would've needed meds for sure if he had been sleeping with her."

"Gee, thanks." Nya knew her so well.

"How are you feeling about your dad?" Concern laced her voice.

She shrugged her shoulders. "He'll always be my dad. I still love him. I'm just pissed, you know?"

Nya nodded. "I get it."

Just then Bria's phone rang and her dad's name appeared on the screen. "Speak of the devil," she said. "We must've talked him up." She answered in a casual tone.

"Pumpkin, would you please stop by the house this evening around six?"

"Everything all right?" She hoped he didn't have any bad news to share with her.

"Yes. Your mom and I are fine."

She didn't really feel like being around her dad because she was still upset with him. But she knew her dad. If she refused to see him or talk to him, he'd show up at her job. He never liked leaving issues unresolved between them. So, she said, "Sure, I'll be there."

She ended the call and Nya was looking so far down her throat she was certain she could see her tonsils. "You already know," Bria told her. Nothing else needed to be said. She didn't have to explain.

***

Bria and Spade showed up at her parents' house at the same time. They stood outside conversing briefly.

"You looking yummy, baby," Spade told her. He held her hand in the air as she twirled in front of him.

"Thanks. I'm glad to see you, but what are you doing here?"

"I want to talk to you and your parents."

"About what?" She displayed some attitude as she placed her hand on her hip.

Pressing the doorbell, he said, "You're such a baby. Wait and see."

Before Bria could get all dramatic, as she was known to do, Mrs. Murray answered the door and greeted them with hugs and kisses. "My favorite young couple. You're right in time for dinner."

"Good, because I'm starving," Spade said. "Nobody cooks better than you, Mrs. Murray." He handed her a card.

"Thank you, sweetie." Mrs. Murray kissed him on the cheek.

Bria playfully elbowed him in the ribs, and he smoothed the spot with his hand. "What did you do that for?"

Touching the tip of her nose, she teased him, "Brown-noser."

He simply shook his head as they followed Mrs. Murray into the dining room.

Mr. Murray exited the half bath. "Hey, you two." He made his way over to Bria and kissed her on the cheek. He gave Spade a manly hug, and they all sat down at the table.

Mrs. Murray served fried chicken, potato salad, collard greens, sweet corn bread, and iced tea. They bowed their heads and blessed the food. Everyone fixed their plates.

Spade didn't even take a bite of food before saying, "I have some good news." All eyes were on him. "The oncologist confirmed that I do not—repeat—do *not* have cancer."

"Glory be to God!" Mrs. Murray praised.

Bria got out of her seat and hugged his neck. "That's the best news." She planted a kiss on his face before taking her seat again.

"I'm happy for you, son," Mr. Murray said.

"So what does this mean for the two of you?" Mrs. Murray pointed her fork at Bria, then Spade.

"I love him," Bria said coolly, stumping everyone at the table, especially Spade.

Spade looked Bria in the eyes and said in the most sincere voice he could manage, "I love you too."

"Well, there you have it," Mrs. Murray announced. She pressed her hands together in a praying position and touched her lips. Her eyes filled with tears. "I know you love my child." Her voice cracked.

"Yes, ma'am, I do."

"You better not hurt her again." A single tear escaped her left eye. "She's our princess . . ."

"And she's my queen," he proclaimed.

The sound of an aircraft could be heard outside. Spade insisted they go out and take a look. They stepped onto the huge deck and saw a plane writing the words: MARRY ME, BRIA.

Bria covered her mouth with her hands. Mr. Murray wrapped his arm around his wife as new tears formed in her eyes. Spade turned to face Bria and retrieved a small velvety box from his pocket. Getting down on bended knee, he said, "Bria Bianca Murray, you are my whole heart. Would you do me the honor of becoming my wife?"

The over-the-top proposal was just the type of exciting and thrilling thing Bria had come to expect from Spade.

He never ceased to amaze her, and everything with him was an adventure. Bria had never met anyone like him before, and not even Kerryngton made her feel the way Spade did.

Bria bobbed her head like a bobble-head doll before squealing, "Yes! Yes, I'll marry you."

Standing to his full height, Spade presented Bria with a much more impressive new engagement ring. It was the nicest ring she had ever laid eyes on. The magnificently beautiful cushion cut diamond engagement ring took Bria's breath away with its beauty, brilliance, and spectacular size.

"How many carats is this ring?"

"Twelve point nine," Spade told her.

Mesmerized, she couldn't stop staring at her hand. The center diamond was near colorless and practically flawless! She admired the spectacular cut and noticed how the ring sparkled tremendously. Flanked by two brilliant cut trapezoids the combination was outstandingly beautiful! The custom-made platinum setting featured round brilliant cut diamonds pave set on all three sides of the shank. The center basket was uniquely crafted with a beautiful design and also studded with round diamonds.

"Let me see your ring," Mrs. Murray requested. When Bria flashed her parents her ring, they gasped. "Magnificent!" Mrs. Murray exclaimed.

"It's breathtaking!" her dad said.

Bria wrapped her arms around Spade's waist and rested her head against his buff chest.

"I would say welcome to the family, but you never left," Mr. Murray said as he patted Spade on the back.

Spade broke away from Bria and peck kissed her lips. He then hugged her mom and dad.

Sensing the love all around them, Bria didn't want to taint the occasion by having unforgiveness in her heart.

She asked God to forgive her for any unforgiveness she harbored in her heart, and then she said, "I forgive you, Dad. I love you."

"All right, all right," Mr. Murray said, wiping his eye. "We'll give the two of you some time alone." He escorted Mrs. Murray back inside and closed the door behind them.

Spade and Bria held hands as they looked up at the spot where the sky writing had been. The aircraft was gone and although the words had faded into the light blue sky, the impression was forever imbedded in Bria's mind.

"How did you even plan that?" she asked completely baffled.

"When we were in London I bought the ring. I knew I'd give it to you one day. The skywriting was spur-of-the-moment, especially after our conversation last night and my doctor's good news this morning, and on top of that, I felt like you loved me. The timing just felt right." He tilted his head to the side and stroked his face. "And your jealous outburst was kinda sexy."

She playfully punched him on the arm. "How did you know I'd say yes?"

"You're not the only one who prays."

Bria smiled at him.

"I don't want to wait to marry you," Spade proclaimed.

Bria felt overjoyed. She didn't want to wait to marry him either. All she needed was a date and location. "Do you think we can pull it together in a month?"

He flashed a grin. "We can get married first thing Monday morning as far as I'm concerned. Courthouse. Vegas. Whatever."

"No courthouse or Vegas. It's our first wedding. It should be special."

"The fact that we love each other and want to spend our lives together should be enough. We should follow our hearts and do what's best for us. It's our first wedding, but it better be the last for both of us. Divorce is not an option as far as I'm concerned." He pulled her closer to him. "As long as I'm marrying you it's already special. None of that other stuff matters to me. People get too caught up in the ceremony." He held up a finger. "Case in point. Remember Kim Kardashian's 72-day marriage? They spent millions of dollars on a fairy-tale wedding."

"True." She could think of many other short-lived celebrity nuptials as well.

"And then you got people like Ice T and Coco eloping in Vegas and having a love stronger than most people. Even if they split up, they had a good ride."

She was not surprised that he'd use a legendary hip-hop gangster rapper as his role model for marital success.

He cupped her face in his hands. "I won't deny you the opportunity to have the wedding of your dreams and to have your daddy walk you down the aisle. Whatever you want to do I'm cool with that."

"Thank you."

They shared a sensual kiss. Bria melted into his arms, imagining the minister pronouncing them husband and wife and saying, "You may now kiss the bride."

Thirty-two

Bria couldn't contain her excitement. She needed to talk to her best friend right away. She checked her watch, and it was close to eleven. She called Nya to let her know she needed to speak with her, and Nya told her to come on over. *Thank God for sisterhood,* Bria thought.

Bria parked her car in Nya's driveway; the porch light was on. She knocked on the door. She didn't want to ring the doorbell and wake Chance up. Chance tended to go to bed early and wake up extra early, whereas Bria and Nya preferred to stay up late and sleep late. Nya immediately let her in.

"Girl, what's up?" Nya asked. "I got the ice cream ready." She studied Bria's tearstained face. "You been crying?"

Bria flopped down on the couch like a rag doll. "Sister, you aren't going to believe what happened after I left the spa. I'm exhausted."

Nya sat next to her with a concerned look on her face. "Talk to me."

Bria started out by giving her a blow by blow of her evening with Spade. She told her about his misdiagnosis, the skywriting marriage proposal, and their subsequent engagement. She held up her finger to show Nya her gigantic rock.

Nya reached out to hug her. Bria could feel wetness on her face. Then Nya sniffled. Bria looked at her and asked, "Why are you crying?"

"Because I'm so happy for you. You deserve this. Spade is a terrific guy, but you know that already. Not only will he give you the world, but you *are* his world. I can tell by the way he looks at you that he's in love with you and always has been." She wiped her face. "I was praying you'd come around and see how right he is for you. Congratulations."

Bria could feel the sincerity in Nya's words. "I love you, sister."

"I love you too. Everything you've told me so far has been good news. I could understand how that could make you cry."

Bria's cell phone rang, and she checked her caller ID. "Spade's Mom" popped up. She showed Nya the phone. "I have to take this."

"Yes, girl. Talk to your mommy-in-law," she giggled.

Bria answered.

Spade's mom skipped the pleasantries and went straight to the point. "Bria, I just got off the phone with my son, and he told me the great news. I'm so happy the two of you are back together. I just wanted to tell you that. Congratulations."

Bria loved Spade's mom. "Thank you. I'm happy and excited."

"Me too. You know I always considered you to be my daughter."

That had always meant something to Bria. "Thanks. I'm at Nya's house now, so I'll talk to you some other time." They said their good-byes and got off the phone.

"Anyway," Nya said, "have you thought about a wedding date? Are you going to re-create the wedding you were supposed to have the first time around?"

"That's a good question. I already have everything. Might as well. One less thing to worry about. We haven't had a chance to set a date just yet, but we both agree we don't want a long engagement. We've waited long enough."

"Whew! Thank goodness." She touched her forehead. "I *know* that's right."

And Bria thought *she* was the dramatic one.

Nya made a face.

"What's that about?" Bria asked.

"Girl, I'm ready for you to get married so we can talk about sex."

Was Nya losing her mind? "We already talk about sex."

"No." She rested her hand on her chest. "*I* talk about sex. You just listen. You have no personal knowledge of it, so you have no idea all the feelings that come along with it."

That got a laugh out of Bria. "I wouldn't mind having an intimate destination wedding. Somewhere on a beach."

"A beach is good. When Chance and I were planning to get married we researched some beach locations. St. Kitts in the Caribbean stood out to me. Their beaches had turquoise water and weren't crowded." She placed her index finger on her cheek and tapped it. "Better yet, have the wedding on Tybee Island. You want to be considerate of people who don't like to fly. And it'll be easier to plan since you want to get married right away."

"The more I think about it, the more I want to be married in three to four weeks."

"Okay, Khloé."

Bria gave her a curious look. "Why did you call me Khloé?"

"If Khloé Kardashian can pull off a wedding in three weeks, why can't you?"

Bria pushed her, and Nya rocked to the side. They both laughed. "I forgot to call Spade." She grabbed her phone and called him. "Hey, handsome."

"You made it home, love?" That was the first time he had ever called her "love" and she liked it.

"No, I'm at Nya's."

"Okay. Tell her I said hello."

She conveyed the message to Nya, and Nya said, "Hi, Spade."

She could hear him laugh into the phone. "Are you spending the night there, or you going home?"

She yawned. "I'm getting tired. I'll probably just crash here for the night." She kept a few outfits and an overnight bag in Nya's guest bedroom. "We were just talking about our wedding."

"I like that."

"She's excited for us. Check your schedule and let me know your first available open weekend."

"I'll let you know something tomorrow."

"Sounds good. By the way, I spoke to your mom."

"I knew she was going to call you. She couldn't help it."

"You know she's my girl. Love her." She chuckled. "Do you want to invite the same people we invited before?"

"That's fine. If we don't, people might get offended."

"Would you mind if we got married on the beach?"

"Not at all. This is your day. Do it up however you want. Everyone knows weddings are all about the bride."

What a sweetheart! she thought, remembering why she chose him again and would choose him every time.

Thirty-three

Bria and Nya didn't get to bed until almost two o'clock in the morning, staying up talking about men. They had to wake up at seven-thirty to get ready for nine-thirty church service, and Bria felt exhausted. She thought about foregoing church in favor of more sleep, but forced herself to get up and get ready.

She met up with Chance at the breakfast nook since Nya was still getting dressed. He had already put on a pot of freshly brewed coffee, cooked scrambled eggs with cheese, chopped red and green bell peppers, and onions along with turkey sausage links.

When he saw Bria he said, "Look what the cat dragged in. Good morning, li'l sis." He saw her bloodshot eyes. "Doesn't look like you got any sleep last night."

"Not really." She poured a cup of coffee and added a couple of teaspoons of sugar before taking a sip. She needed something strong to help her wake up and give her some energy.

"I didn't even hear you come in last night," he told her.

"Of course you didn't. You can't wake up a log." She drank some more.

"Everything okay?" His concern evident.

"Uh-huh. It is now. Spade doesn't have cancer."

"Thank God!" he shouted. "I'm glad to hear that."

She put down her cup and fixed herself a plate of food. She held up her hand and showed him her new engagement ring. "Oh yeah, Spade and I got engaged—re-engaged—last night."

He placed her smaller hand in his larger one and studied the ring. "Homeboy wasn't playing. He came with it. Now *that's* a ring for ya. I don't know how you're able to keep your hand up carrying all that weight around."

Bria laughed at his silliness and took her hand away so that she could eat.

"Spade, huh?"

"That's right."

"You know Spade's my boy, and I was rooting for him."

Bria ate her eggs and cut a piece of sausage.

"Glad to hear you finally came to your senses."

"I love Spade with my whole heart. I can't wait to become his wife," she smiled. "Wife . . . has a nice ring to it, don't you think? Mrs. Bria Spencer."

He nodded. "I'm just curious. What made you give up Mr. Moneybags? A lot of women would've married money no matter what it looked like, smelled like, or acted like."

"Did you just meet me?" She raised a brow. "Money doesn't impress me."

"Very good." He pinched her cheek.

Nya joined them. "Good morning, peeps."

Chance checked his watch. "You only have ten minutes to get something on your stomach before we have to leave."

She fixed a plate and scarfed it down.

"We need to take separate vehicles," Nya told her husband, "because Bria and I are going to the spa right after church." On Sundays, the spa was open for appointments only.

"That's fine."

Bria and Nya arrived at the spa at a quarter to one. When Meagan saw Bria's ring, she let out a scream loud enough for Dani to hurry to the receptionist area.

"Is everything all right?" Dani asked, trying to catch her breath.

Bria laughed and held up her hand.

"Oh my goodness! You're getting married!" Dani yelled. She scurried across the floor and hugged Bria's neck. "Congratulations! Who are you marrying?"

Nya smirked. "Aren't you bold? That's like her saying she's pregnant and you asking, 'By who?'" She shook her head.

A wave of chuckles and girlish giggles filled the room.

"I'm marrying Spade. We worked it out." She came across like a blushing bride.

"How exciting!" Dani exhaled. She complimented Bria on her ring. "Good-looking artist with a recording deal and wants to get married. Lucky you! My faith in black men has been restored. Does he have a brother?"

Some of the ladies laughed.

"He's an only child. Sorry." Bria pretended to pout.

"Have you set a date yet?" Dani asked.

Meagan and Nya quieted the laughter.

"We're working on it," Bria said. "We're trying to get it done in less than a month."

"Wow! I think that's great!" Dani said in her usual up-beat tone. "Let me know if you need help with anything. I'm at your disposal." And with the blink of an eye Dani went back to work.

"Let me see that ring again," Meagan said as she grabbed Bria's hand and put it near her face. "I have to give Spade props. He has good taste."

"I think so." Bria took her hand back and studied her ring for the umpteenth time. She never got tired of looking at it and marveling at the beauty.

Just then Spade walked through the door and became the center of attention.

Meagan said, "Welcome to The Spa Factory. I hear congratulations are in order, sir."

He grinned, unable to contain his enthusiasm. "Yes, indeed. My girl has made me the happiest man in the world by agreeing to become my wife." He gave his fiancée a squeeze and kissed her on the cheek.

The ladies at the spa extended their congratulatory wishes before dispersing. Then Bria and Spade went into her office so that they could be away from everyone else.

"I still can't believe we're getting married," she said. "It feels like a dream."

"For me too. If I had it my way, we'd go to the courthouse tomorrow and get it over with. We could have the big celebration for everybody else later. I want you as my wife now. I want to come home to you every day and have you in my bed every night."

His suggestion sounded good and enticing to her. She liked the thought of coming home to him, and she couldn't wait to make love to Spade for the very first time. His touches were so hard to resist. He sent stimulating impulses through her body every time they got near each other. But she knew her parents would have a fit if they eloped. She didn't want to deny them of a wedding for their only child. So, she'd have to wait a little while longer she resigned.

"Your offer is tempting, but I can't do that to my parents. They'd be so hurt and disappointed."

He stood in front of her and held her hands. "I wrestled with this all night. We've been through so much. We should already be married. I'm tired of waiting." He looked deep into her eyes. He got close to her, and then backed away. "I know what you said about disappointing your parents, but this is torture for me. Not because I can't handle abstaining; that's not the problem.

"My reasons for wanting to marry you are many. You're a part of me. You make me want to be a better man. You're insightful, opinionated, and honest."

Bria laughed. "You think *I'm* opinionated?"

"That's a good thing. You bring out the best in me by challenging me to be the best version of myself. I know I want to spend my life with you. I want to involve you in every aspect of my life." He looked her in the eyes. "When that doctor told me I didn't have long to live, everything changed for me. It taught me not to take anything for granted. Life is meant to be lived every single day. Tomorrow may not come. All we have is now."

Bria felt herself melting like ice cream in sweltering heat.

"By the grace of God I don't have cancer. I have a lipoma, and I can live with that."

She had a concerned look on her face. "Is that serious?"

"No. Lipomas don't generally require treatment. Because they aren't cancerous growths and can't become cancerous, they don't need to be removed. My doctor removed mine because it had grown; that's all. I'm fine. Just a reminder for me to take care of myself. Nothing for either of us to worry about."

"Okay." She touched his cheek.

"Baby, my career is on the rise. I have to travel, and I want my wife to accompany me."

She could understand that. "But I'm a businesswoman. I'm not always going to be able to travel with you. I have to run my company."

"I get it." He held her chin with his thumb and point finger. "And yes, I want to make love to you, but that's only a small part of it. That's definitely not the driving force for wanting to marry you. I'm attracted to you, and it's getting harder and harder to deny my desires. If you make me wait much longer, I'll be all right as long as I'm not close to you. No kissing, no hugging, no touching, no nothing. And when I do see you I want you wearing loose-fitting clothes."

"What? You can't be serious." She hoped he was joking.

"As a heart attack."

She thought about everything he had just said. She could admit that she loved this man, and she believed with every fiber of her being that he loved her too. He gave compelling reasons for why they should get married now, and they all made sense to her. "Okay, let's say we did go down to the courthouse and get married. Can we still have the big wedding anyway?"

"I never said we couldn't."

She mulled it over. "But we'd have to tell people that we're already married. Otherwise, that would be deceptive."

He tilted her face toward him and planted a soft kiss on her lips. "I'm fine with that."

For Bria, Spade brought out a more "throw caution to the wind" type of attitude. He made her feel as though she needed to stop playing life so safe and live a little. She knew that Spade viewed life as an adventure, and she wanted to experience it with him.

She thought about Spade's cancer scare. Even a young and seemingly healthy person couldn't be sure he'd be around the next day, week, or month. She didn't want to live a life of "what-ifs" or regrets. She searched herself and realized she had always lived a life of delayed gratification. It wasn't enough for her to postpone getting married until after she graduated from college, but she had to wait until she finished graduate school. Thinking back, she could've married Spade when they graduated, got a job, and went to grad school part-time. That mind-set spilled over into other aspects of her life as well. Even when she ate she saved the best for last. Nya often teased her that she ate like a little kid, and it was true. She remembered her parents taught her to eat her vegetables first and eat the meat last. She continued to do that to this very day.

Completely out of her character, Bria couldn't believe what she was about to say next. "Okay, let's do it. Let's go down to the courthouse and get married." She had never felt more liberated in her life than she did right now.

"You mean it?" His grin spread across his face.

She nodded her head. "Yes, I do."

"Save that for tomorrow." He picked her up and spun her around.

She laughed as she held on tight. She had come to realize that even the most well thought out plans weren't guaranteed. Look at how her relationship with Spade took unexpected twists and turns, she mused. There was nothing wrong with playing it safe and being cautious, but with Spade, she was able to be spontaneous, which proved to be more fun. She liked the fact that he brought out that side of her. For once, she was doing what she wanted to do and not what everyone else expected her to do.

Thirty-four

Bria called to tell Dani that she would be taking the day off from work and Nya would be in late.

"Why? Are you sick?" Dani asked concerned.

"No, no, nothing like that. We just have some things we need to take care of." It took everything within Bria not to tell Dani that she and Spade were going down to the courthouse to get married and that Nya would be her witness.

"I'll hold it down. Let me know if you need me."

Bria trusted Dani. She knew that she could rely on her to handle business in her absence. They ended the call, and Bria finished getting ready. In the back of her closet, she found a strapless fitted white tea-length dress that she had never worn. She had gotten the dress from Nordstrom and figured the right occasion would present itself for her to wear it. How could she ever have known the dress would turn out to be her wedding dress? she thought.

With a small part on the right side, her hair hung straight down. She applied a coat of lipstick before fastening the strap on her white lace ankle strap heels.

She looked in the mirror and felt excited. She was getting married! Small butterflies danced in her stomach.

Spade called to tell her he was outside. She grabbed her clutch purse and filled it with her compact, lipstick, breath mints, Kleenex, and an envelope containing her driver's license, birth certificate, and Social Security card.

Her overnight bag was packed with lingerie, clothes, shoes, makeup, and toiletries. She picked it up as she hurried to meet her man, her soon-to-be husband.

As she locked her front door she realized that the next time she walked through those doors she'd be a married woman! Mrs. Spade Spencer. What an honor! She looked up at the clear blue sky and thought, what a great day to get married.

Spade held the door open for her. Nya and Chance were parked in front of her house waiting to trail them to the courthouse. She waved at them as Spade placed her bag in the trunk and she slid into the passenger seat.

"You look gorgeous, love," he complimented her as he closed the door behind her.

Dressed in an all-black suit she thought Spade looked handsome and told him so. "You look handsome."

"Thanks, baby."

They held hands for much of the smooth ride until Spade called his mom. When she answered, he placed her on speakerphone and said, "Guess what?"

"What?" She sounded impatient.

"Bria and I are getting married today."

She screamed into the phone. Bria and Spade exchanged glances. "Congratulations, baby. I'm happy for you. Give Bria my love."

"You can do it yourself," he said. "She's right here. I have you on speaker."

"Bria," she said. "I told you he'd come back. I love you. Welcome to the family, baby."

Her warmth exuded through the phone and touched Bria's heart. "Thank you. I love you too."

"Later, Mom," Spade said before ending the call.

They passed a Chick-fil-A on the corner, and Bria's heartbeat sped up. She knew they were literally just moments away from the DeKalb County Courthouse. She closed her eyes, took a deep breath, and exhaled slowly.

"You all right?" he asked.

"This is one of the best days of my life. I couldn't be happier."

"Mine too."

They parked in the garage and waited until Nya and Chance finished parking their car before walking up to the courthouse together.

"You look like a doll," Nya told her as she handed her a small but adorable bouquet. She then pinned a boutonniere on Spade's lapel.

Bria liked the way Nya paid attention to details. She always remembered the little things.

"Yeah, you look a'iight," Chance said, grinning. His big and expensive camera dangled around his neck. He hugged Bria, and then shook Spade's hand. "This is it. Congratulations. When we leave up out of here, you'll be Mr. and Mrs. Spencer. How're you feeling?"

"Ask me afterward," Bria said. She felt the butterflies again.

"I can tell you now," Spade announced. "I'm sitting on top of the world."

"Thanks for agreeing to play amateur photog," Bria said.

"No problem."

The engaged couple walked hand in hand until they reached the security checkpoint. When they finished, they all got on the elevator to the Marriage License Department where Bria and Spade filled out their paper-work to apply for their license. Spade paid the fee, and they received their marriage license right away.

Nya pulled Bria to the side. "You ready for this?" Nya asked her best friend.

"Absolutely."

She lowered her voice. "What about birth control?"

Bria's eyes grew wide. "Remember when you told me I should start taking birth control at least one month before my wedding to give the medication time to work?"

"Yeah."

"Well, I picked up a three-month supply of birth control pills from my gynecologist when I thought Spade and I were getting married the first time, but when he called things off I never started taking them."

Nya gasped. "Oh no. You don't have a choice but to make Spade use condoms until your pills become effective."

"I don't want to use a condom my first time. That'll kill the mood."

"Nothing kills the mood more than a screaming baby." She tapped her head. "Think about it."

Bria sighed. "Fine." She was about to join Spade and Chance but Nya stopped her.

"Did you guys have the STD talk?"

"He doesn't have any sexually transmitted diseases, and you know I don't."

"Did you ask to see the paperwork to prove it?"

"This is Spade, remember?"

Nya dusted a fallen lash off Bria's cheek. "Okay, now we can go."

They got on the elevator again and went to the justice of the peace to perform the ceremony. They had to wait outside of the room while the couple before them finished getting married.

"You getting nervous?" Spade asked his bride-to-be while they waited.

To Bria's surprise she wasn't nervous at all. "No. You?"

"Not even a little bit. I've never been more sure about anything in my life."

They were notified that it was their turn to exchange their vows and went inside the chambers. The officiant greeted all of them and asked for the names of the bride and groom. The judge then performed the ceremony which seemed to take less than five minutes. Chance played amateur photog and snapped pictures with his digital camera.

The judge said, "Today, we are here to join you in marriage and to share in the joy of this occasion, which should be one of the most memorable and happiest days of your life.

"On this day of your marriage, you stand somewhat apart from all other human beings. You stand within the charmed circle of your love; and this is as it should be. But love is not meant to be the possession of two people alone. Rather it would serve as a source of common energy, as a form in which you find strength to live your lives with courage. From this day onward, you must come closer together than ever before, you must love each other in sickness and in health, for better and for worse, but at the same time, your love should give you the strength to stand apart, to seek out your unique destinies, to make your special contribution to the world which is always part of us and more than us.

"Being assured that you are aware of the meaning of this ceremony I will now ask you to repeat the marriage vows.

"Do you, Spade Spencer, take this woman, Bria Murray, to be your lawful wedded wife, to love, honor, and cherish her through sickness and in health, through times of happiness and travail, until death do you part?"

"Yes," Spade said.

"Place this ring upon her finger and repeat after me."

Spade took the ring and slid it on Bria's finger.

The judge said, "With this ring, I thee wed and forever pledge my devotion."

Spade repeated his vow.

The judge spoke to Bria. "Do you, Bria Murray, take this man, Spade Spencer, to be your lawful wedded husband, to love, honor, and cherish him through sickness and in health, through times of happiness and travail, until death do you part?"

She looked dreamy eyed at Spade and responded, "Yes."

"Place this ring upon his finger and repeat after me."

Bria took the ring and slid it on Spade's finger.

The judge said, "With this ring, I thee wed, and forever pledge my devotion."

Bria repeated her vow.

The judge directed them to join hands, and they did. "By the act of joining hands you take to yourself the relation of husband and wife and solemnly promise to love, honor, comfort, and cherish each other so long as you both shall live. Therefore, in accordance with the law of Georgia and by virtue of the authority vested in me by the law of Georgia, I do pronounce you husband and wife."

Bria couldn't believe they were married! Just like that!

The judge continued, "You came to me as two single people and you will now leave as a married couple, united to each other by the binding contract you have just entered. Your cares, your worries, your pleasures and your joys, you must share with each other. The best of good fortune to both of you. You may kiss the bride."

Spade held his bride close to him and gave her a tender French kiss.

When they stopped kissing, the judge announced, "It is my privilege to introduce to you for the first time: Mr. and Mrs. Spencer."

Nya stood there sobbing and blowing her nose. Bria kissed her on the cheek. "Thanks for being here for us."

They all took turns hugging each other and exited the chambers.

"How y'all feeling, Mr. and Mrs. Spencer?" Nya asked them.

"Still on top of the world," Spade said.

"Yeah, what he said," Bria laughed.

They headed to the elevator and pushed the button. While they waited, Bria and Spade held hands and occasionally kissed each other. When the doors opened they pressed the button for the main floor. As soon as the doors opened and they stepped out Bria was horrified to see Kerryngton.

There was an awkward silence until Bria spoke up. "Kerryngton, what are you doing here?"

"Traffic court. Ironically, I got a ticket one night while I was coming to visit you." He eyed her up and down. "Did you get married?" he asked, his stare intent.

She nodded.

"I would say congratulations, but I won't." His tone was harsh. He then proceeded to verbally rip Bria a new one. "I should've known you were nothing but a gold digger. You didn't care about me. You're full of games. I don't have time to entertain some silly—"

Whatever composure Spade had, he lost it. He swung on Kerryngton and before Kerryngton could retaliate, security hemmed Spade up real quick. Spade yelled, "How you gon' disrespect my wife, fool?"

Bria wanted to slink her way back into the elevator and go anywhere but there. She couldn't believe Kerryngton had acted like such a jerk. She looked into his dark eyes hoping that she could see some resemblance of the decent person she once thought he was. Instead, she saw anger. Unbridled, untethered rage!

Kerryngton clenched his fists, but he was lucky that security was there. Spade looked like he wanted to beat Kerryngton within an inch of his life. He touched the spot on his jaw where Spade had punched him. There wasn't any blood.

He said disgustingly, "You can have her."

"Sir, do you want to press charges?" the officer asked.

Kerryngton gave Spade a stern look. Even though the officer had asked the question, Kerryngton spoke directly to Spade. "No, he obviously had a lapse in judgment."

The officer released Spade, who then grabbed Bria by the hand and led her out with Nya and Chance trailing behind.

When they got outside Bria said, "I'm so sorry, babe. Are you okay?"

"I'm fine." He shook his hand, and Bria looked at it. He had punched Kerryngton so hard he cracked the skin on his knuckle.

"We have to get some ice for your hand," she said.

"Kerryngton has lost his mind," Nya said. "You dodged a bullet with that loose cannon."

Chance shook his head. "I can't believe he acted like that. I thought he had more class than that."

"His ego is as bruised as my hand," Spade said. "He lost a great girl, and he's feeling salty about it."

Nya hugged and kissed Bria and Spade on their cheeks. "Please don't let this ruin your day. That was nothing but the devil. The enemy obviously saw a godly union worth attacking. Don't let him win."

"We won't," Bria promised her.

Chance hugged Bria. "Proud of you." He kissed the top of her head. He then gripped hands and bumped shoulders with Spade. "Take it easy, man."

They said their good-byes, and Bria and her new husband got in their car. As soon as they drove off, Spade said, "You know you have to give him that car back."

"No, I don't," she blurted out. "I'm keeping that car. It's mine."

"Are you for real?" He had that "I can't believe you" sound in his voice.

"I'm not a gold digger. I didn't ask him to get me that car. He did that on his own. It was a gift. He gave it to me free and clear. I'm not giving it back. And you shouldn't expect me to. That was before we got married." She felt firm in her position.

He just gave her a side-eyed look. Her head was swimming. This was certainly not how she wanted to start off her married life. She could've strangled Kerryngton for ruining this for her. She agreed with Nya. This was nothing but the devil.

Along the way they stopped off at the store and picked up some peroxide, rubbing alcohol, topical ointment, cotton balls, and an ice pack for Spade's hand. Bria applied the alcohol to the broken skin, and Spade clenched his jaw. She could tell it burned, but there was no way around it. She then applied the topical ointment.

"There," she said. "We'll freeze the ice pack when we get to the hotel."

They arrived at the upscale downtown hotel where they were planning to spend their first night as a married couple. They made their way to the entrance where Spade literally swept his bride off her feet and carried her over the threshold.

The bridal suite had been done up right, complete with a king-size bed, double shower, a Jacuzzi, and a private swimming pool. Bria placed the ice pack in the freezer. She hoped he wouldn't need it, but just in case, it was there.

Spade took the liberty of ordering room service.

Bria and Spade acted like they were addicted to each other. By the time room service arrived they were exhausted from all of their foreplay. Spade had feasted on the buffet of her body to the point where she was begging him to make love to her. He promised he would, but not right then.

She felt embarrassed when Spade opened up the door for the waiter and she was holding her strapless bra and panties in her hand. Her dress was only halfway zipped up, and her hair was completely disheveled. Spade hadn't fared much better. He had taken off his shirt, jacket, and pants. Trying to put them back on proved futile, so when he answered the door, his shirt was on but unbuttoned. His pants were practically falling down because they were unzipped and unbuttoned. Through it all the waiter kept a straight face as they tried to make themselves presentable.

The waiter placed the food on the table and Spade tipped him as he walked out the door.

"I ordered room service because I had a feeling we'd be working up an appetite," Spade told her.

She could agree with that. She had worked up an appetite all right. An appetite for Spade. She was so hungry for him she peeled her body out of her dress and stood before him as naked as the day she was born and probably feeling equally as carefree and said, "I want us to make love in as many areas of the suite as you can handle."

He stripped out of his clothes immediately. "As many as *I* can handle? You're the virgin. I think you meant to say as many as *you* can handle," he chuckled.

"Whatever." She pranced in front of him and got a clear view of the swimming pool looking refreshing and inviting. She pointed. "I want to make love in the pool."

Spade had previously stocked the refrigerator with protein shakes. He grabbed one and guzzled it down. "Let's go, baby."

"Wait!" She remembered Nya's warning about the condoms. She hated to mention it, but she felt he needed to know she wasn't on any birth control. She explained to him about the birth control or lack thereof.

He rubbed his face. "I don't want any barriers between us. I want to feel you. We can use the withdrawal method, or we can take our chances and go half on a baby. You know I want kids, so I wouldn't be mad if you got pregnant."

She wanted to have his babies, but she thought they should spend some time enjoying each other before throwing babies in the mix. She figured she'd be ready to start a family in about a year. She couldn't wrap her mind around the concept of going straight from being a virgin to motherhood.

"Are you sure you can do the withdrawal without slipping up?"

"Trust me." He put on the most romantic, baby-making CD Bria had ever heard.

She took off her purity ring and handed it to him. "I saved myself for you."

"You didn't save yourself for me."

She gave him a questioning look, wondering if he was serious.

"God made you for me."

Once in the pool Spade handled Bria with pure love and tenderness. He took his time with her and made her feel comfortable. Attentive and caring, Spade often asked her if she was okay. If she made a noise or had an expression on her face that indicated she felt any pain or discomfort, he'd stop and try something else. Tears streamed down her face as he deflowered her. Pain turned to pleasure as he felt so good she never wanted him to stop. She could've sworn she'd seen a glimpse of heaven as she cried out, "Oh God!"

Thirty-five

Bria and Spade took a break from their love fest to get some high-protein snacks and rehydrate themselves. Spade had been putting in the work, and Bria was certain he needed to replenish all the fluids he had lost. His cell phone rang, but Bria pressed her chest against his back. "Don't answer that," she said, nibbling on his ear.

He checked the screen. "Sorry, baby, I have to. It's my publicist." He picked up, and she could tell he was getting an earful. He appeared upset when he got off the phone.

"What's the matter?"

He seemed to be thinking of the right words to say. "Nothing. She was just filling me in on my release party this weekend."

She hugged him. "I'm so proud of you!" She gave Spade a seductive look and led him to the kitchenette where he propped her up on the cold counter and had his way with her. Afterward, they made their way to the king-sized bed and had some more fun.

"Now I get what Nya was talking about," she giggled.

When they finished, Bria felt sore and exhausted. They showered together before taking a much-needed nap.

Two hours later, Bria was awakened by Spade groping her. Surely he wasn't ready to go again. Nya had been right. The more men got it, the more they wanted it. She stretched and yawned.

"You look so peaceful when you're sleeping."

She wrapped a bedsheet around her body and snuggled close to him.

He spoke to the top of her head. "I was just thinking we should have our wedding here."

She thought about that for a moment. The hotel was definitely upscale and plush. She doubted she could find another facility more extravagant or lavish. And they certainly had the room to accommodate 250 guests. Plus, she could pull it together faster. She could see it. "Good idea. I like it." Her stomach growled, and she let out a slight chuckle. "I'm famished."

"Me too."

Spade threw on a pair of boxer shorts, and Bria put on his T-shirt. They brushed their teeth before going into the kitchenette to eat some of the leftover room service.

"How's your hand?"

"It's okay."

"Do you need your ice pack?"

"Not really. I don't think it's going to swell."

When they found their meal of crab cakes made with real crab meat, asparagus, and twice baked potatoes, they warmed it up. They had chocolate trifle for dessert, but Spade surprised her with a small fondant all-white wedding cake. They cut a slice of the moist, delicious cake and took turns feeding each other. They topped the evening off with a champagne toast.

Bria thought her husband was the most romantic guy ever. She loved him so much. She looked at him with the most admiring eyes, convinced this was the happiest day of her life.

Rolling over in bed Bria expected to feel Spade's warm body next to her. Instead, her arm fell flat on the cold empty space. She rubbed her sleepy eyes and glanced at the clock on the nightstand. The time read 4:15 a.m. She sat up to see if maybe Spade had gone to the bathroom, but the bathroom door was open and no lights were on.

She went into the separate office area and found her man. He looked up from his computer and said, "Baby, what are you doing up?"

"I noticed you weren't in bed and wanted to check on you."

"I'm fine. I get up every morning between three and four."

Better him than her, she thought. The only thing she did at that hour was turn over in bed and check her eyelids for holes. "Are you coming back to bed when you finish?"

"Afraid not. I like to get an early start on my day. It helps me to get more done."

"Oh, okay."

He pecked on the keys.

She yawned and covered her mouth with her hand. "I'll let you get back to work. I need some more sleep." She went back to bed but couldn't quiet her thoughts long enough to doze back off. Additionally, her enthusiasm about her new life kept her up too. She finally quieted her mind long enough to get some more much-needed rest.

When she did wake up, Spade was still working. He had drawn the curtains and sunlight lit the room. "Are you going to the spa?" he asked.

"No, I want to hang out with you awhile longer." She draped her arms around his neck.

"I ordered us some breakfast."

"Yummy." She licked her lips as she took a seat at the table.

Spade blessed the food. Bria sprinkled pepper on her omelet and used her fork to cut off a piece. "I can't believe we got married." She smiled at him.

He bit into a piece of crunchy toast and chewed. "About time," he teased.

Looking down at her dry toast she decided to spread soft butter on top. "Are we checking out of here today?" She drained her glass of orange juice.

"That was the plan, but if you want us to stay an extra night, we can."

"I would like that. I'm not ready to go out into the real world yet." She dabbed her mouth with a napkin. She looked at her handsome husband and said, "I love you."

"I love you more."

Every time she heard him profess his love for her she felt like the luckiest woman in the world.

"I have about another hour worth of work. After that, it's me and you," Spade told her.

"No problem, honey." She finished up her food.

The clock on the microwave read seven-thirty. *That's it?* Bria thought. Her body felt as though it should've been at least two-thirty in the afternoon. It was too early to call Nya, because she didn't get out of bed before eight o'clock. The only person she knew would be up at that time of the morning was her mother, and she was mostly having her usual morning cup of coffee. She went into the bedroom part of the suite and called her mom while Spade resumed working.

"Good morning," Mrs. Murray said. "You must've read my mind. I was going to call you this morning, but I didn't think you were up yet. What are you doing up this early?" She sounded suspicious.

"Hey, Mom. I-uh . . ." Bria couldn't believe she was tongue-tied. Then she realized her mom had said she was going to call her. "Why were you going to call me this morning? Is everything okay?"

"That's what I wanted to ask you. Last night I had the most bizarre dream about you. I dreamt you and Spade ran off and got married."

Bria could've sworn her heart stopped beating. She then realized it wasn't her heart but her breathing. She really didn't want to tell her mom this over the phone, but how could she not? Here her mom was having intuitive dreams, so Bria had to come clean.

"Ma, you know how much I love you, right?"

"Oh Lord. Let me sit down for this one."

Her mom didn't like for her to skirt around any issues, so she blurted out, "Spade and I got married yesterday, but we're planning to have another ceremony and reception for our family and friends." She didn't want her mom to worry, so she didn't tell her about the encounter at the courthouse.

She heard her mom getting choked up. "My baby is married now? Congratulations."

"Yes, Ma. He makes me happy. Please say you're happy for us."

There was a pregnant pause. "Your dad and I raised you to believe in love and trust your heart. Spade's a good man, and you're fortunate to have each other. I just don't understand why you couldn't wait. You've waited this long, why not wait and have it all?" Bria could tell by the sound of her voice that she was disappointed.

"We love each other and didn't see the point of waiting any longer. All we've ever done is wait. We wanted to start our lives together now."

"I'd be lying if I told you I wasn't disappointed. I would've liked to have been there, but since you're having another ceremony I'll have to accept that." She paused. "My baby's all grown up. I'm proud of you, Bria. And I'm happy to call Spade my son. He's exactly the type of man I prayed you'd end up with."

"Thanks, Mom. That means a lot to me. I just wanted to let you know what was going on. We're staying at a hotel in Buckhead now."

"Okay. Give Spade my love. I'll wring your necks later."
She let out a slight chuckle.

That night, Bria gave Spade a sensual massage complete with oil and candles. When she felt his body relax that's when she kissed him on the side of his neck. He turned over on his back, careful not to knock Bria off of him. She rubbed his muscular chest and shoulders. She flashed her white teeth at him and traced his pecs with her finger.

He folded his arm and placed his hand behind his head. "Feels good, baby." He licked his lips. She could tell by the naughty look in his eyes, and his nature rising beneath her that he was ready for dessert, and not the fresh fruit tart they ordered from room service either.

Thirty-six

Spade couldn't believe how his life had come full circle. A few months ago he was engaged to Bria and signing a record deal. And then he found himself facing his own mortality. Today, he was married to the love of his life, his CD was dropping, and he didn't have a life-threatening illness. Nobody could tell him that God didn't exist; he knew better. He had gotten to know God for himself. He had promised God that if He restored his health and gave him back his woman, he'd thank Him every day for the rest of his life. He also promised to use his life to glorify the kingdom. And he did. Before he even stepped out of bed in the morning Spade thanked God for waking him up. He started and ended every day with prayer and gratitude.

He had started moving some of his belongings into Bria's house. Since the lease for his condo wasn't up for another six weeks he had time to figure out what to do with his belongings. The way Bria had turned up her nose at his furniture she wouldn't have cared if he donated his belongings to Goodwill.

He adjusted his pillow. Bria looked like a doll when she slept, Spade thought. So peaceful and beautiful. He stared at her as she lay next to him. He was still trying to wrap his brain around the fact that Bria was his wife, and he was her husband. He was glad they had finally come together, and she was definitely worth the wait. He prayed that she would never change. He loved her exactly as she was right now.

Bria's eyes fluttered before she opened them and looked into Spade's face.

"Why are you staring at me?" she said, turning her face in the opposite direction.

He smirked. "Girl, ain't nobody staring at you." He touched the small of her back, causing her to move.

She covered her mouth with her hand. "Are you excited that your CD drops today and the release party is tonight?"

"Yeah. I can't believe this is my life. Dreams do come true." As happy as he was, he still wished his grandmother could've been there to see how he turned out. Due to his spiritual beliefs, he chose to believe that she was in heaven and already knew exactly how he was doing.

"You deserve all this and more, honey."

The doorbell chimed, and they didn't appreciate the interruption. Spade got out of bed and threw on a T-shirt and sweat pants. When he got down the stairs to answer the door, he could see his mom through the glass panes. He yanked the door open.

"Mom, what are you doing here?" He pulled her close for a hug. He noticed she had a suitcase with her and a rental car in the driveway.

She rubbed his back. "I wanted to surprise you. Surprise!"

He looked at her. "I'm surprised." He showed her in and grabbed her suitcase.

"Where's Bria?" she asked.

Bria came to the top of the stairs wearing a robe. "I'm right here." She trotted down the stairs and gave her mother-in-law a hug.

The elder Ms. Spencer explained, "I knew that Spade's release party was tonight, and with your recent wedding, I figured now was the perfect time to visit."

"We're so happy to see you," Bria said sincerely.

Ms. Spencer smiled hard.

They went into the kitchen and talked over coffee.

"How was your flight from Detroit?" Bria asked.

"It was fine. Now that the two of you are married," Ms. Spencer said, "I'm thinking about moving to Atlanta. I want to be nearby when you start having kids."

Spade thought that was a hint and a half. "That would be cool." His lips curled upward. "How long are you staying this visit?"

She held up five fingers. "Five days."

"I'll get the spare bedroom ready for you," Bria offered.

"Thank you. That's why you're my favorite daughter-in-law." She pinched Bria's cheek.

"I'm your *only* daughter-in-law," Bria clarified.

"Yeah, yeah, but even if you weren't, you'd still be my favorite." She giggled.

That night, Bria, Spade, and his mother went all-out for the release party. Spade looked debonair in a dark suit and red power tie. Dressed in a bloodred-colored dress, Bria looked striking. Ms. Spencer looked too sexy decked out in a backless black dress to have a grown son. Spade even rented an Aston Martin to arrive in style.

On their way to the event, they heard Spade's song on the radio and turned the volume up. They could hardly hear the song because they were too busy screaming like a car full of teenagers. Spade took that as a good sign. It put him in a party mood.

Once at the event, it was on and poppin'. They walked the red carpet as soon as they got out of the car. The night air felt perfect. Cameras were in their faces, and all they could hear was, "Over here," "Hey, over here." They stopped and posed for the photographers and waited until all of the photographers got their photo ops. Bria and Spade held hands as they walked inside the building.

People treated Spade like he was already a celebrity. He couldn't move two feet without someone giving him hugs or daps or a conversation.

He whispered in his wife's ear, "You're the baddest chick in the room."

Men were eyeballing his wife, making Spade's chest stick out just a little bit further. He felt proud to call her his wife, knowing every guy in the room wished they could have a woman like her. Some guys were even ogling his mother, and he didn't appreciate that.

"I'm going to take a seat," Ms. Spencer said. "I'm only here to support you, baby." She kissed Spade on the cheek and left him with his wife.

Spade encouraged Bria to work the room. He told her to meet people and socialize. He could tell that she was having a good time socializing with celebrities, popular radio personalities, and other industry professionals. She handed out business cards promoting the spa.

Spade had to disappear for a brief spell to meet with some of the people in his camp. When he returned, the chatter that had filled the room suddenly went silent. People stopped talking midconversation and turned to face the door. Spade entered with his entourage and the crowd gave a roaring applause. He loved every minute of it. He stood in front of a huge display poster with his image and his CD cover.

He waved, posed for pictures, and searched the crowd until he found Bria. He felt better knowing where she was.

"Come on, there's some people I want you to meet," he spoke directly into her ear as he grabbed her hand and led her through the crowd. She smelled so good he wanted to take her in the bathroom and handle some serious business. He loved a good-smelling woman.

He introduced her to the members of his team: his publicist, manager, booking agent, record producer, record promoter, music attorney, and the record label's A&R department.

"Guys, I want you to meet my wife, Bria Spencer. We just got married this week," Spade said.

Everyone congratulated them. They were all very nice and welcoming to Bria.

Bria said to Spade, "I have to go to the ladies' room."

She scurried away, and he followed her. Two women rushed out of the bathroom when they saw him. Knowing he had limited time, he paid the bathroom attendant fifty-dollars to clear out everyone except Bria for the next twenty minutes.

Bria exited the stall and washed her hands. "What are you up to?" she asked. She could see his reflection in the mirror.

He locked the door and came up behind her. He kissed her on the neck and hiked up her dress. "You look so good, I couldn't resist, Mrs. Spencer."

She batted her eyes and said in a flirtatious tone, "Mr. Spencer, shouldn't you be out there with your guests? This is *your* party."

"The party's in here." His hands caressed her body. "This is one of my fantasies for you."

She laughed. "Oh, really?" She sounded playful and went along with his plan.

He knew that he didn't have a whole lot of time before people started getting restless about not having access to one of the bathrooms, so he made every moment count. He took his sexy wife right there on the sink.

When they finished they washed up in the sink using paper towels and straightened out their clothes. Bria applied a fresh coat of lip gloss and headed back to the party. She walked out ahead of him, trying not to draw any unwanted attention.

Spade came out just in time to hear his opening act perform. They had just taken to the stage.

"Baby, let's dance," he said to his wife.

She took his hand, and they danced a couple of songs. There was a woman gyrating next to them, and the woman in front of them was backing that thing up.

Spade couldn't overexert himself because he still had to perform.

"I need to take a break. My dogs are killing me," Bria complained.

"All right, while you go take a breather, I have some people I need to talk to before I get changed." He handed her a glass filled with Sprite from the bar, and she carried her drink to the table where Spade's mother was sitting. He disappeared into the crowd.

As soon as Bria sat down, she kicked her shoes off underneath the table, hoping that no one would notice. "Are you having a good time?" she asked Spade's mom.

"The best." Someone tapped Ms. Spencer on the shoulder. "Excuse me, Bria." She moved over, putting some space between the two of them and spoke to the red-haired lady.

Shortly afterward, Kerryngton invited himself to sit next to her at the table, away from her mother-in-law.

She sucked air between her teeth and rolled her eyes. "Ugh," she said with disgust. She resisted the urge to throw her drink on his designer-label attire.

"Calm down. I didn't come over here to fight with you," he said. "I want to apologize. I shouldn't have called you a gold digger."

"You got that right. I never cared about your money. You're the one who acted like money was a love language. All you did was spend money. I didn't ask you for anything." She felt good getting that off her chest.

She noticed that the red-haired lady had left and that her mother-in-law was looking at them. She suddenly felt uncomfortable. She hoped Ms. Spencer couldn't hear their conversation even though there was some space between her and Bria.

"I guess I deserved that," he said. "I'm not going to lie, you messed my head up when you refused my marriage proposal. Talk about a bruise to the ego. No woman had ever rejected me like that before."

She softened her stance, and she could feel her anger melt like the ice cubes in her drink.

"I'm not ready to be your friend, but since Spade is my artist, we at least need to be civil," he explained.

She gave a faint smile and nodded. "I got you."

"Um, Bria."

"Yes."

"Congratulations."

She could tell that was difficult for him to say. "Thanks. I appreciate that."

"Good. Stay tuned. I have an announcement to make before Spade performs." He stood up.

Bria didn't know what that meant, but she was sure Kerryngton wasn't crazy enough to say or do anything embarrassing at Spade's event.

"Bria," he kissed the back of her hand, "as always, you look stunning."

Bria tactfully pulled her hand back and gave him a toothless smile before he walked over and spoke to Spade's mother. Bria couldn't hear what he had said, but whatever it was upset Ms. Spencer. Her eyes welled with tears.

Bria felt protective and moved closer to them. "What's going on? What did you say to her?"

He didn't say anything.

Ms. Spencer got up and went into the bathroom. Bria felt like punching Kerryngton in the throat, but she refrained. Instead, she gave him a mean look before running behind her mother-in-law.

Once in the bathroom, Bria heard sniffling sounds coming from one of the stalls. A stark contrast from what she and Spade had been doing in the ladies' room earlier.

"Please come out and talk to me," Bria pleaded.

Ms. Spencer unlocked the stall and walked out. She dabbed her watery eyes with tissue.

"What's going on? What did Kerryngton say to you?"

A woman washing her hands in the sink looked at their reflections in the mirror. Ms. Spencer waited until she walked out before taking a deep breath and exhaling. "Bria, you're young, and you may not understand what I'm about to tell you. I can only pray that you, and especially my son, can forgive me one day."

Bria felt her heartbeat speed up.

Turning her face away from Bria, she said, "Many years ago I had a drug addiction. Before Spade, I had another son."

Bria gasped. "What?" She covered her hand with her mouth.

"Yes." Tears streamed down her cheeks. "I wasn't in any position to care for a child. I didn't have money for an abortion, so I put the baby up for adoption."

"Oh God." Bria's heart sank.

She sniffled. "About four years ago a young man reached out to me, telling me that he was my son. He wanted to meet me, but I . . . I refused. I didn't want to revisit that time in my life. I was so ashamed. I didn't want to face him or Spade."

Bria swallowed hard, dreading to hear the rest of the story.

"The child I put up for adoption had found me. He knew my name, address, telephone number, everything." She cussed. "Nothing can stay hidden forever. At least not if somebody really wants to find out." Sighing, she said, "A while later I received a letter telling me that he had been locked up." She shook her head. "I know this is going to sound sick, but I felt relieved. I never responded to the letter."

Bria frowned at her. "Why would you feel relieved?"

"Because I didn't have to deal with it, and I hoped he'd forget about it. Then tonight . . ." She closed her eyes and lowered her head. "When I saw you talking to that guy, I had a weird feeling in the pit of my stomach. And when he came over to me, I knew."

"You knew what?"

Her lower lip quivered. "That he was my son."

"Are you sure?" Bria wanted to shake her, because she knew Spade's life was about to change forever.

"Yes, I'm positive." Her voice trembled along with her hands. "He told me. He said, 'Nice to finally meet you, Mom.' And when I looked in his eyes, I had no doubt. A mother knows."

"This is going to devastate Spade. Kerryngton is the president of the label that signed him."

"Oh God." She ran into a stall and threw up.

They could hear that the opening act was wrapping up and Spade was about to take to the stage.

Bria pulled Ms. Spencer's hair away from her face. "It's going to be all right. We'll deal with this. But right now we've got to get out there for Spade."

Ms. Spencer pulled some tissue from the roll and wiped her mouth. She then tossed it in the toilet and flushed. Bria ushered her to the sink so that she could rinse out her mouth. When she finished, Bria gave her a peppermint.

Ms. Spencer touched up her makeup. "Time to face the music."

"Literally and figuratively," Bria said.

They walked out and took their seats.

Spade's energy level was turned up. He wanted to see Bria before his performance because she was like the Adrian to his Rocky. He knew he'd kill it as long as he had her by his side. He couldn't be defeated. He went to her table.

"Tonight's your night, baby," she reminded him. "You've been waiting your whole life for this moment. I'm proud of you. Go represent for the family."

Family . . . That sounded good to him. Spade placed two fingers over his luscious lips, blew her a kiss, and left. She puckered her lips and kissed the air.

The opening act cleared the stage and Spade took over. "Everybody having a good time tonight?" he spoke into the mic.

"Yeah," "Woo hoo," and cheers could be heard from the audience. A round of applause followed.

"I'm so glad everybody turned out tonight to support me and the release of my new CD. Words can't even express how much this means to me. Thanks to all of you, but praises to God for making this possible."

More cheers and applause from the crowd.

"Before I perform tonight, I want to introduce y'all to the two most important people in my life." He gestured toward Bria. "My wife, my heart, the love of my life, Bria."

She waved and people clapped.

He then motioned toward his mom. "And my mom."

Spade felt someone pat him on the back. He turned around when he heard Kerryngton say, "Congratulations, Spade! May I?" He reached for the mic, and Spade let him have it. "Good evening, everyone! For those who don't know, I'm Kerryngton Kruse, the CEO of the label lucky enough to have signed Spade." He faced Spade. "I came out to tell you that your song is number one on iTunes." He held up his index finger.

The news startled Spade. When his eyes initially landed on Mr. Kruse his gut reaction was to clock him again. He didn't know whether that pat on the back was him marking the spot where he wanted to place the knife or a legitimate congratulatory pat on the back.

He had to separate business from personal, because he couldn't go around beating up the head of his record label, he thought. Even though he didn't like Kerryngton because of what he said to Bria, he still had to work with the guy.

He couldn't believe that his song was number one! Inside, he was rejoicing and thanking God.

Kerryngton shook his hand. "You worked hard. You deserve it." He summoned for a waiter to give him and Spade some champagne. They each took a glass. The crowd cheered some more and raised their glasses along with Spade and Kerryngton. Kerryngton led the toast, "Here, here! To Spade!"

Everyone clinked their glasses together and sipped.

Kerryngton turned his attention back to Spade. Away from the open mic he said, "I apologize for the other day at the courthouse. I was out of line and shouldn't have said all that stuff to Bria. She's a good woman and didn't deserve to be treated like that. You're lucky to have her." He grinned. "Now let's get this money." He then placed the mic back in its stand and got off the stage.

Spade took another sip of his sparkling drink and set it on the side of the stage. He winked at his wife and took to the mic again. "My newly released single is number one on iTunes. Nothing but God. Holla at ya boy."

He gave the DJ the signal to begin, and he ripped it. He knew he was killing it so bad that he could've changed his name to Slayer. He was sure Charlie Sheen wouldn't mind if he borrowed "Winning," because that's exactly what he was doing.

After the party was over, Spade was still on an emotional high. He told Bria and his mom, "I feel so good, I don't feel like going home yet."

"That's great, baby," his mom told him, but she seemed nervous.

"Let's get out of here," Bria said, trying to hurry him out.

As they made their way to the door, Kerryngton intersected them. "You ripped it tonight," he told Spade.

"Thanks, man."

"Can I talk to you for a sec?"

Spade shrugged. "Okay."

"Son, wait!" Ms. Spencer said, and both men looked at her. "Let's all go somewhere more private and talk."

Spade raised a brow. "Why would we do that?"

"I have something to tell you. It's important," she told him.

Kerryngton said, "Listen to your mother."

Spade was about to go off, but he didn't want to give Kerryngton the satisfaction of knowing he had gotten to him. He decided to let that slick comment about him listening to his mother slide. "What's up, Momma?"

"We don't need to talk in front of the cleanup crew," Kerryngton said. "No one's on the other side of the building."

They were quiet until they arrived at the more private part of the facility.

"Somebody needs to tell me what's going on," Spade demanded.

Before a word could flow out of her mouth, Ms. Spencer was in tears again.

"Mom, what's wrong?" Spade asked as he wiped her tears with his hand. He hated seeing his mother cry.

She then told him the same thing she had earlier revealed to Bria.

Spade felt as though a boulder had rolled over him. He couldn't look at his mother. Trying to console him, Bria hugged him.

"Son, I'm so sorry. I love you. Please forgive me."

He heard Kerryngton's voice and looked at him. "I knew you were my brother. That's the only reason I didn't press charges against you and drop you from the label."

Spade felt his anger rising again and silently prayed. He was a Gospel artist and didn't need any bad publicity because of his temper. As calmly as he could he said, "If you knew you were my brother, why did you date my girl?"

Bria stepped away from him, and Ms. Spencer grabbed her hand.

Kerryngton looked him square in the eyes. "Because you had everything I wanted."

Reading Group Discussion Questions

1. After Spade received his prognosis, do you agree with the way he handled his relationship with Bria? Why or why not?

2. Spade confided in Mr. Murray and swore him to secrecy. Do you think Mr. Murray was right to keep his confidence? Explain your answer.

3. When Kerryngton came on the scene, what did you think his intentions were?

4. While in London, Bria learned some startling truths. Did you expect her to make the decision she made regarding her relationship with Spade? If so, did you agree? If not, what did you want or expect to happen?

5. As Bria's relationship with Kerryngton progressed, could you feel their love developing? If so, were you for them or against them? Why?

6. Medicine is not an exact science. Were you surprised by Spade's final results? Do you know of anyone who has ever been medically misdiagnosed?

7. It has often been said that good men are hard to find. If you could choose between Kerryngton and Spade, which one would appeal to you most? Explain. If not you, which one would you pick for Bria? Why?

Reading Group Discussion Questions

8. How did you feel when Spade and Kerryngton had their altercation?
9. Did you notice any growth or changes in Bria's character? If so, what?
10. Were you surprised by the outcome of the story?

UC HIS GLORY BOOK CLUB!

www.uchisglorybookclub.net

UC His Glory Book Club is the spirit-inspired brain-child of Joylynn Ross, Author and Acquisitions Editor of Urban Christian, and Kendra Norman-Bellamy, Author for Urban Christian. This is an online book club that hosts authors of Urban Christian. We welcome as members all men and women who have a passion for reading Christian-based fiction.

UC His Glory Book Club pledges our commitment to provide support, positive feedback, encouragement, and a forum whereby members can openly discuss and review the literary works of Urban Christian authors.

There is no membership fee associated with UC His Glory Book Club; however, we do ask that you support the authors through purchasing, encouraging, providing book reviews, and of course, your prayers. We also ask that you respect our beliefs and follow the guidelines of the book club. We hope to receive your valuable input, opinions, and reviews that build up, rather than tear down our authors.

What We Believe:

—We believe that Jesus is the Christ, Son of the Living God.

—We believe the Bible is the true, living Word of God.

—We believe all Urban Christian authors should use their God-given writing abilities to honor God and share the message of the written word God has given to each of them uniquely.

—We believe in supporting Urban Christian authors in their literary endeavors by reading, purchasing and sharing their titles with our online community.

—We believe that in everything we do in our literary arena should be done in a manner that will lead to God being glorified and honored.

We look forward to the online fellowship with you.

Please visit us often at www.uchisglorybookclub.net.

Many Blessing to You!

Shelia E. Lipsey,
President, UC His Glory Book Club